Red Army Faction Blues

Ada Wilson

route

First published by Route in 2012
PO Box 167, Pontefract, WF8 4WW
info@route-online.com
www.route-online.com

ISBN (13): 978-1-901927-48-1

Ada Wilson asserts his moral right to be
identified as the author of this book

A catalogue for this book is available from the British Library

Although some of the scenes in this book are based on actual
events, this is a work of fiction. Any resemblance it might bear to
actual circumstances is coincidental and all characters are
imaginary composite constructs of reportage and myth.

Design:
GOLDEN www.wearegolden.co.uk

Printed and bound by CPI Group (UK) Ltd, Croydon, CR0 4YY

Route is supported by Arts Council England

RED ARMY FACTION BLUES

March 21st 1970. Peter Green steps down from the plane at Munich Airport.

Fleetwood Mac's star.

The Green God.

As a guitarist, many consider him beyond peer – so much feel, such a light touch, so much instinct, so restrained, so modest, so *black*. And as a songwriter he continues to pull out surprises, moving the band far from the twelve bars, giving them the most unlikely string of best-selling songs, but also credibility too; gravitas.

He wears a tailored Biba maxi coat over a Liberty shirt, a long multicoloured scarf dangling, carrying his guitar case. His beard is almost to his navel now.

Things are blurring for him, not just places and faces, but left and right, back and front, the long bus rides and the endless planes. And all the people. Crowds with pens and notebooks, behind cameras, at mixing desks, grinning over cups, squinting through smoke, extending autograph books. At parties and in dressing rooms, on planes and on buses, in the desert, in the wilderness, in front of the five thousand.

He flashes the peace sign at the journalists and photographers, who are all waiting for his words; starts to tell them a little bit about what's on his mind, just a little, but then thinks better of it. They only take his ideas and twist them. Always been the same.

But still they press him for more, because it's only *his* opinions they want, only *his* thoughts that make the front pages. Who cares about the others?

'Do you really want to give all your money away?' they ask him.

'Here in Germany, the young are demanding that all music should be free. They don't like this star system. What do you think about that?'

'They say that Germany should turn to its own music now, not keep relying on that from England and America. Do you agree?'

'What did they think in England when Rudi Dutschke was shot? What was the reaction to that?'

'What are your politics?'

'Are you a Marxist? A communist?'

'Some people say you're better than Jimi Hendrix, better than Eric Clapton, even. Would you like to comment?'

'What do you make of the counter-culture here in Germany? The young are living together, practising free love. The women want to be like the men. Do you think that's right?'

'What about the protests, the actions? Did you hear about the bombs?'

He knows nothing about any of that, Peter Green; flashes the peace sign at them again.

'I believe in freedom,' he says finally, knowing it's hardly enough. 'Wherever it takes you...'

The group's German agent starts to steer him anxiously away by the arm. The others are already in the limousines, ready to be whisked off, indistinct figures behind the tinted windows.

And Peter Green squints across the tarmac now.

Don't look over there, Peter...

He gazes across the runway and sees another group of people waving and smiling at him now.

'Who's that?' he asks.

The agent turns. 'Oh,' he says. 'What can they want... You don't know them? The guy with the John Lennon glasses, that's Rainer Langhans. You know?'

Peter Green looks blank. The agent shrugs.

'The dark-haired girl is Uschi.'

'She's absolutely beautiful,' Peter Green says. 'Isn't she? Just look at her.'

Don't look over there, Peter. Just ignore them. Get in the car. Really, don't walk over there, don't go with them.

PART ONE:
THE NEW CURRENCY OF COMMUNICATION
AND THE GREAT REFUSAL

'The Blues were actually the central committee in Berlin – all of the colourful types were part of it, half counter-culture, half political underground. Just "the Blues" because we had been through the whole long trip, through the wave of the cultural revolution. We were politicised not so much through politics, as through the cultural things which were happening in those years.'

Bommi Baumann

1. BERLIN. EASTER SUNDAY, 1967

Tense? Yes it is.

It's always tense here.

What do *they* want now; what imagined favour is being pulled in?

I stand scowling into the rain on the edge of the Ku'damm waiting for Kurt's man and watching the students going at it again.

Ho, Ho, Ho Chi Minh! Amis out of Vietnam!

A crowd of perhaps three hundred is gathered under tattered banners to stop the bomb – the Free University flotsam who spend most of their days buried under blankets. Pretty boys and girls with their leaflets and principles and anxious concern for peasants on the other side of the world. A few professors and intellectuals too, who ought to know which side their bread's buttered.

For a moment I almost envy them as they do their ritualised dance with the bulls outside the Café Kranzler; must be a thrill with righteousness on your side. A push here, two pushes and a cuff or the swipe of a billy club back. Berlin's security forces have to keep busy – sixty thousand of them on tap in the West Berlin bubble. More security positions than ever before it seems, in this time of peace. SchuPo, BePo, PoPo or KriPo – which level of professional assistance do you need?

Suddenly there's a new splash of colour. One of the SchuPo – the regular grunts on the front line – takes a hollowed-out egg full of red paint straight down his smart tunic. His colleagues sneer. It looks dramatic, I have to admit, but behind the flanks they're already reeling out the hoses from the green vans and the horses are being mounted. Another egg manages to explode across the elevated sign above the Kranzler – a bold slash of tutti-frutti Yank-

Italian flash, its 'f' a dollar sign, its 'z' an English pound symbol. Now dripping blood – direct Commie hit.

I see the tank-grey Mercedes with its official plates approach and turn off down a side street. Compromised and near-soaked to the bone, I trudge over.

Ho, Ho, Ho Chi Minh! Amis out of Vietnam!

I take off my hat as I get in the back as directed. All-leather interior swimming with cigar smoke. Behind steel-rimmed glasses in the front next to the driver, is Kurt's man.

'Mister Urbach,' he says, staring straight ahead as rain pounds at the tinted glass. 'A little blustery out there?'

With Kurt's man, my best response is ever silence; he doesn't joke. He pulls a mottled flask from his leather-trimmed jacket, hair slicked raw white, links glistening from starched cuffs. Bleached, still hungry. Tapered pianist hands that have probed and twisted, blinded, garrotted, castrated. And rain still pounding at the tinted glass.

We slowly circle back on ourselves and watch the demonstration as he talks. About the Grand Coalition and the extra-parliamentary opposition; about Berlin's mayor, Albertz, and the need for the Emergency Laws. Outside, the hoses are being trained on easy targets – observers knocked from walls, girls spreadeagled in puddles. The BePo – the specially-trained riot suppressors – having fun with it now, relaxing, lashing out; their mounted division preparing for a charge, shoes sparking against curbs. The PoPo, the covert political squad, and the serious crime mob, the KriPo, will all be in there somewhere, watching and waiting.

So which of them wants what, exactly, from me?

I glance at our driver's fierce spheres in the rear-view and look away again, then Kurt's man turns on me, his own eyes like gun chambers.

'Peter, tell me,' he demands. 'What do they actually want?'

What do *you* want? That's all I'm wondering.

'It's not as if they're even Berliners,' he continues. 'Not one of them. Don't know our customs or traditions. Don't respect them. Not interested in that, any of it. Just look at them.'

The window slides silently a fraction and I'm back in my sentry box without a weapon. Eyes and ears.

Kurt's man coughs abruptly, point proven.

'Ingratitude is what it's called,' he tells me. 'Insolence. Think they can just arrive with nothing from anywhere and impose their values on us. Driving us back to the Dark Ages this is. Come here, they should try to fit in, become part of this city, this culture, not theirs. Acknowledge the fact that we're the hosts and they're the lucky ones we're letting under our wing. Adopt and adapt. Weren't even here for the last difficulties. If they were, shit, they wouldn't be trying to tempt the Bear back.'

He offers the flask over the seat. I shake my head, examine the crowd.

'You know what they're saying, the real Berliners?' he continues. 'Those who were born here? The ones who respect our traditions and customs and remember? I'll tell you what they're saying, Peter. They're saying things were better before. That this would never have been allowed under Hitler. They're saying get them to camps, throw them over the other side in body bags. And…'

Pauses for effect.

'…I've heard what those crowds are saying, the older ones, the women who can still remember…'

With Kurt's man, my best response is ever silence. But he's going to tell me anyway. As if I don't know already. Turning to me now, behind steel-rimmed glasses, links glistening from starched cuffs, he grins.

'…Gas them. That's what they're saying. That's the voice on the street, from the real Berliners who remember.'

Ho, Ho, Ho Chi Minh! Amis out of Vietnam!

And now there's smoke across the cobbles, a few Free University chemistry lab concoctions, the fumes pushed low by gusts of wind.

Kurt's man turns back and relights his cigar. More smoke.

'Who are they really with and who are they against, the SDS?' he asks me. 'That's what we need to know. The working man is it? Is that who they think they represent? And do the working men even know? Couldn't they kick something off like back in '53 – actually get the workers on their side? Wherever *they* may be these days, over here, the noble workers. Strapped by their belts to the rails of the bars already I expect, save falling into the sawdust and puke. The carpenters, the plasterers, the hod carriers and roofers and brickies. But these *students…*'

He dips and pulls at his tongue with distaste, examines a stray hair between thumb and forefinger.

'…even if they never quite get around to studying, want to tear everything to its roots. Absolutely no idea what they want to replace it all with though, of course, that's the problem. All Nazis, see, our generation. Or Stalinists. The fathers. What other options did we have? Hardly a time for sitting on the fence, was it? So now they throw a few eggs at America House.

'You'd respect your son for such limp gestures would you Peter? Shouldn't they be taking crowns, killing the kings? Isn't that what it's all about? Think they've got a problem with fathers, might find it started with Frederick the Great…'

He smiles at his joke. Frederick the Great's galvanisation, his eureka moment, was when his closest of close friends was executed in front of him. By his father.

Kurt's man turns solemn again, he shakes his head, flicks his fingers, takes a swig.

Ho, Ho, Ho Chi Minh! Amis out of Vietnam!

'It's the young, I know,' he continues. 'The rich young, the pampered young, with their ideals. The educations they're receiving at our expense. And at the expense of the Allies too. Paid for, at the end of the day, in the sweat and toil of the workers they're so keen to represent. You know what they'd also say, the real Berliners? That they don't even want the fucking Free University here, that's what they'd tell you. That's the problem with it all. Too good for service. Low taxes, cheap rents, no curfew. That Dutschke lad for one, wants to stop shooting his mouth off or someone will take matters into their own hands sooner rather than later.

'Anyway,' he says with a sigh, 'in the end, some are born for the bullet, others go on to power. Those lucky enough find a way to steer through it. That's always been the way don't you think? Steering through? Making do? Making the best?'

We stare out at the crowd as the car inches around its loop and rain still pounds at the tinted glass. The police horses have made their first charge but are getting anxious, forced into tricky twists and dips so their riders can get in close with the batons as the penned-in students try to dodge the blows.

Ho, Ho, Ho Chi Minh! Amis out of Vietnam!

'We have files on all the ringleaders. That one there, for example...'

A manicured thumb turns my eyes right. Thick beard and glasses, threadbare suit, pressing leaflets on a middle-aged couple. Mister Respectable Civilian's teeth bared like an Alsatian under a low hat, striking out with his folded brolly. His wife in fur and heels, set to break into a run.

'The urgent message he's peddling, thick with student satire, appears to be giving his marching pals the Virgin Mary's blessing on this holy day,' Kurt's man tells me. 'Urging them to steal. Their Holy Virgin a thief now. Mocking the authorities. Mocking the Church and the beliefs of decent people.

'Shoplifting charge back in February appears to have gone to his head. Butter, shoe polish and two pairs of socks – a little personal protest against the obscenity of private property – fifty marks fine, but his friends rallied round. Like that one, for instance...'

He fingers a wispy ginger beanpole with protruding washboard ribs below a sheepskin, baggy pants tucked into boots, like a village farmer, carrying a papier-mâché model of an atom bomb.

'...no papers, but working an offset litho for Rotaprint in Wedding. *Situationist*, or something like that. Three days ago observed outside the Chinese Embassy with two others. One of them Dutschke again. What could their business be there? That's something you can find out. I'll have the files delivered.'

Kurt's man slowly shakes his head.

'Situationist,' he repeats. 'What a situation. Butter, shoe polish and two pairs of socks – can that really be all this is about?'

KriPo back-up arrive now, a battalion of radio cars and troop carriers, sirens keening. Bodies roll out, barking into megaphones. The BePo horses are charging at anyone who moves.

The students have regrouped and chant louder, more stones start to fly.

'You wouldn't believe how hungry the Allies are for information Peter,' Kurt's man says. 'A constant stream of information. Bloody insatiable they are. And then, of course, you've got to pass it to the other side too. Even unintended gaps lead to mistrust. It's all got to be seamless. Truth doesn't even come into it, one way or the other. I need you to get in close to them, close as you can. You can do that for us can't you?'

'I'll do what I can,' I say, eventually.

'There's one more thing.' He turns now, watching me closely. 'How's work going?'

They fixed it up for me, the job. Railway maintenance. All employees working on the suburban trains of West Berlin have to be members of the West Berlin branch of the East German Socialist Unity Party and carry their red party membership card.

'It's fine,' I tell him.

He turns back to the front.

'Well it's over, I'm afraid, for the foreseeable future. Unfortunately they believe you've been taking things that don't belong to you. You're not happy about it and you'll let everyone know about your grievance with the authorities. I'm sure you can take care of the other details.'

We pull down another side street and the driver gets out and opens my door. Kurt's man doesn't look at me.

'You'll be okay out there,' he barks at the windscreen. 'You know your way around.'

Ho, Ho, Ho Chi Minh!

The tank-grey Mercedes pulls away – nothing to see here, business as usual in the driving rain.

★

I spend the next forty-eight hours back at the apartment, acquainting myself with the files.

Because what you know protects you against what they know and can use against you.

Some of the documents go right back to 1953, when the Soviets crushed the uprising started by the construction workers. Youthful-looking mugshots of the now-ruined ringleaders, the would-be insurgents of a harsher time. Maybe a few managed to escape the six thousand years of penal camp sentencing that was dished out afterwards.

There's a thick dossier on Rudi Dutschke, who seems to scare everyone the most. His speeches are 'incendiary in their call for revolutionising society, highly offensive to the general population'.

The APO – the extra-parliamentary opposition – appears to consist mostly of such energised students, many of them also members of Berlin's young socialist group, the SDS. They're growing in popularity, gaining confidence all the time.

Among other things, they challenge the legitimacy of the Grand Coalition to rule, and they're hardly alone.

'Fucking vanity contest,' Kurt's man opined. 'Neither party gets enough power so they opt to share it. This is our great idea is it, to split all the policies down the middle? Hope everybody likes some of it? Who voted for it, tell me that? How is this democracy or anything approaching it? The Allies are never going to hand things over to this.'

There's even background information on Berlin's mayor, Albertz.

All that Confessing Church anti-Nazi activity during the war still doesn't sit well with some, however strongly they'd deny it.

'Nobody's happy with Albertz,' Kurt's man said. 'Not even his own, clean as his sheet may be. I've met his type often enough. Think they can please everyone with their piety and reason. Puff out their chests and strut around. Pop like balloons the minute they're prodded. End up pleasing nobody, all of the time, that sort. A mayor has to be seen to be dealing with things, especially here in Berlin. Does this look like everything's under control?'

The Emergency Laws, I was informed, had to be re-introduced as soon as possible, but the APO would certainly fight tooth and claw to try and prevent it. The Allies want them back as a basic condition of handing over sovereignty, as much to protect their own troops here as anything else it seems.

The last time the laws were imposed, the consequences were pretty far reaching. February 27th 1933. The Reichstag Fire and all that followed.

But what's really at stake here and now, in 1967?

Freedom of movement – the right to peaceably assemble and be hosed down and pummelled under hooves?

Privacy of communication – the freedom to have your personal details intercepted, your conversations taped and logged and the unfounded allegations of third parties duly recorded in secret files that will almost certainly be used against you?

The right to pursue a career of choice?

I haven't told Annalise I'm jobless just yet, to all extents and purposes. She's patient and keeps the children quiet, but I'm aware of her presence at all times – cautious optimism in her every gesture, the epicentre of our nuclear family.

The sort of family some of these students seem to believe is the root cause of all the problems. The two ringleaders who were pointed out to me are apparently part of a new commune which aims to make a complete break with society. Their ideas – if the police files are at all accurate – are certainly shocking, and I feel a guilty kind of thrill just reading about them. Especially the remarks by this guy Kunzelmann, the Situationist, and his crazy ideas brought back from Amsterdam: the capitalist order is the enemy of primitive human desire and situations must be created to expose our false reality.

What's that all about?

Get in close, Kurt's man said, as close as you can.

And I think, *Butter, shoe polish and two pairs of socks?*

And I also think, *Gas them? That's the voice on the street, from the real Berliners who remember.*

2. APRIL 4th 1967

We sit in the car opposite the house in Niedstrasse, my two tame SchuPos, Hahn and Engel, in the front, me in the back – luxuriating in their smells of cabbage breath and sausage farts, leathery sweat and damp and smoke.

It's a class neighbourhood is Friedenau, though, we're agreed. Not what they expected.

A gated entrance leading to double oak doors below a carved angel's head.

'Belongs to a writer called Uwe Johnson,' I tell them.

Their shrugs are tinged with suspicion – aware this ever so innocent remark is also in part an accusation.

They should know these things.

What you know protects you against what they know and can use against you.

'He's not exactly on the best-sellers list,' I add. 'An intellectual. Günter Grass lives next door, at number thirteen? Don't ask about number fifteen.'

More shrugs, grunts.

'Johnson's in New York. Not sure how much he knows about what's going on.'

Originally an Ossi, Johnson. Moved into town when they wouldn't let him write. Doesn't appear to be doing too badly here in decadent West Berlin...

As luck would have it, his place is already tapped and bugged – his wife suspected of passing things on to the Czechs. Small world of fractured allegiances, here in the bubble.

I have to know these things.

And as we wait and observe, I try to explain the basic ideas of the commune as we know to date – of fascism developing from the nuclear family and being the smallest cell of the state. Ideas, I tell them, formulated in part from the teachings of Marx and Mao.

'Why don't they just fuck off over the Wall then, if they want to be communists?' Hahn sneers, eyes narrowing to piggy slits.

'Half of them are running away from the East to start with,' Engel tells him.

'Either way… I'm sure the Ministry would welcome them with open arms.' Hahn is becoming animated. 'Few days in solitary at Torgau before their re-education starts. Knock all those shit ideas right out of their brains…'

'Because here, there's no draft, and no curfew,' I say. 'Taxes are low, rents are cheap, what could be better?'

'Try calling decent cops Nazis over there, see where it gets them. They fucked us over Christmas and made fools of us on Sunday again, something's got to be done. Albertz has to cut us more slack, give us more power to sort them out once and for all, the weak bastard.'

Nobody's happy with Albertz.

Sixty thousand of them on tap in the Berlin bubble, and all of them clueless.

Hahn's energy subsides, he slumps back in the seat.

I outline the commune's belief in the need for both men and women to develop freely in all areas of their lives.

Engel sighs at the implication.

'Including sex?'

'Don't let your imagination run away with you,' Hahn grins, coming to life again, the folds of skin at his neck rippling as he throws a mock punch at Engel. 'Just because Bettina won't let you have any.'

Engel flushes. Just turned twenty.

'She wants to wait until we're married, that's all.'

Hahn laughs, claps him on the shoulder.

'Well you could always join this commune yourself then. What about that? Get it for free from the hairy freaks? Who knows what you'd catch. Or maybe I'll take you down to my little place in the Steglitz sometime for what you can't get at home.'

A glint of gold tooth in the corner of Hahn's mouth and I'm levitating above some sordid bed in a squalid flat, looking down on his flabby white body crushing the life out of a slender girl, breathing the shame into her...

'How many are there?' Engel asks me.

'At the moment eight – five men and three women – but people come and go.'

The drunken piano of 'Let's Spend the Night Together' – number one – clanks out from AFN, drifting in and out of static from the transistor on my lap. It didn't take long from the Beatles and 'I Want to Hold Your Hand' to get down to the nitty gritty.

'God, listen to that,' Hahn spits. 'I hate this forces rocker music shit. Turn it off will you?'

He'd hate it even more if he understood a word they were saying.

'Why don't they play some good German music?' he continues.

'What, schlager like Roy Black?' I laugh.

'Nothing wrong with Roy Black. At least his songs have a decent tune to them, something you can sing along to.'

God-in-heaven help us – cleft-chinned Roy Black with his corny messages of alles wunderbar. Or worse still – Freddy Quinn. The crooning seafarer from the circus. The accordions and tubas. Fucking oompah oaf.

'It's always Brit music though,' Hahn complains. 'Or Americans...'

'It's a Yank station.'

It has to be said it's mostly the English groups on the radio – the Beatles and the Stones, of course, the Kinks, the Who, the Animals and the rest. Even most of the cheesy chart stuff is English, though it often sounds German – Herman and his Hermits, Engelbert Humperdinck, Kaiser Bill's Batman.

It's the music of victors, in their language, being listened to – perhaps the reason it sounds so alive. The music of winners, from a country ever so proud of itself. A country where even if you rebel against your parents, you aren't ashamed of their pasts. Even if they're murderers – even if they've torched houses or flattened cities, or shovelled bodies – they pin on their medals and march in parades. Grinning and smug side by side, the innocent and the guilty. On the TV, never-ending pictures of Carnaby Street, where the girls wear Union Jack mini skirts and the boys look like cavalrymen. All smiles. Swirling liquid lights. Big Ben and the Houses of Parliament and the red buses in the land of heroes. And the music, made by people who aren't pressed flat by some ever-unspoken burden and whose fathers and mothers are not sucked down to angry husks of shame and fear.

When they beat us in the World Cup last year, England, it was one long festival of masochism here. Bobby Moore. Martin Peters. Geoff Hurst. Bastards all.

London, it seems, crackles with life now, and even if a current is running through West Berlin, it certainly isn't a positive one.

So fuck them, the British.

Now I love you more than ever.

I turn off the radio and stow it in my box.

'The commune believes,' I tell Engel and Hahn, 'that people should be free to explore and express every facet of their personalities… the intellectual, the political, the sexual…'

'You think they might be having an orgy in there now?' Hahn grins, scratching his crotch and pulling on his HB. Throws it out of the window and takes out a vial, starts dabbing it on his teeth. Oil of cloves. Normally nauseating, but in this situation actually an improvement.

'Freedom from the tyranny of sexual roles and stereotypes forms a major pillar of their thinking. All institutions are derived from the oppressive character of the family and consequently, the small family is the cell that has to be shattered.'

'But why,' Engel asks, looking personally insulted and not a little upset, 'would anyone want to do that? Why wouldn't you want

21

to get married and have a family? You know, just be happy, after everything that's happened? After our history?'

Get married and have a family, just like I did. Be happy. Oh yes. It's all so very simple.

'The commune believes,' I repeat, 'people should be free to express every facet of themselves... the intellectual, the political, the sexual, and just as importantly, their pasts, and that of their parents because...'

But suddenly it seems pointless trying to explain anything to these two goons.

And maybe there's something in it, what they're asking for, this lot – the APO, the SDS, even this new commune. Perhaps the so-called economic miracle has been invented to stop us thinking about it all. Maybe consumerism is hammering the nails into the coffin of our history as they say. And maybe those at the top don't want us to know what the past means. We all have to work harder at this forgetting.

I recognise Rainer Langhans coming down the street with another guy, not immediately identifiable, and duck down in my seat. They're laughing hard at something, Langhans with a brace of books under his arm. They stop outside the gates for a while.

This new character is a little different again, slim and dark, probably good looking to women I suppose, a flamboyant silk shirt open almost to the waist, expensive Italian shoes. Looks like he can handle himself a bit.

'Fucking hell, who's that one?' Hahn asks.

'That's Rainer,' I tell them. 'Rainer Langhans. Arrested in the riots over Christmas. Remember, when they tried to set fire to the models of Ulbricht and Johnson?'

Born 1940 in Jena, son of an engineer who moved about a lot. Slippery and declared bankrupt more than once, the father. Ladies' man. Did things his own way. Made decisions.

'What the fuck's that on his head?' asks Hahn. 'Is that hair?'

Like something the press conjured up in a cartoon to personify the decline of civilisation – a burning building, an inferno of hair. Tower of Babel.

'Looks like a bastard darkie,' says Engel.

'A darkie woman, a jungle bunny,' Hahn corrects him.

'And he's wearing an earring.'

'Puffter. Those little brainy glasses, too.'

'A fucking disgrace,' Hahn spits. 'Army would sort him out.'

'He's been in the army,' I inform them. 'Made lieutenant, actually. Trained with the Pioneers. And he's an expert with explosives.'

This last is something of an exaggeration, but I'm a firm believer in telling people what they might want to hear.

The door of 14 Niedstrasse is opened for them.

'And that's Dieter Kunzelmann,' I tell them.

Born in 1938 on the anniversary of the storming of the Bastille. In Bamberg, a bank manager's son in a backward drinker's town, which says a lot. Passionately interested in himself, is Dieter. Doesn't believe in work, in money, in possessions, in property ownership. How could he?

'He's travelled all the way from Munich via Amsterdam to alert every last one of us square idiots to the lies of the free economy – to surprise us into eventually giving a shit. And, of course, there's no draft, no curfew, taxes are low and rents are cheap, and even cheaper in a commune.'

Hahn is open mouthed.

'Hanging is too fucking good…'

3. APRIL 4th 1967

Our observation of 14 Niedstrasse is cut short when Hahn and Engel are called over to some new commotion on the Ku'damm. They let me out on the corner and I turn back. Shielded by tall elms I clank through a gate with my toolbox and tap on the door of number 15.

The spyhole swings back and Frau Kesler opens up for me, wearing rubber gloves and a folksy apron over a mauve dress, hair gathered up under a net. She steers me through the dark hall, unsmiling, without a word. Stuffed birds and stained oak, Catholic tapestries, a smell of over-cooked meat, furniture covered in sheets. Piano music is straining from another room somewhere. Frau Kesler taps on the door of her husband's makeshift 'study' and I walk into a bank of white lights.

Roland Kesler's head is a tiny shrunken and leathery thing under the big black earphones and even bigger black bifocals. His tapes turning, receivers and intercepts blinking, the adjoining wall to number 14 stripped to the bricks and covered in a spaghetti of wires, connection boxes and Tesa tape. A US military flight case the colour of desert leaks drills and hammers and extension cables. Fat manuals and redundant fittings piled around the desk, coated in plaster. Kesler's bottle-brown cardigan has fawn plastic panels at the chest and shoulders, his white goatee streaked with nicotine.

An old standard-issue Luger, worn nubbed grip, next to an ashtray. He clenches his fist, unclenches.

'Advocators of fornication,' he says, his voice a young girl's with an 's' whistle, pipe clenched between his teeth. 'Enemies of common decency. Perverts, these people.'

'Have you got much?'

He stares at me derisively, rolls his eyes.

'The guys want to watch the girls shitting.'

'What?'

'They want to be able to watch the girls when they take a shit.'

'Explain that to me please, if you wouldn't mind.'

I tip my hat.

'The need for privacy is a bourgeois expression of insecurity and greed, Urbach. Private conversations, for instance, should be heard by everyone if they are not to turn into the spreading of rumours and then accelerate into the development of a pack mentality resulting in personal complexes for the weakest. And ultimately, social exclusion. Criticism should be a matter for all. No whispers behind closed doors, everything laid bare. Mind, body and soul.

'Telephone conversations should be made available to all through speakers which Rainer Langhans says he can get help to install,' he continues. 'They don't understand the danger in making what should be private public, and who can hold it against them and use it when they need to. So much trust in human nature.'

His face betrays no amusement, not even a crinkling around the eyes.

'So the need for locks on doors, even toilet doors, implies the need to keep secrets, to evade the communal experience. It's a bourgeois form of divide and conquer. One little secret is where it starts, leading to treachery and betrayal. And the need for this secrecy is instilled by the church and the state in the nuclear family. The private and the personal must become facets of the communal whole. They must think and operate like shoals of fish, think and act communally.'

'What about Humphrey though?'

Hubert Horatio Humphrey, moon-faced vice-president of the United States will visit West Berlin on Thursday. The Happy Warrior – former supporter of liberal causes, arms control and a ban on nuclear testing – now firmly behind Lyndon Johnson and the bombing campaign in Vietnam.

Presidential ambitions.

'They will attempt to get to him somehow,' Kesler says decisively. 'It's vague, though. Last night they discussed it with about a dozen others, but it was hard to decipher. You have to listen between their lines. Today, once again, they are back to discussing their beliefs and their *feelings*… in some depth… sexual frustrations, personal problems. Rainer and his feelings mostly, in his complicated mumble. To someone who hasn't wrestled with such emotions in what, thirty years? But still stiff in the mornings. Some girl called Birgit dumped him. And always this talk of what is in the interests of the community and the revolution, what Mao would say, what Marx would think. As if they are personal friends.

'And I have also strained to eliminate the harsh feedback – this *Beatles music*, from the Penny Lane and to the Strawberry Fields, and back to the Penny Lane and to the Strawberry Fields again. This Beatles. Like a dose of flu. My head rings. They are rich, spoilt students and they know little of the world as yet, but hope to change it all with a few third-hand utopian ideas. Bridging the gap between socialist theory and bourgeois existence. This is something they keep talking about. Cutting the umbilical cord. The personal is political and the political is personal. This kind of crap. The person must change in order to change society, and the society must change to allow the person to change. Circular horseshit.'

There beneath the blue suburban skies

'And anything else?'

'Fritz Teufel said he started off wanting to make people laugh, but increasingly started to wonder why people had so little to laugh about. Marx, he said, hit him like a bolt of lightning.

'And as for this Kunzelmann. How lucky he is to be alive in these times. There is no place in history he wouldn't have been taken out and shot, with his constant calls to arms. But they all seem to look up to him. Unless they sleep through his long rambles. Hard to tell from here. The girls don't say much at all, but I suppose their presence alone is encouragement enough.'

'Last Friday they were at the Chinese Embassy,' I tell Kesler. 'Langhans and Kunzelmann, with Rudi Dutschke. That doesn't sound so innocent.'

'A doomed-to-fail commercial matter,' Kesler says, with a dismissive wave of his pipe. 'They intend to distribute Mao's Little Red Book here. As if we want these things in the time of the economic miracle. Go shopping, let the chambers rust...'

Strokes the Luger. Clenches, unclenches, more smoke.

'Kunzelmann and Hameister have been working shifts at Rotaprint in Wedding for some time, and now Detlef Michel and Fritz Teufel are there too. I imagine all of the parts they need for their illegal press are procured from this honest business, given the collective stance on the obscenity of private property.'

'Should someone speak to the management?' I ask.

Pulls off the earphones and taps the contents of his pipe onto the desk, six inches away from the ashtray. Clenches, unclenches.

A pretty nurse is selling poppies from a tray

'Is that a question that really needs an answer?'

'No, of course not,' I say. 'Anyhow, it's quite clear from what you've got that they're planning something for Humphrey's visit. That's in stone. It's a question of just how serious they are. What exactly was decided last night?'

He shrugs.

'Beer was being drunk by the boys, and the president of the Free Republic of Vietnam toasted, as well as his good friend Mao. Stopped short at Stalin, of course. Who knows, someone might be listening? They were disappointed nothing much happened at the Easter March, that they were dispersed too easily and quickly. That not too many passers-by wanted to talk, let alone join them. Always the same with these little clubs. It's my party and I'll cry. Kunzelmann was arrested for throwing paint, and Dagrun Seehuber of course, and now she's spoiling for more trouble. It's always the girls.'

'Did you get any new names?'

'Klaus Gilgenmann…'

From Kassel – where the Brothers Grimm collected and wrote most of their fairy tales. Born the very year ninety-five per cent of it was destroyed by 1,800 tons of British explosives. Studying sociology and psychology at the Free University.

'…and one other.'

He's what, sixty-four, sixty-five, Roland Kesler? Old enough for both wars somewhere or other, and to know there are no sides worth taking, no positions ultimately worth defending.

I wonder where he came from, what he did, and who ultimately pays him now. But they all buy into his Chinese whispers, one way or another, BePo, KriPo, PoPo, SchuPo, the West Berlin Office for the Constitution. Not to mention Springer's papers and Kurt's men. From department to department, quarter to quarter, his messages shape-shifting to fit agendas, bouncing back and between in the airless bubble.

And though she feels as if she's in a play

Kesler is twisting a thumbscrew-type device into the bowl of his pipe.

'The other new name is Wulf Krause, student at the Institute of Inorganic Chemistry. Tomorrow he'll call next door to show them how to make the bombs they want. A search of his car would probably net incriminating materials, if that's what anyone wants to find at this stage. My guess would be potassium chlorate – which he can always claim is for killing the weeds in his garden – but also, maybe, some silver fulminate. If they find wax-based materials, it's more serious.'

'Can you remember being young, and thinking you could change the world?' I ask, shaking his hand.

'They want to watch the girls,' he says, shaking his head finally. 'Shitting. Springer would like that story.'

The SchuPo are probably getting more down on the Ku'damm, I decide.

I take the tram – its windows smeared in some kind of textile factory foam, tiny bubbles of magenta and lime bursting onto the condensation-streaked glass.

The men smoke into their fists behind their newspapers, some in suits and clean, others in overalls and streaked with black soot or white dust; the stark monochrome interior contrasting with the bubbles on the window, refracted from the glare of the gas-lamps and shopfront displays we pass. Drained and headscarved women prod handbags down between their thighs, as if delaying unwanted births.

Nobody smiles, eyes squint for the familiar landmarks of home. Small dogs – soot black, plaster white – sniff up and down the aisle. And we pour off, in drab file, onto the Ku'damm. The rain's stopped, at least.

Immediately, I see an excited crowd gathering outside number 140, the headquarters of the SDS, onlookers straining and pushing to get a look at what's happening and just as many people moving swiftly away.

Get in close, Kurt's man said, as close as you can.

The police car is surrounded by snarling and intent young men – short-haired, sober-looking types, not my ragged rogue element – who have obviously been riled by something.

I expect to see Hahn and Engel cowering, but as I move in I realise I don't know the two bulls inside the car. They're desperately on the radio for back-up but a stone skims across the windscreen now, making a couple of jagged cracks which obscure them.

More drinkers are veering from taverns to shout encouragement to one side or the other, throwing butts, pulling up belts, palming jacks, dispensing veteran advice.

'Give some truncheon to the gammlers!'

'Shoot the red bastards!'

'Get out and fight the puffs, you puffs!'

'Turn it over!'

The van's antennae are torn off, the kids start to rock it, side to side.

Ho, Ho, Ho Chi Minh!

Go on, turn it right over, I'm thinking. Drop a match in the tank. Why not? Let's get things moving.

I hang around to watch swastikas sprayed on the sides and register a few suddenly familiar faces. At the sound of approaching sirens the attackers stop and lose themselves in the crowd as it melts away. I trail one of them for a couple of minutes, tap him on the arm. He draws back, terrified.

'What was that all about?' I ask him firmly.

He looks at me suspiciously.

'Nothing, we... are you a cop?'

'Do I look like one?'

He sneers now.

'They just keep pushing us further,' he says, 'that's all. They were hassling Rudi again.'

I let him go.

I get back home with my pockets full of coal and potatoes, pilfered from the allotments and yards along the side of the railway – having brandished the special pass I have yet to relinquish at the watchman on the gate.

Over through the cemetery, scooping up a sad clutch of Easter bells as I go, from which I remove the desolate dedication.

Which she likes, anyway.

And I'm in time to kiss the children goodnight.

Klaus has drawn a picture of me – a ragged scarecrow of a man in a battered hat, with sidewards eyes. Lotte had a fall in the playground, a scab on her knee. I examine and kiss it and she smiles without opening her eyes. Somehow, they take my presence as reassurance, even as I feel like some kind of plague. They smell of yeasty contentment on the two bunks. And what do I smell of, I wonder?

Does betrayal seep from my pores; do people sense my fear?

Hopefully not, because I know it hasn't even started yet.

Annalise has made borscht dumplings and the kitchen and living room stink of its beet. A half-bottle of cherry brandy between us – mine from a sherry glass, hers from an egg-cup. One day, we'll have a cabinet full of cut glass, a cellar full of expensive French wine.

We eat in silence.

Finally, she says:

'She's not getting any better. There was a letter today. It had been opened of course.'

I stare into stew the colour of veins. Varicose veins like her mother's.

She turns from the food and coughs.

'My mother I mean.'

'I know. What can I do?'

'I'm just so worried.'

'Well you don't need to worry. At all.'

'What will happen to her though?'

I stare down into the stew.

'If we could go anywhere,' I ask Annalise, 'who knows, maybe even take her with us, where would it be?'

'America, of course,' she says, without hesitation, screwing her face up with a smirk. 'Californ-i-ay.'

And I know I'm going to get a fuck in the next five minutes or so, while her head is full of big cars and open prairies and the taste of imagined freedom.

And I like it that once she's cleared the plates, she wants to do it over the table.

That's not normal is it, for a respectable Catholic woman in Germany today?

But I know it's only because she doesn't want to wake the kids. And it's something to confess to next Sunday.

Drops out of her dress as if it was a towel, hips wide from the children, shoulder blades still like scythes. Skinny bearer.

But it's also not respectable, surely, to want to leave the lights on and look directly into my eyes?

'I wish I was in Dixie,' she sings, as she lays over the tablecloth, with another tucked over her navel for modesty's sake. 'Oh yay, oh ja.'

That's not normal is it?

And she stares into my eyes, trying to read me, and I'm not normal either.

The smell of yeasty contentment. And boiled beets. My smell of betrayal, seeping from my pores, fear on my tongue and teeth.

That's not normal is it?

4. APRIL 5th 1967

She takes the kids to school. I trawl between static for the patrol cars from the children's bedroom, bottom bunk. Friends nowhere to be found across the shortband.

Get in close, Kurt's man said, as close as you can.

Two pig's heads stuck on hooks, both grinning like the foolish, if generous, man I came to know as Father. This is the first happy memory I'm currently rehearsing, for later. Parts of it are real enough.

Immediately after the war, he re-opened his butcher's shop. Not on Potsdamer, that was bombed flat, but over in Kreuzberg. Koch Street.

But how could he do that, they may ask?

I have never asked him. Nor have I ever really enquired as to what part he played in the things that went on, I will say. It just never came up, all that. Just wasn't talked about. And I wasn't going back to the orphanage.

He was not, of course, my real father, but took me in, without questioning anything. So how could I respond with my own questions? And I was too young to know how to explain.

Meat, of course, was scarce for the first few years. I think I can remember – but perhaps, I'll add, with a strained expression, I was too small and just visualise things I've been told or seen afterwards – he carved up the rats caught in elaborate wires from the rubble of our defeated city. Or diced the wings of the dusty starlings and slicked crows that were stunned with slingshots and dumped in dented helmets at our door. But that would only make him foolishly optimistic as far as I can see. And rather thick skinned, or insensitive. Not until I was ten, or maybe eleven, however, did anything hang from that row of hooks set in the glazed blue tiles adjacent to the wooden counter in my new father's little shop.

Before that were pfennig cuts wrapped in rags, piles of unspeakable offal and cartridge shells in rows crammed with pig fat. Or its rough equivalent. And always terrible arguments between the desperate skeletal queues.

We don't talk now, he and I, for all that he did for me – his generation is finally lost to us, and I can't really say this makes me unhappy. There will be sympathy and nods of agreement at this point – all of our parents are lost to us.

But I do wonder at his eagerness to resume a career in cutting and hacking and slicing and stripping meat from bones, and rendering things down to nothing, I'll continue. At a time when it seemed the whole country should have been contemplating turning vegetarian.

It seemed always to rain, or be too cold, back then, I'll say. But not in the crisp and bright German way. Clothes were always too heavy and at the same time never warm enough. Damp. Like the England we had read about, as if they were visiting their weather on us too, after the bombs.

And so my first happy memory must be of the two pig's heads stuck on hooks, white and leathery – shiny and drained of all tone, like plastic, as if they wanted to be part of our new age and not that old one. And as if they too had something to be stubbornly proud of. And afterwards, the shop swelling with carcasses seemed to reflect Berlin getting its breath back, learning how to think again after the madness. The paper mills started running, so that the newly reared livestock could have their parts wrapped in yesterday's useless headlines. The wooden counter turned overnight to steel and could be bleached down.

And for detail, I will add that my father had very distinctive hands. The fingers were thick cut, slightly fleshy, the palms wide and smooth, patterned with scars and blemishes that bore witness to his trade. The soft but powerful hands possessed by all master butchers – soft on account of the animal fats and grease, and powerful, since they were constantly exercised in the daily practice of his craft. Even if they were well worn as he aged, they remained as sensitive as a surgeon's.

That sounds about right. And I'll say nothing about Poland, and keep Annalise and the kids as far out of the picture as I can.

★

Around eleven – saving me no little effort – Engel actually calls me from outside a photographic shop in Charlottenburg, seeking my guidance before sending in his message.

'I thought that was you in trouble last night,' I say.

'Where?' he asks.

'On the Ku'damm of course, outside Rudi Dutschke's headquarters.'

'No,' he tells me, 'not us. We drove down but there was nothing happening then. They were looking for Dutschke, wanted to arrest him. Anyway, Hahn had done his shift and wanted to get off, so we didn't hang about.'

In the kingdom of the blind, the one-eyed man is king.

Dieter Kunzelmann left 14 Niedstrasse at approximately 10am this morning, he tells me next.

'He's just purchased a chemistry set and the stupid assistant asked for no ID, nothing. What should I do?'

'Like what, for instance?'

'Potassium chlorate…'

'To be handled with care,' I say, 'reacts vigorously, sometimes ignites or explodes when mixed. Burns too.'

'I see, thanks. Natrium peroxide?'

'They use that to bleach wood pulp in paper mills. It's harmless enough.'

'Something called, diat, diatom…'

'Diatomite?'

'That's it.'

'Interesting, Engel. A white powder. Silica, sodium, magnesium and iron. From the fossilised remains of a type of hard-shelled algae. What about that then, Engel? Imagine – brainless to start with, laid to rest all those millions of years ago, then suddenly resurrected as a component of dynamite. The past always comes back to destroy you, eh? Anything else?'

'Lactose.'

'Sugar from milk. No idea, but then I'm no chemist.'

'Ammonium chloride?'

'Now we're talking. Volcanic. More natural products waiting to blast us to oblivion. Feed the cows with it, get your old man to cough his lungs out or just to piss properly. Or again, make explosives with it.'

'Something called Sudan Three.'

A harmless dye, as far as I know.

'Hmm, interesting.'

'Could that be Chinese d'you think?'

'Sudan's in Africa, Engel.'

'Just thinking,' he replies. 'Putting two and two together.'

The kingdom of the blind.

'Any wax of any kind?'

'I don't think so. Is that what we should be looking for?'

'Why not let your superiors know in any case?' I suggest.

'You're right, I should shouldn't I? This is more serious than they realise.'

I want to laugh.

'You could be right I'm afraid Engel.'

Kunzelmann returns to Niedstrasse at midday, only a few minutes after I slide into position at Kesler's place.

'They know the route Humphrey's cavalcade intends to take,' he tells me. Clenches, unclenches.

We sit and listen in silence. About half an hour later, Wulf Krause cruises up in a battered VW, goes inside.

Two hours pass, in which the rain never lets up. Dieter leaves again.

Then Hahn – surprising me by not already being schnapped or seeded out down in the Steglitz – passes in his tail an hour later.

'Using an alibi – Mister Bollman – in the photo shop on Salzsufer,' he informs his base via Kesler's intercept. 'What's this Sudan Three? That's what he was buying. Ammonium chloride and something called diatomite? Sounds bloody dangerous to me.'

Next, Dorothea, Dagmar and Dagrun, the three commune girls, with Hans-Joachim Hameister and Fritz Teufel, emerge, giggling and glancing furtively around, heading off in the direction of the S-Bahn, seemingly oblivious to at least three tails moving at intervals in their wake. So young.

And now somebody's big stick has poked the ants. Kesler switches from message to message between the bursts of static, unblinking behind a blanket of Danish tobacco smoke. Clenches, unclenches.

BePo, go.

KriPo, go.

PoPo, go.

SchuPo, go.

West Berlin Office for the Constitution, go.

Stasi, go.

Springer Press, go.

But where the Yanks are, is a mystery, even as they stir this nest.

I slip out the back and watch from around the corner as the battalion pulls up and the sledgehammers smash into the door.

Uwe Johnson, the absent writer, won't be pleased for one. Or his cheating Czech wife.

5. APRIL 6th 1967

And so here they are now, in the harshest of headlines. And not inconsiderable column inches.

Eleven Little Oswalds.
Dieter Kunzelmann
Rainer Langhans
Fritz Teufel
Dorothea Ridder
Hans-Joachim Hameister
Ulrich Enzensberger
Volker Gebbert
Klaus Gilgenmann
Dagmar Seehuber
Dagrun Enzensberger
Wulf Kraus

Eleven Little Oswalds rounded up on Niedstrasse, some dragged from the SDS headquarters on the Ku'damm. The rest apprehended at the café in the S-Bahn station in Nikolassee, on the edges of the Grunewald where five of them had tested their *deadly lethal concoctions*. Bags of paint and crude smoke bombs against a convoy of five thousand troops, eighty US secret service agents, a CIA helicopter.

Eleven Little Oswalds cuffed and transported to the KriPo centre at Tempelhof Airport. Land of the Knights Templar, Hitler's intended gateway to Germania, the new European capital.

Eleven Little Oswalds dumped in revolving chairs and snapped in monochrome from all angles. Bulls – decent and upstanding West Berliners – twitching to give them a going-over.

A *China-backed assassination plot* scuppered. All involved in the reconnaissance and search operation deserving a huge pat on the back. Berlin's special debt to the USA once more underlined.

Mao's embassy in East Berlin supplied the bombs intended for an attempt on the life of US vice-president Humphrey with *deadly Sudan III*.

East Berlin supplied the bombs intended for US vice-president Humphrey with *deadly Sudan III*.

Russia supplied the bombs intended for US vice-president Humphrey with *deadly Sudan III*.

Act of national treachery by *layabout nuclear-opposing Maoists*. Cardboard cores packed tight with ammonium chloride, potassium chlorate, lactose and diatomite.

Fuses and wicks discovered, a pair of weighing scales hidden under a bed, parts of bells as essential triggers. Several clock toggles. The glow head of a gas lighter. Rolls of Tesa tape. Literature from Russia, from China. Hate materials from around the globe.

A bound notebook with a red cover listing household meetings. A catalogue of small jealousies and tensions. Domestic grumbling. A part-illegible debate on the boundaries of the private and political, breaking with the civil society. The words 'action' and 'Humphrey' pencilled in the margin of a page.

Ho, Ho, Ho Chi Minh!

★

Our evening meal. Herring, potatoes. Annalise prods at that morning's copy of *Bild Zeitung*.

'It's just not safe here,' she appeals. 'I don't know why you could think it is, or why we came. There are too many crazies. Nobody knows where anyone came from, what they've done. And everyone who's in charge is still some kind of Nazi. Even if they weren't party members they went along with it all, or closed their eyes to it.'

We are not going to fuck tonight, over the table, with the second tablecloth pulled up to her navel. For modesty's sake, so I can't see what I'm doing. But her eyes are wide open, trying to read me.

And I think about Springer's papers, *Bild*, *BZ*, *Berliner Morning Post*, *The World*. The soot-black marks they leave on the fingers, word-traces smeared on knives and spoons, on linen and door handles. An infection that spreads through this city, its silent spores spooling out from the Springer Building – beacon of the Free West, slap bang up against the Wall – creeping under doorways and through open windows, shape-shifting, resulting in a range of symptoms:

Anxiety

Discomfort

Fear

Shame

Lies

All these things I think I now smell on myself.

And gazing out from East to West and back again from the top of his tower – with a raised middle finger to Moscow – Axel Cäsar Springer, guardian of traditional German values. Though by now on his fourth wife.

His rise a symbol of our economic miracle. A champion of the free economy which provides him with his monopoly on information. Fencing-in the 'German Democratic Republic' with his quotation marks, refusing to acknowledge its validity.

Well-connected Axel Springer, unfit for service, a permanent military incompetent and, like Berlin's poor mayor Heinrich Albertz, without Nazi blemish – although Axel liked the uniform. A business empire backed by the British out of Hamburg, based on the principles of upholding liberty and the law and furthering the unification of West Europe.

A supporter of our vital transatlantic alliance and solidarity with the United States, Springer, and also a promoter of the vital rights of the State of Israel.

Freemason. Grand Orient. The old boys' strain that went very silent after 1933 – accused by Goebbels himself of conspiring with Jews and rounded up for liquidation with the gypsies and priests. Inverted red stars sewn to their prison rags.

But not the Old Prussian networks – not the Three Globes, not the Grand Land Lodge, not the Royal York of Friendship.

AH himself liked their style:

All the supposed abominations, the skeletons and death's head, the coffins and the mysteries, are mere bogeys for children. But there is one dangerous element and that is the element I have copied from them. They form a sort of priestly nobility. They have developed an esoteric doctrine more than merely formulated, but imparted through the symbols and mysteries in degrees of initiation. The hierarchical organisation and the initiation through symbolic rites, that is to say, without bothering the brain by working on the imagination through magic and the symbols of a cult, all this has a dangerous element, and this is the element I have taken over. Don't you see that our party must be of this character? An Order, the hierarchical Order of a secular priesthood.

★

Inevitably, as a result of all the fuss, Rainer Langhans, Dieter Kunzelmann and the rest have to leave Uwe Johnson's flat, having all eventually been released without charge, although not without considerable paperwork to be noted and filed. Springer's reporters mug them on the doorstep, expecting lowered heads and hands shielding faces. Even the television cameras are there.

Instead they dress up for the occasion, like young teachers and salesmen, dutiful daughters and hard-working sons, with well-prepared lines. Laugh and joke. Mug for the cameras.

The television crew drags away Dieter, Ulrich, Hameister, Dorothea and Dagmar to re-enact their bomb throwing in the Grunewald, smother a few more trees with flour and paint.

For now they're homeless, reliant on their friends, but in two or three days' time will be offered the perfect place to enable them to continue their social experiment – to pick apart their egos and tear down the barriers between each other. In pursuit of the coming revolution.

Langhans will be able to strong-arm his father into stumping up the modest rent, for the time being.

Stuttgarter Place is perfect, Kurt's man thinks, and for some reason the Office for the Constitution does too.

It may offend the buried middle-class sensibilities of our students somewhat, scare them a little, to be down there with the lost. But where better for them to rub shoulders with the proletariat they so wish to liberate from the chains? To observe them at leisure?

And where better for pitifully paid surveillance, for loose mouths to be found, than above the Western on the corner of Kaiser-Friedrich Street with its most desperate of clientele and workers? Its tired, tired tarts, its resigned and compromised landlord and its half-invisible Maltese pimps.

So now they laugh and joke, pose for the cameras. Famous, for having done very little really. But it's a start.

What does Dieter Kunzelmann care about the Vietnam War when he has orgasm problems?

This is a new game, a new ball for them to run with. A better flour bomb for them to throw.

Sex. The kind of sex the pack with the pads and pencils demands. The unspoken sex the city had already read of between the lines in the story of deadly Sudan III in the hands of layabout nuclear-opposing Maoists. What do they care about such things?

Seven men and three women, the papers all casually noted. Seven men and three women all living together, getting to know each other. Breaking down the barriers between themselves.

And how does that read over the breakfast tables?

Sex.

Soot-black marks on the fingers, word-traces smeared on knives and spoons, on linen and door handles.

Sex.

With Axel Cäsar Springer, gazing down from his tower, ready to reject all forms of political extremism and uphold the principles of the free social market economy. And sell the city sex. Anti-intellectual, highly conservative, Germany's leading Cold Warrior. Divorced Martha in 1938, one daughter, Barbara. Married Erna 1939, one son, Axel Junior. Married Rose Marie 1953, then Helga in 1962, who has given him two more sons.

Noted and filed.

6. MAY 25th 1967

I accidentally-on-purpose run into Rainer Langhans on the street just outside the Western, bluff a double-take and gently block his path. I'm all smiles, palms-wide reassurance. He's nervous though, I can tell.

'Hey, I know you, you're one of those guys in the paper, the gammlers, the bombers, pretty mad stunt that was…'

He inches back.

'But at least you're doing something,' I continue quickly, 'because somebody has to shake it up a bit. We can all grok that. What are you doing down here?'

He looks at me uncertainly, taking in the dusty boiler suit, the toolbox, the copy of *The Truth* rolled under my arm. I tip my hat.

Just moved in, he mumbles. The wild curls that so upset Hahn have become even longer, exploding outwards.

'Up there on the fourth floor,' he gestures, squinting into the weak morning sun behind his glasses. 'It's pretty run down at the moment, we need to get the water on and the stove working, get the damp out.'

A strange kind of calm assurance comes from him, something I'm not used to.

'That's the landlord's job, you should be on his case,' I tell him. 'I know that crooked old bastard, anything to avoid the hassle, but won't drop the rent. They never do.'

'The rent's pretty good really,' he says.

'Well it's not exactly the most salubrious of neighbourhoods is it? You've got to be on your toes around here. All the same, landlords still have responsibilities. I do a few jobs for him from time to time, little coal for the back pocket if you know what I mean? And I think I'm going to need that now. I could come up and have a look at it for you if you want.'

'It's okay...'

'No really let me take a look, they don't call me The Fixer for nothing around here. I'm not going to charge you... this time. I just want to see where you plan to have all these orgies.'

He smiles.

'Well that's what I read in *Bild*, so it has to be true doesn't it?'

'Of course,' Rainer says.

'But listen to this...' I take the paper from under my arm, thumb through a few pages, fan it out and read:

'"Freedom is not and cannot be where a tiny minority of the society possesses the overwhelming majority of the newspapers, magazines and other instruments of public opinion, and uses them to incite the hatreds of the Cold War." What about that?'

I wave the paper about and nod my head, fold it back up.

'They have a point, of course,' Rainer says, grinning again.

'That's why it's called *The Truth*.'

He hesitates, trying to figure me out.

'I think you might be disappointed,' he says.

'Well anyway, let's have a look around and I'll sort the water out for you at least.' I offer my hand. 'Peter.'

Fisher of men.

'Rainer.'

As we climb the creaking stairs I start to tell him about the dispute with my employers.

'It's been a tough few weeks for me, I can tell you,' I say, and explain about my job as a railwayman and the recent unfortunate incident. 'Everybody does a little pilfering, that's understood. Perks of the trade, but I think I need somebody to represent me on this now.'

'You should get in touch with Horst Mahler,' he suggests.

Noted and filed.

A sign on the door:

FIRST PAY, THEN TALK

'That's for the journalists,' Rainer tells me. 'They continue to hound us. We decided if we're going to provide them with all the ideas, they should at least pay us for them. And we've got plenty of ideas now.'

I fan my paper in front of him.

'The re-establishment of monopoly capital and militarism in West Germany,' I read, 'has resulted in a newspaper and publishing system in which the magnates of financial capital have regained their positions as the all-powerful rulers of public opinion. What about that? How can you fight it?'

'I'll show you,' he says.

We pass a series of bedrooms with mattresses on bare boards and candles burned away to stubs, trailing stalactites of wax. There's a living area with three big, bright windows and a pale wooden table at its centre, heaped with plates and cups, bottles and books. There are more books along shelves and even more in battered suitcases, posters on the walls, Mao, Che Guevara, Rosa Luxemburg. Damp. Rippled wallpaper, stained ceiling, growth around the skirting boards.

Eric Burdon droning from a hi-fi.

'The Animals,' I say, 'really cool.'

'This is Peter,' Rainer announces. 'Offered to try and get the water on for us.'

Dieter Kunzelmann, naked to the waist, sucking on a pipe on a rickety chair, surveys me with steely interest.

The dusty boiler suit, the toolbox, the copy of *The Truth* rolled under my arm. A genuine representative of the proletariat, no less. I tip my hat.

Ulrich Enzensberger sprawled on a battered sofa, looks up for a second, goes back to his reading below a long fringe. Dostoyevsky, *Crime and Punishment*. Dagmar Seehuber and Dorothea Ridder filing through a scrapbook of newspaper cuttings on the floor, giggle and whisper something.

'He's been working on the railways but they sacked him,' Rainer tells them. 'Misappropriating company property wasn't it?'

They laugh at this. Seemingly I've just gone up in their estimation.

Rainer crosses the room and picks up some leaflets from a low table, handing them to me.

'See what you think of this.'

On May 22, 1967, during an American Week featuring products from the US, a fire broke out in a department store in Brussels that claimed 300 lives. This was a mass happening organised by Belgian activists protesting against the Vietnam War.

A burning department store with burning people conveyed, for the first time in a major European city, the sizzling Vietnam feeling – being there and burning too.

They're watching my reaction as I read. Am I their target audience? A worker, wherever we may be these days?

'That sizzling Vietnam feeling,' I say aloud, grinning and shaking my head, pushing my hat back, reading very slowly. 'That's a bit naughty.'

They smile proudly.

None of us need shed more tears for the poor Vietnamese people while reading the morning paper. From now on, we can simply go to the clothing department of KaDeWe, Hertie, Woolworth, Bilka or Neckermann and discreetly light a cigarette in the dressing room.

If fires erupt in the near future, if barracks blow up somewhere, if the grandstands in a stadium collapse, don't be surprised. No more so than when the Americans marched over the line of demarcation, when Hanoi's city centre was bombed, or when the Marines invaded China. Brussels gave us the only answer to that: burn, department store, burn!

'So what does…' I begin, looking puzzled. 'I mean, how…'

'A way of getting people to think about what they consume and how they consume it,' Dieter offers.

'Well don't pull your punches will you? If the press get hold of this... I mean...'

'That's exactly what we want,' Rainer says.

'Are you sure about that?'

He nods.

'This is how we can get things done, move things forward. Bringing it all out into the open.'

'It's sickening the way this Brussels fire is portrayed as such a big tragedy,' Dagmar speaks up, 'when the bombs in Vietnam are normally tucked away, as if it's an obligation to report them. As if everybody's bored with those repetitive deaths and that same story. Like at the end of the day, those lives don't count.'

'Boys and guns and war,' Dorothea adds. 'That's what's got to change.'

I shrug.

'Not much anyone can do though.'

'Come and look at this.'

Dieter gets up and takes me to a box room, shows me the off-set litho printer, fenced in by inky plates and spotted rags reeking of chemicals.

'Our secret weapon,' he says.

'That whole Humphrey thing, shitty as it was, taught us something,' Rainer explains at Dieter's side. 'Just a small story that was blown up out of all proportion like that, but it went around the world in a matter of days – left Berlin to reach Paris, London, New York. Only in the end, it didn't spread the message they wanted at all. It spread our message to the people who were really listening for it.'

'So we think we can learn from that, build on it and use it,' Dieter says, 'fight the fascists with their own weapons, turn their weapons of propaganda around on them. Use them to make things change.'

Want to tear everything to its roots. No idea what they want to replace it all with though, that's the problem.

'I don't think I really understand,' I say. 'How will it change? I mean where would you even start here? It's the same old Nazis running the show, the politicians and the judges. The former SS running all the bulls. And what about your lecturers and professors? At least over the Wall they don't have that.'

They both nod, still weighing me up.

'We don't agree with what's happening in the East either, that's for sure,' Dieter says.

'You should come on the demo on Friday,' Rainer tells me. 'We're preparing a little welcome for Iran's Shah.'

Noted and filed.

'I don't know,' I say, feigning embarrassment now. 'Things to do, you know. It's not for my type all that.'

They're embarrassed now, as if they've crossed a line. I love it. God forbid you insult a prole like me.

'Let me look at the water for you,' I say, brightening, 'see if I can get it sorted.'

I go through to the kitchen and get out the tools, locate the stop valve under the sink and of course it's rusted rigid, like it is in all these places. Two turns with the spanner and brackish water gushes from the tap. Want to change the world for the workers but can't even use a spanner. Then I unblock the stove's flu and in no time we're sitting around drinking hot tea, joined by Fritz Teufel and Detlef Michel, back from Wedding.

Both subject me to the same haughty examination.

'What's he doing here?'

They've been fired from their jobs at Rotaprint.

'Should someone speak to the management?'

Bound to happen after the Humphrey thing, we're in general agreement, but leaving them somewhat strapped. To add to their woes, the SDS has also opted to expel them all, for dragging its reputation through the mud.

I tell them a little more about my own situation, impress them with a few details of my personal protests against the obscenity of private property, offer to fix a few more things around the place. They give me the number of Horst Mahler's office.

I look around the room one more time. They're all watching me awkwardly.

'A lot of books...' I gesture. 'I should read more.'

'I know something you'd like, I think.'

Rainer goes to one of the suitcases, pulls out a volume.

One-Dimensional Man, Herbert Marcuse.

'What's it about then?'

Dieter and Rainer exchange a glance.

'The false needs that are created by advanced industrial society,' Dieter says.

'Methods of control and the desperate need for the great refusal,' Rainer adds.

'A thriller then?'

They laugh.

'You don't need to bring it back, we'll steal another,' Dieter tells me, with a wink.

Give it a go, they say, see what you think, they say. I take my leave.

Noted and filed.

Get in close, Kurt's man said, as close as you can.

7. JUNE 2nd 1967

The Savak – the National Intelligence and Security Organisation of Iran – are in town, haughtily erect behind the red-and-white crash barriers outside Berlin's Schöneberg City Hall.

Today Vietnam's on the back burner and there's a different chant: *Mo, Mo, Mossadegh!*

Not as snappy, it has to be said, but going out to Iran's plucky former prime minister, who died this March while still under house arrest, having really upset the applecart with his plans for privatising the country's oil reserves back in the Fifties.

Back then it was all about Anglo-Iranian Oil – the victors laying claim to everything; planting their flags again. First there was a small uprising in Iran. Churchill – of the ash-mottled waistcoat and brandy jowls – eventually had to tap up big brother to throw some fuel on it. More enticements followed – CIA agents stashed in car-boots, with cases full of precious dollars for the Peacock Throne.

This is what we know about the Savak: when General Teymur Bakhtiar was appointed military governor of Iran, in December 1953, he immediately started to assemble the nucleus of a new intelligence organisation. A US Army colonel working for the CIA was sent to work with his men, training them in basic intelligence techniques – surveillance and interrogation methods, the use of networks, organisational security. The first effective intelligence service to operate in Persia for centuries. After the colonel was replaced with a more permanent team of CIA officers – specialists in covert operations – the agency was given the name Savak – the National Intelligence and Security Organisation. At the beginning of the Sixties the CIA trainers left and were replaced by a team of instructors from Israel's Mossad. They had unlimited powers of arrest and detention, the power to censor the media, to screen applicants for government jobs and to use all means necessary to hunt down dissidents.

And now here they are, our government's special guests, straight across from us in this old Berlin square.

Consumerism putting the lid back on history…

And the leaflet that's being passed around, written by the young journalist Ulrike Meinhof – who's making a name for herself on TV now – alleges electric shock, whipping, beating, inserting broken glass and pouring boiling water into the rectum, tying weights to the testicles, and the extraction of teeth and nails.

Anyway, increasingly active in the face of rising Shia and Communist militancy over there, is the Savak.

Under a darkening sky, where Kennedy made his famous speech in '63, we're waiting to welcome Iran's Shah, Mohammad Reza.

He too can now be a Berliner, it seems. Didn't his father remain Germany's loyal friend even in those dark days when it had very few indeed? And wasn't even the mighty Springer muzzled by emergency legislation for offering criticism of the regime?

Mohammad Reza, who's given the workers shares in their fields and factories and set up literacy courses in the remote villages throughout his country, if you read the reports. Even though eighty per cent remain illiterate.

And has been so generous and understanding about the oil reserves.

And has eaten only from silver plates and issued his commands down a golden telephone, pinning on his ornamentations above his bullet-proof vest, forever looking over his shoulder; watching the eyes of his five thousand bodyguards.

And his second wife, Farah Diba, who's so outraged certain sections of the Berlin population with her lifestyle profile in *New Review* – empty-headed gush about summers on the Persian Riviera by the Caspian Sea.

The students are here to shout at Reza as Mo Mo's traitor and

America's special puppet friend. King of Kings dangling on strings, Head of the Warriors, Light of the Aryans.

A pamphlet is passed to me by the girl crushed to my right, who doesn't look older than sixteen, but tells me she's at the Free University. White mac, pedal pushers, boating pumps. Short blonde hair and a bee-stung bottom lip. Nervous blinking gestures under a long fringe.

'It's just terrible what he gets away with over there,' she mumbles, as if she's reading a message her mother has sent her with to school, squinting, looking down at her pumps. 'What are we doing rolling out the red carpet to him? A mass murderer? And his father was in league with all our cronies too. The train stations are blocked and there are restrictions at the airport. Did you hear they rounded up all of his opponents from Iran who live within fifty miles of here? How is this happening?'

More democracy, less memory, less justice.

'But at least he's not dropping bombs on people, like they are in Vietnam,' I say.

She nods gravely.

'So where does it stop, if you excuse one fascist?'

She summons the courage to look up at me. Angrily, accusingly.

'It might have escaped your notice but we have quite a few ourselves.'

'You think I don't know that? Think everyone's happy about the situation?'

I tip my hat in surrender.

'Anyway,' I say. 'So you like it, up at the university? Sorry, what's your name?'

'Marina.' She nods. 'It's pretty good, there's always something going on. That lot over there…' she gestures without looking up to the source of most of the noise.

My new friends. Brown paper shopping bags over their heads, with infantile depictions of the Shah and his wife on them, slits for eyes and makeshift megaphones between jagged, ripped mouths.

Like characters from an underfunded science fiction film. Rainer, ever the dandy in a long fur coat.

Mo, Mo, Mossadegh
Shah, Shah, murderer

'…they're pretty crazy really. But cute and funny too,' Marina says. 'I don't think many of them are actually students though. They're pretty famous now, after that Humphrey story and now the Brussels arson thing.'

'If I were them, I wouldn't be so keen on putting my face out in front of all those bulls,' I say.

She looks at me appalled.

'So what should they do, hide? Run away? All the students get what they're trying to say, even if the public doesn't and even if the rest of us think they should be using the attention to make more serious points.'

I shrug.

'Like what?'

'Like the limited options for women in this society, for one thing,' she fires back.

I smile.

'Ah, I see.'

She scowls.

'I'm not sure you do. Not sure any of you do. The press won't let it drop now anyhow, not after they've been made to look so stupid. We all know there's nothing funny about people burning to death. That's what we've been protesting about all along. And the reaction just shows how the authorities want to treat us all like idiots or fools, capable of throwing ourselves into the flames. They just hate anything that's different, anything that's at all cool. Or if it's approaching problems from a new angle.'

She gazes down at her pumps again, left eye still twitching. Pretty beautiful.

I nod thoughtfully, appraisingly.

'Fritz Teufel though, I think he's the real crazy one,' she mumbles.

Teufel. Where, I wonder, did such a family name come from? It could be taken to simply mean mischievous, I suppose, as in 'cheeky devil', and there are families who bear it proudly. Although maybe not anymore; Fritz Teufel is Satan personified for Springer's press, his name a gift for the headline writers.

'I worry for him and that Kunzelmann, how far they might go,' Marina says. 'You know, he broke into the Rector's office, stole his gowns and chains and cigars? Took off on some little kid's bike and drove it honking into the university's auditorium and onto the podium. There was an SDS conference going on and Rudi Dutschke was speaking…'

'Rudi?'

'Have you met him?' she asks.

'Once or twice,' I say. 'He's cool.'

'He's gorgeous too, but too serious. Very serious. Married too, isn't he? I don't think the students' council should have expelled the commune. We all have to work things out together because we all have the same enemies.'

'And what's he studying, Teufel? Any idea?'

She shrugs.

'Literature, I think, or history. Philosophy maybe. The fun guerrilla, that's his idea, but I'm not so sure myself. You can't just make fun of everything.'

'So what about you?'

'Medicine.'

'Great.'

She shrugs, smiles.

'Healing's the only way,' I cajole. 'I'd like to wake up sometime thinking I'd actually saved somebody's life, eased somebody's pain. Not sure I'd feel quite as good about throwing eggs.'

'So what do you do, then?'

'Work on the railway, but right now I'm in dispute over conditions.'

'So you read *The Truth*?'

'Of course, got my red party card too. Not that you have a great deal of choice if you want the job.'

'A proper worker then. I thought you all hated us students?'

'That's a pretty patronising generalisation, Miss,' I tell her, seeing her colour instantly and enjoying it. 'I'm joking. Ninety-nine times out of a hundred it probably hits the nail on the head.'

'So you're the exception that proves the rule are you?'

I shrug.

'Suppose I must be, I've met some of them too…'

I gesture across at my new friends. Getting excited now, in their costumes.

'Gave me a book that one, Rainer. *One-Dimensional Man*, it's called. That's me, I think. Haven't read it yet. I will do though. It's about all this, well…'

She looks up at me and smiles, chews her bottom lip, blinks down at the ground a couple of times.

I start to read the pamphlet she gave me, aware already of its contents and of who wrote it. And who paid for it. But I need to be seen to be reading it now, here, and I need someone like Marina to see me doing it.

It bangs on about starvation and poverty and disease, about illiterate children going blind, knotting carpets for fourteen hours a day. About Mo Mo's Minister of Justice having his eyes torn out, illegal trials, everyday torture, hot plates and truncheons dipped in acid. About nothing anyone assembled here could ever do anything about.

The Shah's authorised faithful are already in position outside the building – a flank of Savak in their black suits hold up welcoming banners, turning occasionally with anger at the taunting crowd behind them. Our crowd is now separated from them by a line of police.

'I don't like the way they're looking at us,' I say to Marina.

'It's okay, the police are here between us.'

Christ, can't she read eyes, doesn't she register the set snarls below those helmets? Can't she feel the *hate*?

'That's who I mean.'

The motorcade arrives, a convoy of bikes surrounding the Shah's Mercedes 600. He emerges, straight-backed and imperious, white tunic hung heavy with self-awarded medals, elaborate braiding and epaulettes, Farah Diba in her tiara and sash. They smile and wave for a moment, the cries of 'Murderer!' and 'Mo Mo' smothered by the cheering and chanting of the imperial faithful and the Savak goons.

An egg full of paint succeeds in hitting one of the guards on the leg as the visiting royals are escorted into the building.

Mo, Mo, Mossadegh!

The Savak man turns and I can see his jaws grinding, eyes narrowing. At home in these situations. He snaps off his banner and seems to just melt through the police line; brings the pole smashing down on the head of some unfortunate about twenty yards to our left. I put my arm around Marina.

'I told you this didn't feel right.'

The crowd gasps and writhes, trying to move in all directions at once. More Savak turn and follow now, suddenly tearing at the barriers and swinging at the penned-in crowd. More cracks, women scream.

The temptation is to panic, and for disbelief to blur your vision.

A man in a leather jacket rushes forward in front of the Savak, appealing to a bull, gets a truncheon across the nose for his trouble.

Women shield young children clinging on to tiny German flags.

The police have completely broken their line and stare on.

A smoke bomb from somewhere.

I bundle Marina forward and we scrabble over the struts. Keeping my distance, I appeal to a bull:

'You have to do something. Get those goons away from here. They're not even German.'

Lips turn into a snarl. He reaches for the truncheon at his belt, I dip forward and grasp his wrist, whisper low:

'Protection of the Constitution, and this is madness. Get me and this girl away now or I'll fucking stab you myself, you prick.'

Inspiration, the mother of invention. And we're free, through a scrum of uniforms. I pull Marina towards the S-Bahn, the chants and shouts receding.

And I start to laugh between shallow, grateful gasps of air.

'What did you say to him?' she asks.

'I pay his wages, he works for me, that's all I said. We're West Berliners, and innocent, let us through, that's all.'

She smiles and shakes her head. Hasn't let go of my hand.

And away from it, everything is order and calm. Couples sitting outside the cafés with their purchases, the shop windows bulging. Bakeries full of fat brown loaves and elaborately iced cakes, alabaster dummies draped with the latest mini-skirts and furs in the boutiques, electrical stores crammed with toasters and tumble dryers and new televisions.

'You know what they want Marina,' I say, gesturing at the shops. 'They want to give you all this stuff. Don't you think that's just great? Don't you think they're so thoughtful and generous? All of it. As long as you just keep on doing what you're asked.'

Her head rests on my shoulder now.

'It's all about power, isn't it,' she says. I feel her breath on my neck.

'And control,' I say. 'And forgetting.'

We don't have to say anything else and head back for coffee to the flat she shares with three girlfriends, to whom she breathlessly explains what's happened.

The boyfriends of two of the girls are there too, and examine me with suspicion, as if they already know my type. Inferior, too old and certainly not part of their clique. I can imagine the conversation they'll have when I go.

'He's reading Marcuse,' Marina says, defensively, and something inside me melts.

I say little.

'What, and the police just stood there and watched?'

Yes they did.

'And the Persians could just hit anyone they liked?'

58

They are all planning to be outside the Opera House tonight, where the Iranian royals will be accompanied by West Germany's president himself, Heinrich Lübke, along with his wife, our unpopular mayor Albertz and other dignitaries. A command performance of Mozart's *Magic Flute*.

'Please be careful Marina,' I say. 'I have a bad feeling about all this.'

'Something really different is happening to us now isn't it?' she asks me.

'In what way?'

She purses her lips, the tic in her left eye intensifies.

'Just… I don't know, I can just tell that we're part of something, and it's not just here in Berlin. I mean something bigger, that's going on around the world all at the same time. Different cultures with nothing much in common, they're all feeling the same. Like a breaking with the past. Something that's not connected to everything that's happened in the past, but is connecting all of us. But it's as if only the young can sense it, or even want it, believe it's even possible.

'We're protesting, for instance, today about Persia, somewhere we've never been – or at least I haven't – and I'm not sure I could even locate it on a map. Or like Vietnam… it's hard to explain, just that something feels exciting and good. And it makes me happy about the future, the way things will turn out. Like there is a greater good. And we can't do anything to stop it. But neither can the people who want to, whatever weapons they use.'

I make my exit.

*

By early evening the crowds are gathering on Bismarck Street, the bulls steering and cajoling them all onto the pavements behind Hamburg barriers, effectively clearing the long, wide road, which is completely closed to traffic.

Half an hour before the cavalcade is due to arrive, Fritz Teufel attempts to sit down slap in the middle of the road. He's barefoot and in a bright red shirt, his beard getting ever longer. They immediately drag him up and carry him away.

He's building quite a band of followers.

I find Hahn down a side street in an unmarked car, slide in alongside him with my head down.

'I see they've already arrested the Devil,' I say.

Grunts an acknowledgement.

'Won't be the last tonight either,' he tells me. 'We're taking all those bloody people. Those fucking commune clowns. That puff with his beads, and the ginger nutter too. First Christmas, then Easter. Ruining all the holidays and they think we're gonna forget. Anyway, Albertz has finally seen sense and given us the go ahead for us to get tough. Not that he'll be commanding the action, he'll be lording it with the toffs listening to the fucking opera.'

'I forgot what a great music fan you are,' I say.

'Sounds like an orphanage burning down to me, worse than the bloody Beatles. I know where I'd rather be.'

And Mozart, another Mason of course, admitted as an apprentice to the Beneficence Lodge in 1784, promoted to journeyman a year later, and later still, a master. The best of the musical Brothers, welcomed in all the lodges.

And *The Magic Flute*. I have a programme for the performance tonight. Madness begins with the legends and stories.

Coaches full of the Shah's loyal supporters start to stream past us.

'They've got reserved places up front,' Hahn says. 'Bait the crowd a bit, stir them up.'

'I fucking hate those people,' I say.

'Me too,' he agrees, 'but who cares? Your enemy's enemy is your friend. Duensing's plan is that we keep the kids all crammed in behind the barriers until the good people are safely seated in their royal boxes and that's when the music really starts. Operation Foxhunt. First, they're gonna charge the middle so all the kids push to the sides. He calls it the liver sausage method. Push it in the middle so it splits at the ends. Only there'll be a lot more of us waiting for them at either end. We're reinforced. All four branches. Water cannon, horses, green ambulances, the lot. There's something you could do…'

Very soon, Mohammad Reza and Farah Diba and their very important German friends – the Lübkes, Duensing, Albertz and the rest – will be settling in to hear the story of a handsome prince, lost in a distant land, being pursued by a serpent. The strangling of the serpent, the rapes and the abductions, the slaves and the priests. The enchantment. The Gates of Nature and Reason and Wisdom. The council of priests in solemn march.

An Order, the hierarchical Order of a secular priesthood.

The rapture and the daggers and the silences. The Temple of the Ordeal. The grove of palms and the pyramids. The magic flute, taming beasts, promising ecstasy.

If it were that simple.

The traitor listening to the magic bells and hearing only: an orphanage burning down.

★

I should go home, back to Annalise, back to the kids, with my pockets full of potatoes and coal from the sidings, clutching my Easter bells.

But these things won't pay for the new uniform Klaus needs, the piano lessons Lotte is keen to start, the new shoes for both of them. I think of the picture he drew – a ragged scarecrow of a man in a battered hat, with sidewards eyes – the scab on her knee. Klaus and Lotte, warm in their bunks. Smells of yeast and beets.

And my wife's mother, who's not getting any younger, or any better, over there in her crumbling apartment where the electricity is always off and the shops out of bread, still pining for her husband, missing her only daughter, her only grandchildren.

Not missing me, the one who took them away.

So we'd only argue again, me and Annalise. Or even worse, she'd withdraw into herself even more.

I find a small bar down a different side street, playing the Beatles and the Stones, the Kinks, the Who and the rest. Herman and his Hermits, Engelbert Humperdinck. Sit and chase a beer down with a schnapps, and then another.

And when a victorious song from the land of red buses and Carnaby Street and cavalrymen stops, I hear the other music from Bismarck Street. The sausage being split, the grab gangs, in plain clothes, fox hunting.

The magic flute, taming beasts, promising ecstasy.

Beer number three, schnapps number three.

And then I'm out on the corner, with the ex-soldiers in string vests, the ex-sailors with heavy belts holding up their guts, the plasterers and the hod carriers with their tattoos and all the old hate. The old, old hate. The hate of our mothers, the hate of our fathers. Fathers and mothers who are sucked down to angry husks of shame and fear.

And I tell the ex-soldiers and the ex-sailors, the plasterers and the painters and the brickies, just why all of the police — every single one of them here in the bubble — the BePo, the KriPo, the PoPo and the SchuPo — are so angry.

'You know what it's all for don't you, all of this? One of the students stabbed a copper. Imagine? Just walked straight up and stuck the knife in his chest.'

A Maoist with instructions from the Chinese Embassy...

A communist layabout under instruction from the Ossies...

A fornicating long-haired spy with a hotline straight to Moscow...

And as we survey the scene — the pounding feet, the clatter of hooves, the sirens, the streams of water, the shouts and the screams, the thump of people falling, the sausage splitting — I watch this message pass down the line, from ex-soldier to ex-sailor and from ex-sailor to ex-soldier. From cupped hand to ear.

And now they're tearing up their own stones from the pavement, pulling out their own crude weapons and wading in, more pounding feet...

The clatter of hooves on the cobbles, the sirens, the shouts and the screams, the truncheons against metal, the truncheons against skulls, the thump of people falling.

And I think of new uniforms and shoes and piano lessons.

And I think of Annalise. Cautious optimism in her every gesture, the epicentre of our nuclear family.

And her head full of big cars and open prairies and the taste of imagined freedom. And once she'd cleared the plates, we did it over the table. Dropping out of her dress as if it was a towel, hips wide from the children, shoulder blades still like scythes. Borscht dumplings and cherry brandy.

One of the students stabbed a copper. Imagine? Just walked straight up and stuck the knife in his chest.

I should go home, back to Annalise, back to the kids.

The Gates of Nature and Reason and Wisdom.

And I tell more ex-soldiers and ex-sailors, more plasterers and brickies, why all of the respectable police officers are so angry.

And they're tearing up stones from the pavement, pulling out their weapons and wading into it all, finding their places.

And the children will be on the two bunks, the smell of yeasty contentment. And betrayal seeps from my pores like sweat through my suit. Fear pumps out from my mouth, to everyone I speak to.

I know it hasn't even started yet.

And I go back to the bar.

Beer number four, schnapps number four.

And I think about Marina, out there somewhere, in the middle of it all.

The false needs that are created by advanced industrial society.
Methods of control and the desperate need for the great refusal.
Something really different is happening to us now isn't it?

8. JUNE 6th 1967

Following the murder of Benno Ohnesorg by Karl–Heinz Kurras on June 2nd, Marina and her flatmates are wearing black armbands.

On Friday night they heard Berlin's mayor, Heinrich Albertz, declare the city's patience to be exhausted, to bestow upon the demonstrators the unfortunate distinction of not only having abused and insulted an honoured guest, but having caused the death of Benno Ohnesorg and the injuries of many others.

A mayor has to be seen to be dealing with things, especially here.

Marina and her friends are just so young, and over the past few days emotions have been pummelled and tenderised. The old certainties have melted away. New anxieties have appeared and irrational fears of a conspiracy against them. The stakes have been raised. Something has changed forever.

They've heard Mayor Albertz say that Benno Ohnesorg, who was shot by a plain clothes police officer, is the victim of an extremist minority.

The police have plastered their own posters all along the Ku'damm, appealing for help in rounding up the minority of radicals who for months have terrorised the people of Berlin, through the abuse of freedom.

They have heard Albertz tell the city of Berlin that these extremists have abused freedom in order to overthrow the democratic rule of law.

But they are hearing something else.

And I think I can hear it too.

Something's happening now isn't it? It's hard to explain, just that something feels exciting and good. And it makes me happy about the future, the way things will turn out.

They are hearing something else when Berlin's chief of police, Erich Duensing, makes his liver sausage analogy and talks of cutting out the part which stinks, slicing into the middle to take away the rankness. They have already heard through their grapevines about Friday's Operation Foxhunt. Now they are hearing something else.

Marina and her flatmates stand under a flag of black ribbons on the Ku'damm and try to explain how they're feeling to anyone who'll listen.

In the *World on Sunday* they have read of the rowdies and hordes, the communist street fighters who use hooliganism as an argument. They have read that Karl-Heinz Kurras was pushed into a car park by students who then pulled out their knives.

They are hearing something else.

Just as they read about the China-backed assassination plot that was scuppered, the bombs intended for US vice-president Humphrey with deadly Sudan III, the act of national treachery by layabout nuclear-opposing Maoists, back in April.

The students surrounded Karl-Heinz Kurras and kicked him to the ground, the *World on Sunday* tells them. Fritz Teufel was the leader of another group which wounded two officers with stones.

But Marina and her flatmates already know there was no China-backed assassination plot, no deadly Sudan III, no act of national treachery by layabout nuclear-opposing Maoists. Just as they know that Fritz Teufel, barefoot and in a bright red shirt, attempted to sit in the middle of the road and was immediately dragged up and carried away half an hour before the Shah's cavalcade arrived.

The Shah and his wife have now flown home. To eat from silver plates and bark commands down golden telephones. Things like this happen in Iran every day, the Shah tells the *World on Sunday* with a shrug.

Like all of Springer's papers though, *World on Sunday* sends out other messages it is not aware of, for those who every day become more adept at reading between the lines.

They are hearing something else, Marina and her flatmates –

like many others, not only in West Berlin now – and they know that Fritz Teufel has not been granted bail, is languishing in a cell in the Moabit even as Karl-Heinz Kurras enjoys paroled freedom.

At the SDS student's centre on Saturday, Marina and her flatmates listened to the shrill proclamations of a woman with mascara-streaked cheeks called Gudrun Ensslin, who had yet to take part in a demonstration. A preacher woman, a dervish. The fascist state was preparing their mass extermination, she told them, weeping uncontrollably. Violence is the only answer to such violence, since there can be no arguing with the Auschwitz generation. And it seemed to them that there could be some truth in this. But they are hearing something else and know her way is not the right way.

Every day they become more adept at reading between the lines, even as the stakes have been raised and something has changed forever.

Over loudspeakers blasting across the campus from the packed auditorium in the Free University, they listened to repeated calls for calm, calls to descend in small groups on the city centre to discuss what happened with anyone willing to talk, to restrain themselves from any further radical action and avoid being provoked by their fellow citizens.

And they listened to the words of Rudi Dutschke – Red Rudi, fire burning in his eyes – who has told them if they don't continue with their resistance they are turning themselves into Jews. And it seems to them there could be some truth in this too. But the words of Rudi Dutschke are always saying two things at once. They are saying you cannot change anything and they are saying you must change everything.

That Dutschke lad for one, wants to stop shooting his mouth off.

There will be no lectures this week, but there will also be no retaliation, no escalation of violence. The students will engage with the people, win them round with logic and reasonable arguments, with sensible discussion.

Marina and her flatmates stand under a flag of black streamers on the Ku'damm and talk to passers-by. This is what has been agreed. And I stand with them, their prole bouncer.

And all along the Ku'damm are clusters of students, in black armbands under black flags, engaging passers-by in these conversations. The police move in pairs, but don't intervene.

The civilians are hostile and uncomfortable in their straight-jackets of sympathy and respect – the students are shocked and in mourning and I am a worker at their side. Palming a blackjack, a copy of *The Truth* under my arm.

Marina's black armband is over her white mac, buttoned up to her throat, and she looks more beautiful than ever in her frustration, in her anxiety. Cropped hair on end, blotches on her cheeks, clogged mascara around her eyes, baggy from too little sleep, like Gudrun Ensslin's. She chews her bottom lip, chews her nails and the tic in her left eye is more intense than ever. She clutches at the pole of the black flag with her chewed fingers and it's as if she's trying to steer a ship through a violent storm, bending into the eddies of hostility, the currents of accusation. Oh yes.

And I can be her anchor, or her rudder. It's hard to say which.

'He's reading Marcuse,' she told them, clinging on to what she wants me to be, what I might even yet become, just as she grips the pole of the black flag.

I turn away and feel like I might retch.

And the public lets Marina and her friends and me know it doesn't really want these discussions.

The public wants a return to quiet, discipline and order. None of this would have happened under Hitler. The public believes armed force should be used against all protestors and all those who take part in demonstrations should be immediately thrown out of their universities. It wants an even bigger wall, and the protestors and students at the other side of it.

And I want Marina now. Badly.

★

Karl-Heinz Kurras, sometimes known as Otto Bohl, and his Walther PPK 7.65 millimetre, in the shadows.

I know him.

We know him.

Karl-Heinz Kurras in the car park on Krumme Strasse, the crooked street, with his Walther PPK 7.65 millimetre. Department 1 PoPo in plain clothes, with a flat full of disordered documents relating to West Berlin security, gathered intelligence and defectors. His disordered files for his courier at the Zoo. His file on the Stasi defector Bernd Ohnesorge amongst them. It's a very similar name.

Karl-Heinz Kurras with his miniature camera, his listening devices, his ammunition, his gulag paranoia, his traded guns, his deals. He saw knives all around him.

The pounding feet, the clatter of hooves on the cobbles, the sirens, the cannons of water, the shouts and the screams, the truncheons against metal, the truncheons against skulls, the thump of people falling. The grab gangs, in plain clothes, fox hunting. But Karl-Heinz Kurras, in plain clothes, saw only knives all around him, in the darkness of the crooked street.

Maoists with instructions from the Chinese Embassy. Communist layabouts under instruction from the East. Fornicating long-haired spies with a hotline straight to Moscow. And knives.

Coming for your food, coming for your water.

Karl-Heinz Kurras with torn loyalties, the wild card, hearing voices. Knives in the hands of the students being beaten, knives in the hands of the onlookers, in the hand of Benno Ohnesorg. And they were surrounding him, moving towards him.

One of the students stabbed a copper. Imagine? Just walked straight up and stuck the knife in his chest.

His brain rotted, pulling out his Walther PPK 7.65 millimetre and pointing it at the head of Benno Ohnesorg. Benno Ohnesorg who was being beaten to the ground by fellow officers.

'What's your name?' he demanded.

'Ohnesorg.'

With his listening devices, his ammunition, Karl-Heinz Kurras had made a file on a Stasi defector.

And on the crooked street, when they were closing in with their knives it was an easy mistake to make. The names were almost identical.

The hand of Karl-Heinz Kurras did not shake. He fired a warning shot, two warning shots, a warning shot and an accidental shot. Who knows?

A fatal shot.

Benno Ohnesorg – who was no relation to Bernd Ohnesorge, but how could you be expected to know? – was wearing a red shirt like Fritz Teufel that night. And he fell instantly to the concrete floor of the car park.

There was a long silence, before one of his colleagues said:

'Are you crazy? Shooting here?'

Berlin's mayor Heinrich Albertz has no doubt about it being self-defence, since an order for the use of firearms was not given.

Does this look like everything's under control?

9. JULY 6th 1967

Who's on trial here today?

They are hearing something else again, these spoiled children of the economic miracle, as they fidget and chatter now, smile and wave and cheer and sigh in the public seats of the Moabit courtroom.

June was a long month.

In their black armbands, small cars trailing black flags and streamers, they followed the coffin of Benno Ohnesorg to his home town of Hannover, given free passage through the German Democratic Republic, with young boys in uniform waving down from the hills. No tolls, no queues. A guard of honour at the cemetery. Because the German Democratic Republic not only cares for its people, but does everything thoroughly. And the entire world welcomes that.

They have heard about the new incidents in West Germany, in Hannover, but also spontaneously, in Munich and Frankfurt, in Göttigen and Freiburg too. A new community is coming together – they have all followed Benno's coffin to logical conclusions, however separate, however different. They're a community in that, a community in their grief and anger and surprise and hurt. A new community ready to cut the cord.

In Hannover, at a congress attended by five thousand students the day after the funeral, Rudi Dutschke spoke of the ban slapped on a coming demonstration in West Berlin.

The time for observing such rules was now over, he appeared to be suggesting – the starting point of real change would be in a deliberate breach of such rules, a new strategy of provocation.

Rudi Dutschke – a refugee from the East and a conscientious

objector, allowed to study in West Berlin thanks to its master, the USA.

Now declaring some kind of war.

That Dutschke lad for one, wants to stop shooting his mouth off.

Later, he spoke to certain newspapers of his new vision for West Berlin – as a free city with open borders, with both East and West Germans at complete liberty to move within and through it. Fuelled by the production of corporations from both the East and the West. A city with individuals directly elected in all areas of social life. A city based on a new sense of communities.

Utopian Socialism. A democracy that would be a role model not just for West and East Germany, but for the world.

As if.

And elsewhere, on the last day of the war in the Middle East, Axel Springer spoke too, of reunified Jerusalem as a different example of a model democracy for Berlin.

Axel Cäsar Springer, champion of the free economy which provides him with his monopoly on information. Supporter of our vital transatlantic alliance and solidarity with the United States. Promoter of the vital rights of the State of Israel. Freemason. Grand Orient.

June 10th marked the end of the Six Day War after Israel had completed its final offensive in the Golan Heights. It seized the Gaza Strip, the Sinai Peninsula, the West Bank of the Jordan River and the Golan Heights, tripling its territory and placing around a million Arabs under its direct control.

'Two and a half million Israelis have taught the world that you sometimes have to act for yourself and not wait for Big Brother,' said a Springer editorial. 'Will Europe ever understand this, or will the doves simply kneel down before the Communist tanks?'

Silent spores, spooling out from the Springer Building – beacon of the Free West, slap bang up against the Wall – creeping under doorways and through open windows, shape-shifting.

In the event, the demonstration in Berlin passed without incident.

Leaflets rained down on the crowds from the Europa Centre below the revolving Mercedes star. Choreographed students in a line, Gudrun Ensslin amongst them, did a synchronised dance with letters on both sides of their shirts. Subliminal protest, innocent and trusting despite the hurt and uncertainty and sense of betrayal. Resign, Albertz.

Albertz has finally seen sense and given us the go ahead to get tough. Not that he'll be commanding the action, he'll be lording it with the toffs listening to the fucking opera.

★

The spoiled children of the economic miracle in the Moabit today know, too, that the case they are here to witness has little to do with a burning department store in Brussels.

The members and supporters of the first of the new communities have become increasingly intent on acts of resistance, it is claimed. Their actions are no longer limited to the university campuses, but spill out onto the streets as their themes become ever broader. They are fuelling argument and dissent, but also drawing innocent bystanders into their protests, interfering with traffic, causing congestion. Tempers are raised, fistfights break out wherever they go.

The spoiled children see Rainer blowing bubbles on the stairs of the courtroom, the ushers and guards marching past, oblivious to this tramp, this effeminate bum. Blowing bubbles from tubes pocketed in toy shops by Dieter Kunzelmann and intended for his two young children, Grisha and Nessim. Who have been deposited by their Dutch mother at the first of the new communities on the corner of Kaiser-Friedrich Street. Products of free love. Products of the shattering of the nuclear family.

Something's happening now isn't it? It's hard to explain, just that something feels exciting and good.

Marina sits beside me in the Moabit courtroom, and today I am something else too. I'm clean shaven and in the only suit I possess, and with a clean shirt under it. Marina is happening to me and it feels exciting and good.

So who's on trial here today?

In the Moabit courtroom, the guilty are arranged according to the level of their crimes – their complicity and involvement – a symbolic pyramid of ascending shame.

To the side, at eye level, are the penitent reporters with their pens and pads, in detention, doing lines, in their cheap overcoats, with their nicotine moustaches, scoured beerhall complexions and Springer stains. Smelling the guillotine in the air, thinking of heads on sticks. Here to scribble down accounts of their own misdeeds.

Still at eye level with the students are the faceless ushers, the ghostwalkers who've forgotten everything – only doing their jobs, just small cogs in the machinery of justice, simply obeying orders as always. And the guards. Who stop us from forgetting like we should. Two guards lead in Fritz Teufel direct from his barred cell, to wild applause and the angry hammering of a gavel from up high.

Fritz the Devil, leader of a group which wounded two officers with stones, barefoot and in a bright red shirt, attempting to sit in the middle of the road, dragged up and carried away to his present place of residence, behind the iron slats, on the wooden crib with the lice and the rats and the barked commands of other small cogs. In the machinery of justice, listening to the echoes along corridors of damp stone.

And Karl-Heinz Kurras, sometimes known as Otto Bohl, already acquitted.

Resting back home, relieved of his Walther PPK 7.65 millimetre. At leisure in his disordered flat full of other guns and disordered documents relating to West Berlin security. Gathering intelligence on defectors, his files for his courier at the Zoo.

Erich Duensing too, West Berlin's chief of police, has embarked on a long holiday.

They are hearing something else, the young spectators.

On a platform raised above them like a stage are the lawyers and clerks in their punishing uniforms, itchy wigs, tight collars and coarse gowns. With their old books and files, their sacred texts passed down from one generation of leaders to the next. Books of order and authority, essence of the machinery of the state. The elevated tier.

Raised higher still, below the flags and plaques, on the high chair below the emblem of the spread eagle, is Judge Schwerdtner, who opens proceedings by requesting an adjournment for the old books and files to be further consulted.

Horst Mahler, who is versed in their brutal language and customs, can only object strongly on behalf of Rainer and Fritz.

Horst Mahler – stamped in the mould of the hierarchical Order of the secular priesthood, in his dark uniform, with his thinning hair, his heavy framed glasses. Older than me, and old enough to know the difference between children's games and the real world. Who's taken an interest in my own case too – *everybody does a little pilfering, that's understood, perks of the trade* – but not quite as diligently as I've taken an interest in his.

Horst Mahler with his tight collar and widow's peak – an unlikely defender of the little man. A Robin Hood versed in the brutal language and customs? Or an entirely different animal? How deep, I wonder, do his sympathies lie? Father committed suicide at the end of the war, life without his Führer being unbearable. Not exactly a walking advertisement for the nuclear family, then.

So now, the penitent press, from their bench of shame, look at Rainer Langhans and Fritz the Devil and scribble. Do their lines, sit their detentions. Scribble about not only a burning building in Brussels, but an inferno of hair, an explosion of new colour, flower power blowing into West Berlin on a California breeze – a pink jacket, free love, a red Chairman Mao pin, Jesus sandals, dirty jeans, beards and disrespect and the decline of civilisation. The reporters smell the fear of the new, the guillotine in the air, the heads on sticks.

And they scribble in their margins:

Rainer Langhans.
Bastard darkie.
Darkie woman, jungle bunny.
An earring, Jesus sandals.
Puff.
Little brainy glasses.
Fucking disgrace.
Army would sort him out.

Fritz Teufel.
Thief.
The guerrilla of fun.
Bearded stone thrower.
Myopic gibberish talker.
Pied Piper of anarchy.
Deflowerer of German Maidens.
Bitten by the snake of rebellion.
Puff.
Fucking disgrace.
Army wouldn't take him.

Seven men and three women all living together, getting to know each other. Breaking down the barriers between themselves.

Sex.

'The guys want to watch the girls taking a shit.'

Rainer and Fritz smile and wave beatifically. They are both happy to talk about their backgrounds and beliefs.

Rainer admits he volunteered as an officer cadet, but found it boring, and that plenty of the people he mixes with came to Berlin to escape similar destinies.

Fritz suggests to them he was a bit lazy – perhaps to try and assuage the embarrassment of his accusers a little. His shortsightedness saved him from the draft, he shrugs, and he was attracted to the big city from the little town of Ludwigsburg near Stuttgart – home, since 1958, of the Central Office of the State of Justice to investigate Nazi crimes – where his father worked for the local tax office.

Quite openly, he volunteers to the court his earlier, vague ambition of becoming a humorous writer. Of the sadness that political awareness has given him. Of losing his humour and the sorrow he feels at knowing that for his parents, such awareness is not possible, after all they experienced.

He speaks, too, of the need to eventually abolish property, and of how this can be achieved through the establishment of the new communities.

The lawyers bristle at his next suggestion, that they might be somehow complacent, a little self-satisfied – that having gassed Jews they are now selling weapons to Jews to kill Arabs, in the name of a higher democracy.

Fritz shrugs again. Perhaps – his body language suggests – he's being a bit harsh. They hate this. The old hate.

They can't be expected to understand such things. Fritz nods at them in sympathy, invites them to visit the first of the new communities once they finally understand the need for the great refusal.

Nobody else, of course, is willing to supply any details of their own pasts. Why confess? Only understandable, given the circumstances.

The journalists look down at their notebooks, the ushers and guards at their shoes, the lawyers and clerks at the sacred texts. Judge Schwerdtner at his fingernails.

What is there to be afraid of? they are all asking themselves. Where is it coming from? this fear, they wonder.

It depends where you're standing, what your crimes are.

And to supplement the sacred books, specialists are invited to take the stage.

Doctor Jacob Taubes, an Austrian-born philosophy professor, now a US citizen, talks of the surrealist André Breton imagining himself walking down Parisian streets with pistols in each fist, ridding the world forever of painters and sculptors and composers. No more art, Breton demanded, back in 1920, Taubes tells the court. No religion, was what he wanted, no armies, no police. No Republicans and no Royalists. No Bolsheviks and no Nazis. Nothing. Pistols in each fist, Breton imagined himself annihilating all traces of an external world of thought.

There is nothing with which it is so dangerous to take liberties as liberty itself, Taubes reminds the court, quoting Breton again. To reduce the imagination to a state of slavery – even though it would mean the elimination of what is commonly called happiness – is to betray all sense of absolute justice.

Could Breton make these remarks in West Berlin in 1967, Taubes asks the court, and escape being labelled a terrorist?

Werner Richter, head of the esteemed collection of left-wing writers, Group 47, approaches the problem from a different angle.

The leaflet about the Brussels fire, he suggests, is pompous, stupid, arrogant and tasteless. An insult to revolutionary aspirations.

Rainer grins and waves.

Fritz smirks.

Finally, Günter Grass, arguably the most famous member of Group 47, author of *The Tin Drum* and neighbour of Uwe Johnson on Niedstrasse in Friedenau, takes the stand.

'I do not want this court to consider the output of some confused, adolescent boys – if already a bit too old to be considered such – to be taken seriously as a call for arson,' he says, unlit pipe in his fist.

Another refugee, from Danzig. Believer in the Willy Brandt snail's pace of reform. Brandt, the Coalition's Foreign Minister, somehow, people sense, is open to new ideas, ready for change. Impeccable credentials as an anti-fascist. Grass, meanwhile, missed the Nazi draft by a whisker, is his story.

'This fanatical document says a lot about the insanity of their situation in the cause of new communities,' he tells the court.

If fires erupt in the near future, if barracks blow up somewhere, if the grandstands in a stadium collapse, don't be surprised.

Marina watches the proceedings intently. She's part of this now, too.

And sometimes, now, I find I forget. For a while.

Klaus and Lotte have new shoes. Lotte's scab has disappeared from her knee. Klaus has his new uniform and Lotte will start her piano lessons this week.

And sometimes I find I forget, for a while, such as this moment when, in the Moabit courtroom, Judge Schwerdtner shocks his audience by demanding psychiatric examinations.

On the raised platform heads are bowed now, the lawyers and clerks deep in their old books and files, their sacred texts passed down from one generation of leaders to the next, books of order and authority, essence of the machinery of the state. The elevated tier.

But Rainer and Fritz are extremely relaxed – virtually horizontal in the dock, as it happens – and suggest that psychiatric tests for all involved, even the judge himself, would be an agreeable and revealing aid to the proceedings. Perhaps intelligence tests too.

Every outcome has been rehearsed. This is another ball to run with, another paint bomb to throw. Another situation.

The journalists looking down at their notebooks, the ushers and guards at their shoes, the lawyers and clerks at the sacred texts, Judge Schwerdtner at his fingernails – naturally refuse to recognise the authority of their accusers.

The case is adjourned, Fritz dragged back to his cell in the former Gestapo detention centre, as the spoiled children of the economic miracle boo and jeer.

'Free Teufel,' they start to chant.

The ushers and the guards – only doing their jobs – ascend the triangle, seeking guidance.

'Free Teufel! Free the Devil!'

Stamping feet. A slow handclap.

'Free Teufel!'

Police, assembled along the sides of the court, in their peaked caps, inch forward.

The lawyers and clerks are impassive beneath their wigs. Black crows.

'Free Teufel!'

The stamping and chanting becomes more insistent. The small cogs in the machinery of justice start to move in from the sides.

Marina hugs me, takes my hand. I look at her bitten fingernails.

'It's not simple is it?' I say to her. 'Nothing's very simple at all, is it? I don't think you should keep holding my hand, really.'

She lets go, looks at me uncertainly, for a moment, but the remark doesn't seem to trouble her for long.

Soon we're outside, with Rainer and Dieter and Ulrich, Dagmar and Dorothea and the rest. Rudi Dutschke, a scarecrow in a baggy jumper, grinning. Horst Mahler looking awkward.

And Dieter leans across to Rainer, a mad glint in his eye, and says: 'You could have pushed it even further, after all we talked about.'

Dieter Kunzelmann, born 1938 on the anniversary of the storming of the Bastille. In Bamberg, a bank manager's son in a backward drinker's town. Passionately interested in himself. And all the fun of the fight.

Noted and filed.

Flashbulbs splutter, microphones thrust like goading spears, and they're even signing autographs. I tip my hat low over my eyes. There are famous writers, musicians and artists. There are factory girls and schoolchildren who've bunked off for the day to be here. And everybody's suddenly smiling and happy and not pressed flat by some ever-unspoken burden.

Rainer puts his hand around Marina's shoulder, shakes my hand again.

'We have to keep being faster,' he says, 'and more organised, and to have no fear. You can help us more than you think with these actions. We need you.'

And Marina's hand is in mine again, despite what I said. And right then, I think: It's not my fault Annalise, not really. We were tricked into it, don't you see? Tricked into thinking that's what it was all about, the only way of doing things?

The need for both men and women to develop freely in all areas of their lives. People should be free to explore and express every facet of their personalities... the intellectual, the political, the sexual. All institutions are derived from the oppressive character of the family and consequently, the small family is the cell that has to be shattered.

Because I'm already apologising, as if I can read the future.

10. JULY 6th 1967

Outside the Western, our entourage meets the postman with a fat sack – all mail for the occupants of the communal flat on the fourth floor.

Fan mail.

Dieter jokes with the postman, Marina flirts with him, tries on his hat. 'Wait a minute Mister Postman,' the girls sing, teasing him. Invite him in, tell him not to work so hard, to insist on better pay, or just pack it in. Not doing anything is much more fun, they giggle, pecking him on his beetroot-red cheeks.

Dieter and I haul the postbag up the stairs – it tips and tilts as if there's a body in it – the rest of them charging up behind us, chanting and laughing, the girls still singing the old Marvelettes song – Tamla Motown's first Number One – the boys trumpeting and grunting the theme tune to the US Western show, *Bonanza*. Young and fast and without fear, Rainer said. He's right.

We hurl the contents of the sack out onto the floor around the table.

Everyone cheers, adrenalin still pumping, imagining many other such symbolic victories to come.

We stare at it all for a minute – the massed longings of a generation that is hearing something else, out there in front of us. Confirmation that the messages between the lines are being read and understood. The possibilities, the new communities ready to come together.

Somebody puts on Frank Zappa. Angular jazz guitars and falsetto doo-wop. The room fills with crush and conversation and smoke. Someone passes me a beer.

And the talk, initially, is of this courtroom performance. What it means, and how to push it further. Of what messages it has sent out across the world, to those who are listening for them. Of other actions, of new and better actions to come.

A group of prominent SDS members, for instance, has been on hunger strike, to draw attention to the incarceration of Fritz. Rainer and Dieter find this extremely funny. Fritz is one of their own, but they're not going to starve for him. Not about to deny themselves a single crumb. It's the last thing he'd want. And they joke about Rudi Dutschke's approach to it all. Serious, earnest Rudi, the man of word and deed, the good Protestant, and the man of appetites – hiding sausages and bread rolls up his sleeves. The storming of a church too, and Rudi taking the pulpit. A Marxist Martin Luther. Looking for martyrdom, unable to laugh at himself, to laugh at it all. Which could well be what is required.

And the room is thick with many sources of laughter tonight. A laughter that is somehow being conveyed between the lines of the reports in Springer's papers. Contagious, generous, holding nothing sacred, merciless.

But I'm watching him here amongst them, Rudi. He's part of this, for all his seriousness – wants with all his heart to laugh and joke with these friends from the first of the new communities. Doesn't want to believe for a moment that you can defeat your enemies with laughter; with jokes and mockery. Can't buy in to their high-minded method of just taking the piss.

Noted and filed.

West German handwriting, as a rule, I note as I shuffle a clutch of envelopes, is spiky and insistent, claustrophobic, cramped. That from France often at a tight liquid slant. Letters from the UK bear voluptuous and loose words. Those from the USA are often entirely in capitals. Reflecting different degrees of freedom? Or as Fritz suggested, self-satisfaction, complacency?

I gaze at the envelopes, see patterns in the marks I never noticed before. Think of the letters the soldiers sent from their fronts, those that were sent back the other way. Those from in and out of the camps. The photographs of children, locks of hair. Letters scored with black lines on military orders. Letters torn open, sliced with knives. Like bodies in trenches. Sacks of letters thrown into incinerators, dropped into the sea. Letters started and torn up. The massed longings of generations, always hearing something else.

Mao, Che Guevara, Rosa Luxemburg on the walls. Rippled wallpaper, stained roof, growth around the skirting boards – you don't notice such things in a full room. And now the water runs, and the boiler is working. And I have the toolbox over with me, in any case.

Rainer brushes against me, talking to four people at once, but mostly to Rudi – an energy wave in his exhilaration, coming down from the excitement in court.

'It's like a new kind of currency,' I say to him, from the corner of my mouth.

He turns, and grins, arms pawing for his attention.

'The new currency of communication, Peter, it's waiting for us. You see, Rudi,' he turns, 'everybody's buying into it, those old ways are over. But we've got to get Fritz out somehow, that's the important thing. All actions have got to be directed to that.'

Pick up another handful of mail, thinking of what Kurt's man said:

Drugs are the new thing. Make people lose their inhibitions, feel free to say things they otherwise wouldn't. It's not like getting them pissed in the old days. There are all sorts of possibilities.

I feel detached now.

I've lost Marina somewhere in the crowd, take a reefer from my jacket, light it and pass it on.

Another new currency for them, another channel of communication. I see the girls examine it with curiosity, wrinkle their noses, boys trying to look knowledgeable. Turning on.

Snatches of a dozen different conversations wash around me – politics, art, music, from the haughty to the banal – a compartment in my brain logs the comments, puts them to a name, a personal history wherever possible, as I continue to examine the stamps.

'What we need is music made by non-musicians to make a utopia solid, a different world with different sounds...'

'But the Beatles are shit compared to the Stones...'

'The historical second front for Vietnam...'

'But there has to be focus, a point to the actions...'

'...in *Against the Murderous, Thieving Hordes of Peasants*...'

'...getting all those collectives together...'

Noted and filed.

Here in West Germany we are abandoned, unable to escape from a world of fairy tales. Our stamps, when not extolling the efficiency of Deutsche Post, its horn and lightning waves, have illustrations from the Brothers Grimm – Hansel and Gretel, the Wolf and the Seven Kids, The Frog Prince.

Frau Holle, covering little girls in gold and tar.

'Art that promises there is a way out of this society...'

'The Animals, that's the best band...'

'We have no money anyway, that's why we asked to be arrested, as a collective...'

'...violence as the Devil's work and called for the nobles to put down the rebels like mad dogs...'

'...they don't know what to do if it's not written down for them...'

'...the non-binding nature of an exclusive avant-garde...'

Noted and filed.

I'm lost – to all extents and purposes, to anyone who may be watching me back – in the details of the stamps, their delicacy, their infinite promise of a united world, of oceans that can be bridged and continents spanned. New communities.

I take out a second joint, light it and pass it to someone else. Its sweet scent starts to fill the room. The boys are nodding with authority now, the girls, still squinting, but starting to smile and relax. Turning on, like simple connections in a circuit. My circuit.

We are lost in the forest here in Berlin and the past is approaching. We are threading a trail of berries backwards, trying to avoid the inevitable, covering little girls in gold and tar.

Packages and letters from England, overloaded with images of the Queen, her castles, but also those celebrating radar, penicillin, the jet engine and television in shillings and pence. A country where even if you rebel against your parents, you aren't ashamed of their pasts.

What should we send back?

The music of the victors, in their language, being listened to. The music of winners, from countries ever so proud of themselves.

Actions. That's what we do. Not music, not art.

Frau Holle, covering little girls in gold and tar.

'It's like schlager, stupid music with stupid words and a stupid melody, which on the surface shouldn't be music at all, but its stupidity is political…'

'…rejected people guilty of the murder of Christ…'

'As Marcuse points out, liberated sexuality has nothing to do with promiscuity…'

'You men are all led by what's between your legs…'

Noted and filed.

From the US, thin airmail letters and others which have crossed the Atlantic more hopefully, on which the stamps are colour-coded, placing a value on achievement and status.

Thomas Jefferson, a cent and green. Frank Lloyd Wright two, dark-blue grey.

'…withdrawn tenderness from above, directly related to the movement of goods…'

'Stupidity is political…'

'Elvis Presley, he's schlager now…'

'Phallic symbols…'

'Well what about the Beatles then?'

'…civil disobedience as a potentially liberating source…'

Noted and filed.

'… taken his gun away and that's the extent of it…'

'It's like what Stockhausen's doing with sine wave generators and filters from the radio stations…'

'…violence in the highly industrialised cities…'

'…and as Rudi's said for ages now…'

Noted and filed.

George Washington five cents, blue. Roosevelt six cents, grey-brown.

'We need music that you hear in a different way, that breaks with the past completely. To escape the tyranny of rock and blues.'

Henry Ford, thirteen cents, brown. John F. Kennedy, twenty cents, brown.

★

'What's wrong with the blues?'

It's Marina, her voice cutting through. She's talking to Dieter and the guy I watched with Rainer from the car with Hahn and Engel on Niedstrasse.

Who I now know is called Andy.

Andy Baader. Loudmouth. Show-off.

Until recently ensconced in a damaging ménage à trois with a bohemian called Manfred and his wife Ello, painter of the Naïve School. Ello has a child to Baader. Huge apartment in Schönberg. Rub shoulders with art dealers and psychiatrists, lawyers, journalists. Baader's dark, good-looking, compelling. Once again he's dressed at odds with the rest of them, making no attempt to fit in. A tailored suit and starched white shirt. Slicked hair. Smooths down his hems, flicks at his collar. A dandy. Self-love.

Eyes a little glazed tonight, stumbling over his words.

Noted and filed.

And Eugene O'Neill, a dollar, dull purple.

'The blues,' Dieter laughs and shakes his fist at the roof. 'The fucking blues. When will us slaves be free of it?'

Andy looks at Marina with disdain, rolls his eyes and makes a pistol gesture at his head, playing to his audience.

The room goes quiet, everyone sensing confrontation, a sudden, tangible undercurrent in my sweet smoke and the record in the player stuck, dragging on the end groove.

And then he does a curious thing, this Baader – takes out a small make-up compact and starts to apply mascara to his eyes. Without, he seems to want to demonstrate, the slightest hint of self-consciousness. Camp.

Noted and filed.

Here's someone they can use, someone who really doesn't give a fuck. An actor. A charlatan. A potential liability. But such a feminine thing. It's truly frightening.

I picture him doing this in the beerhalls, waiting for a reaction from the men in the vests, with their belts strapped to the rails – the ex-soldiers and the ex-sailors, the plasterers and the painters and the brickies. Heavy belts holding up their guts, the metalworkers and the hod carriers with their tattoos and all the old hate. The old, old hate.

Noted and filed.

'The English groups who play the blues are simply stealing their music from the American blacks,' Baader sneers. 'It's just another form of exploitation. And ironic. A music which originated from the slaves, from the cotton pickers on the plantations, taken away to make even more profit for the fascists.'

Gudrun Ensslin, I notice, is staring at him with something like awe, but right now he only has eyes for Marina.

'All rich musicians,' Dieter declares now, animated, eyes rolling with glee, not wanting to be overshadowed, 'especially English ones – oh yes, most especially them – are parasites and failures, given the opportunity to do great things but opting for comforts and distractions.'

He's fidgeting with a toy kaleidoscope, oblivious to his small son Nessim around his ankles, pleading for it.

'Like demanding children on a school stage,' he rails. 'All these entertainers will be taken out into the street and shot when the time is right, and their money donated to the fight against the Imperialist Repressors in Vietnam. This is the logical conclusion of understanding your readings of Marx and Mao.'

Dope-tight grins on faces, watching this performance now.

'What about Jimi Hendrix?' Marina asks, incredulously.

Andy grabs her by the wrist and looks into her eyes.

'Yes, even him, that Uncle Tom – why isn't he with the Panthers anyway? And what do the Viet Cong care about the blues music?'

Dieter puts a calming arm on his shoulder. Marina stares at him.

'Get off.'

He lets go of her wrist, sashays away from her.

'There can be no heroes anymore,' he shouts, searching for eye contact in the crowd that's inching back around him. 'It's all shit. Destroy it all and start again…'

I pull another rolled joint from my pocket, light it and walk across to him.

Eye contact.

'Here,' I say, grabbing his wrist the way he did hers, turning him around to a halt.

He grins. A knowing sneer.

I lean in close.

'If you want to do proper actions, we should talk,' I say, out of earshot of everyone else. 'Something a little more, let's say, adventurous? Light up the Berlin sky?'

Raises his eyes.

'I have to go,' he says, passing the joint back, looking over my shoulder and staring into Marina's eyes as he backs away. Mocking, knowing.

Slams the door behind him, the addled room breathes a sigh. A connection.

'Who's that?' I ask Rainer.

'Oh, that's Andy. He's okay.'

'A crazy guy,' says Dieter. 'But you don't want to take him too seriously.'

'He's an arsehole, talks a bag of shit,' Marina says.

'Not really when you think it through,' says Rainer.

And it's all off again.

'Art and music are deceptions, pretty things to delude people, to make the ugliness underneath the surface acceptable...'

I look across at Marina. She smiles back at me.

Noted and filed.

11. AUGUST 9th 1967

As the long, hot summer stretches on, I keep things – a lot of things – under my hat.

I lie down beside my wife and I think about Marina.

I lay beside Annalise on nights when I'm there and we listen to each other breathe.

I no longer have any idea what she's really thinking, below the surface of her day-to-day preoccupations. I'm not sure I even care.

'Don't tell me about what you do,' she tells me, these days. 'I don't want to know anything.'

And her mother, on the other side of the Wall, far to the east. Who's not getting any younger, or any better, over there in her crumbling apartment where the electricity is always off and the shops out of bread.

Still pining for her only daughter and her grandchildren. For her husband too, who of course was a brave man, honest and hard working. Broken by quotas and guidelines and jealous neighbours with loose tongues. Who saw the inside of their cells and understood what might await him. Who was a bit too simple for that. Who shuddered at the length of the forms they pushed on him instead. Whose tools and machines were gradually stripped from his smallholding. Whose meagre crops were never enough to satisfy the needs of his collective. Who was accused of stubborn individuality and capitalist tendencies by jealous neighbours with loose tongues. Whose soil grew barren. Who eked his last years out on their coupons.

Because the German Democratic Republic not only cares for its people, but does everything thoroughly. And the entire world welcomes that.

Sometimes now, I just sleep in my suit on the sofa, the hat over my eyes.

I read the book Rainer gave me, again and again:

Advanced industrial society has created false needs, which have integrated individuals into the existing system of production and consumption, via mass media and industrial management. This results in a one-dimensional universe of thought and behaviour in which aptitude and the ability for critical thought and oppositional behaviour are withering away.

A great refusal is the only adequate opposition to these all-encompassing methods of control.

Klaus and Lotte sleep on their bunks.

Klaus has been fighting, his mother informs me.

'The father came round.'

'Tell him I'll show him what a real hiding is if he bothers you again. Drop him in the Landwehr Canal.'

'You'll have to talk to Klaus, he's going off the rails I think.'

'I will, I will. But you worry too much. All kids fight. It's part of growing up.'

'He keeps things to himself.'

'That too. All part of it. What do you expect?'

'Like you.'

'I'll sort it out.'

I lie down beside my wife and I think about Marina.

'But when? You're never here to do it. And Lotte's suddenly so quiet, too. Why can't you be here for us more?'

Because I can't argue with this, I say nothing, and the silence grows long again.

★

I leave before they wake up, go and pick up some hardboard and nails, insulating tape and detonators.

My new second home is on the corner of Kaiser-Friedrich Street as the campaign to free Fritz Teufel intensifies.

The weather warms up and the days stretch out. For the students, it's the time for bonfires and barbecues, for swimming in the Schlachtensee, sunbathing on the university lawn, and running from the bulls in their riot gear.

The student population of the Free University of Berlin starts to thin out, the lucky ones off to holiday with their families and friends – in the mountains of Fichtelgebirge or the forests of Sauerland, maybe even Rimini. It's a chance to study, of course, and Marina stays away, burying her head in the medical textbooks. But for the residents and many of the friends of the first new community, things are past that.

On the hot cobbles, the demands for decisive action are growing ever louder. They come from above and below, from the street and the closed rooms, from the East and from the West, from gleeful, mad-eyed Dieter, from thoughtful, wavering Rudi, from sober Horst Mahler and from Kurt's man, and those above him.

On the trams, the local men smoke into their fists behind newspapers and women struggle handbags down. The BePo, the KriPo, the PoPo and the SchuPo on the Ku'damm. The men in bare rooms with wire taps and those making clandestine plans. And the leaders, behind closed doors referring to the old books and files.

And on the fourth floor of the communal block on the corner of Kaiser-Friedrich Street, people come and go as they please now, the young and the fast and the fearless. The door is always open.

And we're here again today, back for more. Another action, a happening, a celebration for which meticulous plans have been laid.

Today they plan to celebrate the death of West Berlin MP and newspaperman Paul Löbe, for whose funeral most of West Germany's dignitaries will be in town. Löbe who was arrested in '33 by the Nazis and again in '44 following the attempted assassination of Hitler. Löbe who for some reason is now deemed as tainted as the rest and fair game.

The conversation which resulted in the decision for this dubious action went something like this – although who said what is not really worth noting, not anymore:

'Taking the festivals where we can get them.'

'A fancy dress parade.'

'What's Löbe ever done wrong?'

'It's nothing to do with him.'

'He's the poor sod who just died.'

'It's the pomp and ceremony we want to draw attention to. Doesn't matter who it is. The bourgeois piety. Make it all look ridiculous.'

'The nauseous way they all pretend to give a shit and the continuation of traditions that should have ended.'

'Hiding behind grief as a pretext for a show of authority.'

'An excuse to put on their swords.'

'Strictly ceremonial, of course.'

'Nobody gave a monkey's when they put him in a camp. He only survived the war because he was a crony of Göring's.'

'It's pretty stupid in any case, celebrating somebody's ashes being blown up a chimney,' I said, finally.

At which they all burst out laughing.

'What?'

'Don't you realise what that implies?' Ulrich protested. 'Bodies and chimneys? You can't say that.'

'So now there are things you can't say?' I said. 'Who says so? I think you'll find it's the same people you want to disrespect.'

And rushing to my defence was Andy Baader.

'He's right,' he said. 'Fuck them. We can say what we want. Fuck those old Nazis, you don't ask permission to declare war. And war's coming.'

Some were unhappy about it, naturally, but couldn't dodge the logic, and the off-set litho was cranked into action once more.

We hope Paul Löbe won't be the last up the chimney, our new leaflets declare, and that other notable dignitaries will follow him.

The boards I brought along have been fashioned into a passable coffin, draped in black cloth embroidered with the slogan 'Supreme Court Justice' on the lid. Rainer wears a petticoat and construction worker's helmet decked with American flags.

'Taking the festivals where we can get them.'

Manfred Henkel, artist husband of Andy's lover, is also in a dress.

'A fancy dress parade.'

Dieter's in a nightgown, a bib hung around his neck, embroidered with the slogan 'Always in Berlin'.

'Make it all look ridiculous.'

Andy is not interested in dressing up – always adheres to his own very personal and diligent dress code – but he's impressed with the equipment; the two heavy-duty smoke bombs, the electric timer and automatic ignition triggers. Gudrun touches them all and swoons at him.

After our initial antagonism, we appear to be becoming friends me and Andy – especially since he suddenly only has eyes for Gudrun.

The two of them plan to install the devices in the surviving bell tower of the bombed-out Ceremonial Church on the Ku'damm, as Löbe's mournful procession files into the new church beside it.

We haul the coffin down the four floors and into the rented Fiat van, crammed full of the young and the fast and the fearless, all banging on pot lids with wooden spoons. An action, what it's all about. Rainer drives us to the Schöneberg City Hall.

The crowds are gathered outside, straight-backed lines of police salute as the mourners file in. Ceremonial chains and sashes. Top hats and long coats. Flags at half-mast. Incense swirled. The strains of a hymn can be heard from inside. The institutional. The ingrained. Terribly pious and respectful.

And as the six pantomime pallbearers from the first of the new communities move into the crowd bearing their own body, the police instantly intercept, spurred on by the crowd.

'Never have been allowed under Hitler!'

Some pushing and pulling and truncheons are raised again.

'Get them to camps!'

In the jostling, the coffin, still held aloft, tips to its side and bursts open.

'Throw them over the other side in body bags.'

And out pops Dieter, a manic figure with a long straggly beard in a nightgown, hurling handfuls of leaflets up into the air above the crowd.

Contagious, generous, holding nothing sacred, merciless.

'Gas them!'

I quietly take my leave before the arrests begin.

★

Marina is waiting for me in the Kranzler on the Ku'damm, sipping hot chocolate, surrounded by the good shoppers. Her smile of acknowledgement is tight and brief.

I whistle as I make my order, joke with the ladies behind the counter, still light-headed.

'You really missed something today,' I whisper to Marina as I sit down opposite her. 'Something really special. Best so far, I think.'

Another tight, brief smile. She continues carefully making notes with a fountain pen into a spiral-bound book as I talk. I feel betrayed, wanting an audience, wanting admiration and respect. Her admiration.

Her handwriting, I notice, is tiny and precise, no angular insistence. Her hair is pushed back behind an Alice band and she wears a sleeveless navy smock dress. No make-up, which makes her look even younger than she usually does.

Her response, though, isn't what I was expecting. In fact, as I pile on the details, elaborating as appropriate, her lack of enthusiasm causes me to stall and it all suddenly starts to sound a little ridiculous. My temples start to pound.

'So they've arrested them all again?' she deigns to say, finally, looking up and across at me.

Her pale blue eyes.

'Pretty much, I think,' I say. 'Dieter and Rainer and Ulrich certainly. Andy and Gudrun were over at the other side of the crowd.'

'Doing what?'

I shrug.

'Not sure.'

Her bare arms.

'It was so funny though, Rainer and Dieter and Manny were all dressed as women.'

'That's funny is it? Women are just a joke, is that it?'

Her lovely lips, her tiny, even teeth. Looking younger than she should do.

And what do we do with innocence and optimism here? What's it for?

'I don't get it,' she says.

'Don't get what?'

'The whole thing. Haven't you heard the latest from the United States? Riots in fifty cities? Twenty-seven people shot dead by the National Guard in Newark, another forty-three killed in Detroit and thousands injured? That's something to get angry about. I would understand protest about that. It makes your action seem rather trivial, don't you think? Selfish even. Small minded and mean spirited? What was it supposed to prove?'

'Well,' I try, 'the idea was to, you know, expose the stupidity of it all.'

My words sound hollow, useless.

'Of a funeral?'

'The machinations of the state…'

'A funeral? And this?'

She slides one of our leaflets out from her notebook.

'Celebrate Paul Löbe *going up the chimney… bury a few smart corpses that are slowly stinking to high heaven…* Whose stupid idea was that exactly? Who would write such things?'

'I don't know, maybe Rainer or Ulrich I guess.'

'Why would you take anyone who wrote such things seriously? It's just undermining everything the SDS is trying to achieve. The papers can laugh at it, and then nothing gets taken seriously.'

A silence hangs. Her lovely lips, her tiny, even teeth.

'Your reaction's a bit bourgeois, if you don't mind me saying,' I try, eventually.

She laughs, shakes her head.

'Nothing bourgeois about it, unless it's bourgeois to be getting an education now? And to want to take this society forward? To want to better yourself, do good things? Löbe was a victim, it's pretty simple. Attack the institutions by all means, but at least identify the right targets, and know what you're attacking them for.'

I'm smiling at her and my head's somewhere else.

That dress, her hair pushed back behind that Alice band.

'Like what then?'

'Marriage, for instance. That's one institution that needs examining. To honour and obey? Where's the equality in that, hmm? Being given away by a man to another man. Being *given away*? Like property?'

Women don't talk to men like this. Not here. But I decide to be reasonable.

'Well I don't think men are often that keen on the idea themselves,' I try. 'It's what most women want, that's all.'

Her eyes blaze.

'Really? You don't think it's some convenient male arrangement? Procreate, spread the seed, bring up more men to kill other men. Get a grateful cleaner into the bargain?'

'Whoa…'

My fist slams down on the table. Heads are turning. But women don't talk to men like this.

What would Hahn do; what would real men do? The men who represent our history, who shaped it all? Would Kurt's man even spare her life?

97

Her perfect bitten nails, that nervous tic in her eye. Her bee-stung bottom lip.

Take her out and rape her.

That's what they'd do, Kurt's man, Hahn, all the others.

It's what this city was built on.

What does that make me then?

Tense? Yes it is. It's always tense here.

'It's always the men isn't it, doing these actions?' she's saying now. 'All this talk about a new way of living but it's not really serious… it's like Antje says…'

'I wouldn't listen too much to Antje,' I protest.

'No, you wouldn't would you? Stop smirking like that, I'm not stupid and I won't put up with being treated as if I am.'

She gets up to leave.

I grab her arm and have a flash of that scene with Andy Baader.

'If you want to do proper actions, we should talk.'

Marina sits back down, closes her book.

'Nobody listens to any of us. What women want.'

'Oh, we know what you all want,' I try again, knowing there's a paralysed grin on my face now.

What do men want? What do real men do?

She stares me down.

'All boys together. That's what it's about, all this. The sons of the fathers, wanting to prove something.'

She's out of sorts today, that's all it is. Too much pressure, too many books. Could be her time of the month, I think. That's what Hahn and the rest would say anyway. It's making me out of sorts too, but in a different way.

'I'm getting sick of it all,' she says. 'Listening to all of them. All of you. This idea about confrontation, about the old guys being Nazis and beyond excuse. It's just not enough. They did what they did then, and now they're here. I don't see how Marx would have helped. All this talk and endless talk and now these stupid actions.'

I could take her away from it, I think. We could leave Berlin.

Take her out and rape her. That's what men do. It's what this city was built on.

I could take her away from here, we could get out. Go to France, to England, or maybe somewhere more simple, Asia, Africa, where it's cheap.

But she's going to be a doctor. Heal people, make them well.

That dress, her hair pushed back behind that Alice band. That seriousness.

What do you do with innocence and optimism? What's it for? You rape it, defile it, destroy it. There's no space for it here.

And part of her would acquiesce, I think. Part of her would shrug and submit. And expect it here.

Because we are the protectors, us men, and we stay alert by taking up weapons, taking revenge, or just taking because we can.

But some part of me wants something more, I realise. It's a chink of light.

I'm not them. This is not a war. We are breaking with that history, some of us, or trying to. I didn't get it up to now. I don't have to be part of that old, old hate. Not anymore.

I push my arm across the table, and hold her hand.

'I'm sorry,' I tell her, but my face still feels plastic. 'Really sorry. All of these ideas are a bit new for me. It's not as if I've read all those books you all talk about.'

She smiles. Tight, brief, but she smiles.

And suddenly I realise I don't have to be like them at all, and what I can be, if I choose. And the muscles in my face relax.

12. AUGUST 12th 1967

A new sign, spray-painted on a bedsheet, is draped from the window of the fourth floor of the communal building on the corner of Kaiser-Friedrich Street looking over Stuttgarter Place:
'NOW THE DEVIL IS FREE'

Fritz walked from the Moabit on Thursday, the day after the funeral. On the Ku'damm, he and his colleagues are once again at liberty to taunt the citizens of West Berlin as they go about filling up their abundant leisure time with pointless consumerism. Fritz and his colleagues goading them, not letting them settle. Stirring up a hornet's nest.

But my business today is elsewhere, on the other side.

Alexanderplatz, like most of Mitte, is a building site.

The architects of the German Democratic Republic have a golden vision for their future showcase. All is fervent activity – cranes and cement mixers, lines of brickies and baton teams of carriers. From the window of the small beige-panelled room I see tiny figures abseiling down the sides of the new television tower with their drills and spanners. For the dedicated comrades of the German Democratic Republic there is no time for bars and street fights.

Plan, work and govern together, the slogans in every train station suggest. No mistakes – are you doing your part? they ask. Quality begins with thought, they say, even as they seek to take away the need to think about anything.

Kurt's man gestures at the scene.

'What is scientific socialism without the workers' movement?' he asks, seemingly in party line mode too. 'I'll tell you. A useless compass that would only rust and be thrown overboard. And what's the workers' movement without socialism? A ship without a compass. Bring them together… But you know this. We care for our people, listen to all of our people.'

He draws down the blinds to muffle the drills.

'The revolution in the West, if it is to have any chance of succeeding, must be armed, that's always been a given,' he says. 'Rudi Dutschke must know that. Horst Mahler must know that. The students – if that's what you call them, the APO in any case – have replaced the workers as the new proletariat. Have you heard that said, Peter?'

He grins at my silence.

'You know when not to speak and that's good, but you're probably wondering about Kurras in any case, I imagine?'

Karl-Heinz Kurras, sometimes known as Otto Bohl, and his Walther PPK 7.65 millimetre, in the shadows.

We know him.

'Small fish in a big pond. There's nothing on him, not a shred to be found in files anywhere,' Kurt's man tells me. 'We're certain of that. It's unfortunate, of course it is, but things could certainly have been worse. Albertz is holding on by his fingernails now, and starting to sound like Rudi Dutschke himself, with all this talk of a free Berlin.'

A free city with open borders, with both East and West Germans at complete liberty to move within and through it. A city with individuals directly elected in all areas of social life. A city based on a new sense of communities. As if.

'And as for your new friends,' he continues, 'it looks to me as if all this attention they're receiving is not entirely having the desired effect. Have you noticed a change in the tone?'

I tell him all I know, or all I want him to know.

'You're good Peter, very good,' Kurt's man tells me. 'We're going to look after you, see if we don't. And you'll be glad we did in the long term, believe me.'

I stare out of the window over Alexanderplatz. Tiny figures

abseiling down the sides of the new television tower. Progress. The Socialist Future.

I should go home, back to Annalise, back to the kids.

But it's too late for that now.

'Something good will happen for you very soon,' Kurt's man says. 'I won't say any more now. But when it happens, you'll realise that we made it happen, because we look after our people.'

*

At my new second home above the Western, there has been much celebration. Fritz is free, but nowhere to be seen tonight.

Marina and I are the last remaining guests. Dieter has followed a group out into the night, looking for more action.

Rippled wallpaper, the stained ceiling, the growth around the skirting boards.

Just me and her and Rainer and Antje, who I know little about, as yet.

It's always the men isn't it, doing these actions? All this talk about a new way of living but it's not really serious… it's like Antje says.

And Ulrich, in a far corner, reading another book, eyes shielded by his long fringe.

Confessions of a Beautiful Mind, Goethe.

We sit around talking and smoking, sinking into the battered sofas surrounded by the boxes of leaflets and books.

Mao, Che Guevara and Rosa Luxemburg stare down from the shadows. Rain starts to lash against the windows. The radio's tuned in to some big band music. It's warm, quiet. Nobody can be bothered putting records on. The booze has run out long ago, and there's no milk. We drink black tea.

Rainer, quite stoned now, talks of his childhood. Life at a strange school run by monks in the hush of the countryside. And of his family. His father, Hartwig – a man of brilliant businesses doomed to fail, just like his love affairs and his fast cars. Latin good looks which obliged him more than once, in the old, dark days, to prove his Aryan credentials to the black crows. But an enthusiast for a future of possibilities and, especially, an early proponent of the possibilities of film and moving media.

'It's all there, this little kid that I was, that's what's unusual,' Rainer says. 'I have the proof of the first steps I ever took. My childhood exists outside me on these films, lying on beds, playing in the garden. It's all on film, everything. That's why the media is so important.'

'What do you think it means?' Marina asks, taking a sip from a mug and then deliberately laying back beside me, resting her head against my shoulder now.

Some part of me wanted something more with Marina. And I think I'm glad about that now. In the Kranzler, a black screen was coming down over a bright scene and I pushed out my arm to stop it across the table, and held her hand.

Thinking about what men, real men who shape history, have been brought up to do, as they protect and take revenge.

One hundred thousand women raped here, in 1945.

I should go home, back to Annalise, back to the kids.

'You have something that so far, very few people on the planet have,' Marina tells Rainer. 'Not even the kings and queens of the past, the emperors – in fact hardly anybody in history has such documentation. What about all those lives that were lived that have never been documented in any way?'

One hundred thousand women raped. No film.

'Where's the film of Jesus, of Buddha or Mohammed?' Marina is saying. 'Nobody before this century has ever lived their life on film.'

'There are no films of Hitler, even, at the age of two,' Rainer says, puzzled. 'My childhood could live in the collective memory much longer than his. In theory, you understand. It's an extension somehow of what we currently consider to be our mortality.'

'Why is it important for your existence to be documented then?' Antje asks.

'I haven't quite figured that out yet,' Rainer admits. 'I'm not saying it's important, it probably isn't. Just that it will come to be accepted.'

'But if everything is being documented, then we'd all be better protected,' Marina suggests. 'If everything's on film they can't get away with anything.'

'Someone is always watching over you,' Ulrich suggests, without looking up.

'Guardian angels,' Antje suggests as she builds another joint.

'Hardly,' Ulrich replies.

'Depends who's holding the camera, who's controlling it,' Rainer suggests. 'It has to be a two-way street. The media has the potential to free the population from manipulation. Whether it wants to or not. I really believe that. And not just because of what's happened to us. Look at Vietnam. How would anyone know what was going on if the media wasn't there? Compare it to the last war, when nobody in Charlottenburg would even know what was going on in Wedding, for instance.'

'I think you'll find we know very little about anything that's going on in a large part of this city,' Ulrich reminds him. 'There's a bloody big pile of concrete and razor wire and some very nasty looking men in uniforms with machine guns and dogs in front of the camera.'

'Spies,' I can't help myself saying. 'That's all it's about. Why would somebody be bothered taking the time to watch you if they didn't want to know what you know?'

Antje looks across at Marina. There's a nod of complicity between them.

'That's because men…' she begins.

'…always see things in terms of control and domination, and themselves as the centre of attention,' Marina adds. And the two lean across and chink mugs.

Here we go again, I think.

'I'm guessing that somehow it is more important, only I can't visualise exactly why yet, what it all means, except that I already live forever on that film as an infant,' Rainer says. 'Anyhow, as I was telling you – and it links in with what you just said Marina – my mother was constantly undermining the authoritarian nature of Hartwig, my father, with a wink, a shake of the head behind his back. Kind of in the way we use actions to make the authorities look stupid, to deflate them. They were chalk and cheese, but somehow a team. Though sometimes, it seemed my mother and us children were just tolerating him.'

'You should develop more theory about your childhood being documented, being filmed,' Marina says now. 'I think you're right that it's important.'

'What if everything's documented somewhere?' I hear myself saying.

Rainer leans up and grins at me.

'The new currency of communication, Peter,' he says. 'You said that.'

'I bet there's no film of Peter's childhood,' Marina replies. 'So where did you come from?' she asks, nudging me lazily in the ribs.

And so I tell them.

*

'Two pig's heads stuck on hooks, both grinning like the foolish, if generous, man I came to know as my father. That's the first thing I remember.

'Immediately after the war, he re-opened his butcher's shop. Not on Potsdamer Street where it was before, obviously,' I say. 'They flattened that. Moved over to Kreuzberg, found a place on Koch Street.'

'It's a wasteland now, Potsdamer,' Antje says.

'Why would he want to do that though?' Marina asks dreamily at my side. 'Start again?'

'That's what you have to do isn't it? What else is there? But it was what he knew, I suppose,' I tell her, 'the way he made a living. But I never asked him. Or what part he played in the things that went on. It just never came up, all that. Just wasn't talked about.'

'That's true,' Rainer says, arms folded behind his head, staring at the ceiling. 'And nothing much of it is on film.'

Antje is teasing his hair now.

Glenn Miller's Big Band is playing 'Little Brown Jug' on the radio, but of course nobody can be bothered to get up and switch it off.

We discuss photographs and how the characters in them are forever frozen in time.

'Like butterflies pinned into books,' Ulrich offers from the corner. 'What can they tell you? Frozen. But if you could watch them move, see their wings fluttering, you'd know what they did, what the point of them was…'

'Film's different.'

'Motion.'

'Actions…'

'I think I know how it's going to end,' Rainer declares. 'With a different kind of democracy, based on what people are watching. We'll all be watching each other, taking cues. And the watching will become what people do. More important than actions, more important than politics.'

'You better not tell Rudi or Dieter that,' Ulrich mumbles, without looking up from his book.

There's a pause as everyone tries to get their heads around these ideas.

'We should get a camera,' Rainer says. 'Make our own films…'

'You were telling us, Peter,' Marina says, finally, pats my hand.

'I wasn't going back to the orphanage,' I repeat. 'Not for anything. He wasn't, of course, my real father, but he took me in, without questioning anything. So how could I respond with my own questions? And I was too young to know how to explain.

'Meat was scarce for the first few years, but I think…'

'Little Brown Jug' farts along, but I let the silence hang.

'What?' Marina nudges me again.

'He carved up rats,' I say.

'You're joking.'

'There were worse things happening. And birds. Birds too. They caught them with slingshots and dumped them at our door to collect later.'

Rainer stares up at the ceiling. Antje is falling asleep now. Ulrich lost in his corner, in his book.

'I was maybe ten, or eleven, when meat started to hang on the hooks again. Glazed blue tiles and a little wooden counter, the shop had. And before that, small cuts wrapped in rags, unspeakable offal and cartridge shells in rows crammed with fat. And always terrible arguments between the desperate queues. There were worse things happening.'

I know I've got them. Everyone loves these poor little orphan details.

I tell them about my fictional father's eagerness to resume a career in cutting and hacking and slicing and stripping meat from bones, and rendering things down to nothing, at that very moment in time.

How it always seemed to rain back then, or be too cold, but not in the crisp and bright German way. Clothes were always too heavy and at the same time never warm enough. Damp. Like the England we had read about, as if they were visiting their weather on us too, after the bombs.

'My father had very distinctive hands,' I hear myself saying. 'The fingers, thick cut, slightly fleshy, the palms wide and smooth – patterned with scars and blemishes that bore witness to his trade. The soft but powerful hands possessed by all master butchers – soft on account of the animal fats and grease, and powerful, since they were constantly exercised in the daily practice of his craft. Even if they were well worn as he aged, they remained as sensitive as a surgeon's.'

'Or a blues guitarist,' Marina says. The twitch in her left eye. Her beautiful swollen bottom lip. 'They all seem to have beautiful hands if you've ever noticed. Is it still there?'

'What?'

'The butcher's shop? Is it still there?'

'I think so,' I say. 'I try and avoid going past. We haven't talked for years, me and him, and I can't really say it makes me unhappy.'

Marina sits up.

'Let's go see him then,' she says, 'me and you. Tomorrow.'

'Jesus, Marina...' I start to say, but she puts a finger to my lips and kisses me.

It's right, it's all wrong.

13. AUGUST 18th 1967

The conditional release of Fritz is soon seen as an unsatisfactory result for all of us, in not going far enough to establish his innocence without question.

The conditions imposed on him – reporting back to the police every couple of days, being refused a work permit – suggest he is still guilty of something. That they are not about to strike it from records or let it go anytime soon. The implication, as always, is that he should be grateful for his freedom – dispensed by the lawyers and clerks, with their old books and files, essence of the machinery of the state, the old ways.

Suggesting that Fritz should continue to show his contrition to the Black Crows.

We want something more from them.

Rainer, Dieter and the rest of the guys – even Rudi – are chomping at the bit to hit back somehow. At first, they attempt once again to taunt Berlin's shoppers with leaflets:

A risk is about in Berlin! Rather than report twice weekly to the judiciary as ordered, he romps around drunk on the Ku'damm. The Devil is running around freely, as if a policeman had never been stabbed. As if a department store had never burned down. As if Benno Ohnesorg were still alive. As if.

But the written word is somehow losing its potency, and Dieter starts to lose interest in the off-set litho in the back room of the apartment on Kaiser-Friedrich Street, talking increasingly of the need for confrontation.

Others, though, are hearing something else.

Fritz, meanwhile, is indeed, romping around drunk. Not only

that – he's bedding every young girl from the procession who come seeking him out from their schools or dead-end factories, at the dwelling-place of the first of the new communities. Free love has finally reached Berlin, ushered in by the most shy, articulate ex-convict, who suddenly reveals insatiable appetites.

The young girls love Fritz, love his serious gentleness, his optimism, his lack of respect and his merciless contempt for pomposity in any guise. They want all their men to be like him – free and not guilty, sensitive too, but fun most of all. Perhaps, more than anyone else, after his long and pointless incarceration, he's in a position to talk with more authority on the wonderful nature of freedom, of the absolute need for the great refusal.

And he never reports back once, so it's only a question of time before the paperwork is processed and a warrant for his re-arrest issued.

The only way then, it's decided, is to pre-empt the inevitable machinations of the fascist bureaucracy with another action.

And now the women are coming into their own, and suddenly Marina – spurred on, it has to be said, by Antje and the other girls – is getting into the fun of the potential provocation as well.

Antje has been a kindergarten teacher and has strong ideas about how important the formative experiences of kids are – the need to make children sensitive to recognising authoritarian behaviour and not to imitate or be intimidated by it. The early years set the scene for all that will follow.

And of course, as an orphan – spare a mark mister? – how can I disagree? And she and Marina both unconsciously glance over at me when they're discussing these things. They have this idea about starting their own socialist kindergarten – to enable as many politically active women as possible to become involved in as many spheres of Berlin's day-to-day structures as they can. To have an influence on every level.

And I can't argue with that really, and I have to say, I don't think about Annalise too much, when I'm here.

I'm free, for a little while. Society made me who I am, and society has to take responsibility from time to time.

Antje, who never stays at Kaiser-Friedrich Street, is also qualified in arts and crafts, and together the two of us put our practical skills into creating the most symbolic action yet – the driving of Fritz Teufel back to his rightful place in jail.

The idea is some kind of harsh medieval re-enactment of a public spectacle. Antje makes the costumes – long robes and pointed hats, with a nod to the Ku-Klux Klan and the Grand Inquisitors. I put together the cart in which Fritz will be dragged along by us all – an old railway trolley stripped of its heavy wheels and built up with plywood slats.

And today we wheel Fritz – dressed in rags in the cage, bound in papier mâché chains – down to the Moabit. He's laughing, indifferent.

And we demand his reincarceration, justice to be done, according to the sacred books and files in the machinery of justice.

The small cog at the gates doesn't get it at all, below his peaked cap, in his uniform. There is no paperwork. How is it possible, to admit someone into prison without paperwork? Where is the warrant? There are rules that have to be followed. It's not simply a question of right and wrong, the guilty and the innocent. To be criminal, is to be processed properly.

So turned away, I go with them all, stomping through the District Court, singing defiant songs, distributing the leaflets.

And we laugh constantly. And back at base, with the Devil still free for the time being, I lay under a blanket with Marina and Antje – somewhat compromised by my own supply – and everything is blurred, and I can't tell where one of them starts and the other ends, who's speaking, who's touching me, who I'm touching, whose lips I kiss, whose eyes I'm looking into.

But do I love these people this incredible summer?

Yes I do, very much.

And will I betray them?

Yes.

14. DECEMBER 17th 1967

Her mother is here.

'Something good will happen for you very soon,' Kurt's man told me.

It snows and snows, it's going to be a white Christmas. The kids are full of excitement and expectation. Klaus wants a bike, Lotte just wants us all to have a nice time, to be together as a family; doesn't care about presents.

But Annalise's mother is here with all of her belongings in a cardboard suitcase and a vinyl shopping basket on wheels. Our early Christmas present.

She's arranging her lucky horseshoes and grim sepia photographs along the mantelpiece, hanging her tapestries on our walls.

Because the German Democratic Republic cares for its people, listens to all of its people. Answered the prayers of Annalise and her mother.

Her mother is here and for the first few days was full of gratitude and wonder, amazed at the branded breakfast cereals and potted luxuries, the fresh milk, the chocolate and grapefruit. Amazed at the washing machine and the vacuum cleaner, the glossy magazines full of new fashions, the availability of coffee and cigarettes. Full of praise for what the Americans continue to provide, reminding us of the debt of gratitude that is owed to them by everyone here in the Free West. But the cars, she says, so many cars, scare her. And the young people are scary too, the students, with their long hair and strange clothes.

The German Democratic Republic knows nothing of crumbling apartments where the electricity is always off and the shops out of bread, but her mother is here with us now in West

Berlin, her papers in order, stamped and signed. Ushered through the Friedrichstrasse Bahnhof with her cardboard suitcase and vinyl shopping basket on wheels, surrendering her passport under the glaring bulbs and the picture of the MBB helicopter factory in Rostock. And not a word or twitch from the bored VoPos, the national police of the German Democratic Republic.

And I have the bottom bunk now, much of my equipment stowed below. Klaus and Lotte are on the top, dreaming of this wonderful Christmas.

Annalise sleeps on the sofa, in the living room next to the table where we once made love and were not ourselves for a while.

And her mother sleeps in the bed where we seldom made love. She has a stout stick she bangs against the wall when she wants something. Reunited now, with her only daughter and her grandchildren, but missing her husband, who was honest and hard working.

Her mother squints at me and she sees, or at least senses:

Anxiety
Discomfort
Fear
Shame
Lies

'He smells of another woman,' I hear her tell Annalise through the wall. 'You can see it in his eyes. Why do you think he's out so much? What do you think he gets up to?'

And within a week she's found a valuable ally and guide in Axel Springer, poring over the pages of *Bild* with increasing bewilderment.

'What's happening on this side of the city?' she asks Annalise. 'What's happening here? Why are the authorities allowing it? It's a disgrace. Don't they remember anything? Don't they teach them about the airlift in schools these days? This Rudi Dutschke, why do they allow him to say these things? And the students, throwing things at the police and fighting. Where's the discipline? Where's the respect? Why do they allow this long hair and those clothes?'

Her mother is now aware of the scandalous price of things, that every mark West is worth four marks East. What good is making things available if they're too expensive to buy?

And at the same time she scares the kids half to death with her stories from over the other side.

'You know what they'd do to Red Rudi and all the other troublemakers over there don't you?' she asks, with a snaggle-toothed laugh, running her finger across her neck, followed by the sign of the cross.

'When is he going to get a proper job?' I hear her ask Annalise. 'What must your neighbours think, with him coming and going at all hours? And where's he getting his money if he's not working? Things aren't cheap here, I know that much.'

Her mother is here and Springer's papers are gloating that the revolution is all finished.

Berlin's first new community is now a one-man operation, they report, Rainer Langhans alone among the mattresses. The others have either left, retired from the action or are in jail. All that remains is the memory of the colourful summer of 1967, the papers say.

There were beatings and more arrests at the annual Military Parade of the Western Allies at the end of August, demonstrators sitting in front of the tanks.

Ho, Ho, Ho Chi Minh! Amis out of Vietnam!

In September, at a Frankfurt assembly of student groups from across West Germany, Rudi Dutschke openly called for provocation – an escalation of the great refusal.

Troop carriers surrounded the building searching for Fritz. Now beardless and scrubbed up, he was finally recognised and arrested a week later, at yet another protest outside the Schöneberg City Hall back in Berlin.

At the end of the month, Mayor Albertz finally resigned, as predicted.

But October was marked by the news of Che Guevara's death in Bolivia. It prompted a symbolic storming of the Pentagon and demonstrations in San Francisco, Paris, Rome, Oslo, Amsterdam and Tokyo.

In Berlin, 7,000 people flooded the Ku'damm and the city's new mayor, Klaus Schütz – brought in by Willy Brandt as an antidote to the perceived weakness of Albertz – ordered restraint from his new police force.

Dieter Kunzelmann was arrested and given three weeks in Tegel, and border police of the German Democratic Republic seized a package of 24 pounds of explosives and 50 detonators en route from Munich to Kaiser-Friedrich Street.

'We will not shoot sparrows with cannons,' promised Mayor Schütz, 'but rioters will now be reined in. What Berlin has seen over this summer cannot and will not be repeated. A Berlin with a population which wants order will survive, and can do without a university and students if necessary.'

And Axel Springer, too, spoke of the smear campaign against his newspapers.

'It comes from over the Wall and is being mouthed by many strange groups,' he said. 'One day I will talk publicly about their relationships and financial backers.'

On November 3rd, Karl-Heinz Kurras was acquitted of the murder of Benno Ohnesorg. With slicked hair, in a midnight-blue suit, he flicked constantly at his creases as he told the court of his ordeal. His gun, he said, was licensed by the Allies and it was not within the court's jurisdiction to take it away from him.

More democracy, less memory, less justice.

And at the new trial of Fritz at the end of November, 1000 students clashed with 750 police in the freezing sleet.

Since then, it has snowed and snowed.

★

Marina will be back in Erfurt now, back with her family for the Christmas holidays, but she will no longer speak to me in any case.

I've had it with women, all of them.

We met last week, for the last time, in Kreuzberg, at her suggestion. And I failed to see the significance, to make the connection.

She was not alone. Thick with Antje now, arm in arm, and her two flatmates too, all in a conspiratorial huddle of whispers and insinuation together, waiting for me under the shadow of the Springer Building – beacon of the Free West, slap bang up against the Wall.

Creeping under doorways and through open windows, shape-shifting, resulting in a range of symptoms:

Anxiety

Discomfort

Fear

Shame

Lies

Marina and the new women are waiting for me on Koch Street. Not on Potsdamer. They flattened that.

And gazing down on us, perhaps, and out from East to West and back again from the top of his tower – a raised middle finger to Moscow – Axel Cäsar Springer, guardian of traditional German values.

They let me buy them all coffee and they are guarded and knowing, mocking, conspiratorial. And in a coffee bar it all starts again, their talk.

We are all the same, us men. They want their say, they're not being taken seriously. Kitchen, church and children is no longer enough, they say. Emancipation is the new word on their lips and men have to realise that women are the same as other oppressed groups. And they are thinking about forming not just a kindergarten now, but their own community.

Until finally, I've heard enough and suggest they talk about something else. Maybe I'm rude about it. Maybe they don't think I'm taking them seriously.

They are silent for a while, watching me closely. Antje whispers something behind her hand to Marina. Marina stares at me.

Her pale blue eyes.

Antje nudges Marina insistently.

Marina's bare arms, her tiny, even teeth.

'Don't you know why I wanted to meet here?' she asks me finally.

Her hair pushed back behind that Alice band again. That seriousness.

The three other girls stare on. Reinforcements. I shrug. The seconds stretch out.

'You don't, do you?'

Merciless pale blue eyes.

Antje shakes her head with irritation.

'The butcher's shop,' she says to me. 'Your father's butcher's shop. You were telling us all about it. All about your poor childhood here in Berlin.'

'I suggested we should go and see him,' Marina says.

Pitying pale blue eyes.

'Only there isn't any butcher's shop is there Peter?' Antje says. 'There is no butcher who took you in. Nothing you said was true was it? I was talking to someone who knows you. Someone who knows your wife as well.'

Marina just looks at me.

The twitch in her left eye. She knows it's all true and that Antje's right. Her beautiful swollen bottom lip, her pale blue eyes.

We are all the same, us men.

All liars.

PART TWO:
GET OUT OF HIS HOUSE
OR HE'LL KILL YOU

'The music coming up from below was bad news.
This was like the final nail in the coffin.'

Mick Fleetwood

15. NOVEMBER 9th 1989

They're tearing down the Wall.

I should be there, have to be there – it finally woke me up, slapped me from my stupor – the first TV reports of something stirring back in my homeland.

How wrong we all were.

The consumer society was destined for a violent death we believed – not just a few of us, millions – and social alienation must surely vanish from history. A new and original world was being invented in which imagination would seize power.

But imagination is seizing nothing.

And how right Marcuse was:

The people recognise themselves in their commodities – they find their soul in their automobile, hi-fi set, split-level home, kitchen equipment. The very mechanism which ties the individual to his society has changed, and social control is anchored in the new needs which it has produced.

Advocates of consumerism are holding all the cards, taking everything that remains now. Nobody will be able to fight back because the reasons to do so have finally been forgotten.

The cracks started to show before the summer. First Poland – the shipworkers throwing down their tools, Lech Walesa, the electrician, and his Solidarity, voted in by free election. And then Hungary – a Communist administration already abolished.

Can it really happen in Berlin, in Germany? The papers are full of exhilaration, but there's apprehension too – the prospect of reunification at its core. The old, old hate.

I should be there, they can't deny me. To reconnect, make the past real. Now I'm the right side of the Atlantic at least, most of the actual distance covered. But as far as I feel I should go. For now.

And already it feels like a mistake. Jet lag and disorientation, flashbacks in the night and bad, bad dreams. Of course it's a fucking mistake. I should be back on the hammock on the porch, south of Coconut Grove, growing fat and stupid in a Miami backwater. Minding my own business. Under the radar. Waiting for a call, a little courier job – anything – some sign they haven't forgotten me completely, that I haven't been happily written out of history forever.

Watching the haze over the waves and playing those scratchy old Fleetwood Mac records again and again – hardly the soundtrack to my time in Berlin, but over the years working its way into the cracks in memory like a kind of cement, to become something with a solid shape only I can recognise. Is it just because of what I read happened to him?

No. There's something else in the ancient-wise guitar and already-beaten voice of Peter Green – who I met only once, and for less than five minutes – that resonates beyond time, beyond meaning. His anger and sadness, his self-pity and rootless longing feel like they're mine too.

His songs:

Man of the World.
I just wish that I had never been born.

Oh Well.
Don't ask me what I think of you,
I might not give the answer that you want me to.

Green Manalishi.
When you come creeping around,
making me do things I don't want to do…

And then the other music, his guitar crying, screaming, dying. That was mine too.

Too much time to think and brood, that's been the problem. Too much inaction. Action is everything, isn't that what we used to say?

I should have known better, should be back on that hammock, instead of here, in this one-star hotel room in Sussex Gardens, London, with its stained mattress and blocked sink, the tarts and johns in and out and up and down at all hours, making me jump from sleep that's never long or deep enough.

Wondering how they're going to take it, what they might do.

I switch on the TV without sound. On the screen floodlights dance behind the hooves of Victoria's horses on top of the Brandenburg Gate, bathing the line of police, a crowd at a distance. From behind the Wall, a crane hauls out an entire concrete section, its rebar like talons.

I can't go back, but I have to. That's all there is to it. When did I stop following hunches?

When I left, I suppose. It seemed like the end of something, but I realise now it was too early. And I never made an American – lost much more there than I ever did in Berlin. Maybe I just never liked taking orders. Who does?

Fuck Kurt's man and all of them – they put me in a cell and pretended they were giving me the keys. Just following orders.

When did I stop moving on instinct, living on my wits? Or have my wits abandoned me? Is my instinct now propelling me towards some equivalent of walking into the path of a tank, like those poor Chinese kids on Tiananmen Square?

On the TV, the scene shifts to other sections of the Wall, lingering on its panels – the word 'Freedom' in blood red letters, a list of dates since 1961 marked off in five-bar gates, a Trabant smashing open a gap below Brezhnev and Honecker, locked in a passionate kiss. And Rosa Luxemburg is there too, below black stencilled capitals: 'I AM A TERRORIST'. Aztec butterflies and flowers, jigsaw totem poles. Vague symbols of freedom, simplicity.

I will not be alone in my fear today. Desks are surely being emptied, papers burned, pins torn from ties and lapels – bonfires of insignia and incriminating evidence, throughout Berlin and across all of the German Democratic Republic. And in West Germany too. All will be accusation and denial behind the façade of freedom in the making. Blinds will be drawn. An invisible wall will be put up in place of what's coming down, between the haves and have-nots this time. Like before, nobody will be responsible. Everyone just obeying orders, doing their jobs. Scored lines on typed sheets, file after file, and shredders too. Because after the celebrations, along with the hangovers, it will be time to grind the axes again. For scores to be settled. And there is a price that has to be paid.

And what will they make of me, a relic from that distant age, tanned from the Miami sun, if I ever get there? What will they remember of the currency of communication and the great refusal now?

Maybe they'll get me here first. Here in England, where else? That would make sense. Shut me up for good, here in the land of the victors, the country ever so proud of itself. The country that for almost two centuries – from George I to Queen Victoria – was ruled by the House of Hanover, with dashing British royals invariably paired off with princesses, margravines and duchesses from obscure German provinces.

The country where, after the last war, even if you rebelled against your parents, you were never ashamed of their pasts. So maybe I'll die here, in the land of heroes, the land of Big Ben and the Houses of Parliament and the red buses, where the music was once made. And where money is now made instead, by people who aren't pressed flat by some ever-unspoken burden and whose fathers and mothers were not sucked down to angry husks of shame and fear.

Can they really be afraid of anything I could say after all this time? Shredding and shitting themselves as I speak, looking over their shoulders now. Bonfires in back gardens.

I should be there, in Berlin, but here is as far as I've managed on this historic date.

It's a one-way ticket, they told me after the trial. Did I understand?

I understood. I understood the rules of the game, but this changes everything.

They understood too, Andy and Gudrun, and all of those fellow travellers through that time, willing or not.

And I still see them now, of course. Courtroom. Staring at me, staring at the judges in their wigs and gowns under the spread eagle, laughing at me, laughing at the old Nazis too – the children they deserved. Chewing gum, smirking, sprawling, smoking. Kissing. Andy and Gudrun. In love with themselves and each other. Beyond fear by then.

'Have you personally offered pistols, machine guns, mortars and grenades to certain individuals standing before this court?'

I couldn't answer. I was instructed not to answer. When everything seemed to have gone too far, before it even did.

Nobody died from anything I did. Nobody suffered any long-term damage. That's what I keep telling myself. Apart from maybe Peter Green. But he was on a journey; it would have happened anyway, wouldn't it? That's what I need to know, what I need him to tell me, if he can.

It's not as if I can change anything, or even particularly want to apologise. It's just as if I left something important behind somewhere and I need to know what it was, that's all. And the things that go missing are never to be found again in the obvious places.

There are totems I carry with me at all times, clues to my puzzle and also confirmation and reassurance.

There are old leaflets which provide snatches of the truth, and the first begins:

SHALOM & NAPALM
We have gassed the Jews, and now must save the Jews from Jew genocide.

The crudely printed sheet – Rotaprint, off-set litho, the new currency of communication – is thumbed and faded now, the type worn down like sand on a beach. The second, no less bleached, begins:

PANT-SHITTERS AND RED-CABBAGE EATERS
Build Up the Red Army!
Let the Class Struggle unfold!
Let the Proletariat organise!
Let the Armed Resistance begin!

And the third, which doesn't quite fit – handed to me by a vacant, shaven-headed child on Miami's Ocean Boulevard:

THE WICKED WORLD
BEHIND THE SCENES OF ROCK & ROLL!
The last time I talked to people who knew Peter Green, they told me that now his fingernails are two inches long, he doesn't wash and he sometimes crawls around on his hands and knees like Nebuchadnezzar did. (Daniel 4.33)

One time he was scratching at the door of an ex-girlfriend's house late one night. She thought there was an animal outside her door but when she looked, she saw it was him on his hands and knees scratching at the door and making noises like an animal!

The kids named him 'the Werewolf of Richmond' because he prowls around at night in this horrible state and scares people. They say he was never the same after one time in Germany when he took too much LSD.

It's pitiful to think that a man who was a millionaire and had all that fame and glory is now just a beast!

Those are the wages of sin and entertaining the Devil and his evil spirits!

The images on the TV have turned monochrome, back to '61, '62, and the cranes haul the slabs into place. A man in white overalls dances along the top with a shovel of cement, a woman holding a baby waves a handkerchief, bricks seal up a window from the inside, the lines of tanks and barbed wire and the white crosses of those shot by the guards. The famous footage of the man on the ladder pulled in both directions by his arms and feet. And it's much too long ago.

I look out of the window and of course it's raining in London and I miss the haze over the waves, the hammock on the porch.

I pull up the cord to the phone and tap the wall next to the connection. Old habits die hard.

Do they know where I am? Are they even that good? Won't they have other things on their minds? Do they know the significance of this date?

Kurt's man would know.

On this night, November 9th, 259 years ago now, Frederick the Second of Prussia – Frederick the Great – played his flute in the tower of the fortress of Küstrin, in western Poland.

'Think they've got a problem with fathers, they might find it started with Frederick the Great...' I remember Kurt's man saying to me, long ago.

As the notes danced from his instrument on that night in 1730 – through the bars into the darkness – Frederick recited the fifty-four movements of the Prussian Drill Code in his head.

Remorseless, three to a line, spread out. Precision timing. Stand and shoot. Reload. Move forward. Stand again and shoot. Third movement, finish off with bayonets.

Music and war – so far apart and seemingly inseparable.

On this night Frederick vowed never to speak of his beautiful friend Hans Hermann von Katte again.

The friend he'd watched beheaded three days ago, out there on the square at fortified Küstrin. On the instructions of his own father.

Together, he and Hans planned to escape to England, to defect to the service of George II – his maternal uncle – and to one day return. With a vengeance.

Move forward. Stand again and shoot.

On this day seventy-one years ago, the Free Socialist Republic of Germany was proclaimed by Karl Liebknecht from the balcony of Berlin's palace, with Rosa Luxemburg nodding her approval.

Rosa and Karl – figureheads of the Spartacus League – believed the masses to be the rock on which the final victory of the revolution would be built. The stronger social democracy developed and grew, they thought, the more those enlightened masses would take their destinies into their own hands.

There can only be luxury if it is bought with another's labour, Rosa wrote.

A time will come, no doubt, when our descendants will condemn us as barbarians because we have left the working classes without security, just as we already condemn as barbarian the nations who reduced those same classes to slavery.

Less than six weeks later, her decapitated corpse lay at the bottom of the Landwehr Canal.

Berlin would not be swayed, however, from its dream of social harmony, until Goebbels himself was dispatched by Hitler to the city; elected regional party leader there on November 9th 1926. The little man in the big picture, with his poisonous pen, his love of the theatrical and of abrupt curtain calls. Seeking to obliterate his own disfigurement in the shortcomings of others – a longer nose here, a darker skin there.

Goebbels who looked at clouds and saw swastikas reflected, and masturbated behind curtains as his beautiful people smashed all the mirrors and lay waste. And it turned very dark.

Still, by 1969, on this day in Berlin when a bomb was planted in the Jewish Community Centre, Rosa Luxemburg's name, and Karl's too, were known again in the city – proclaimed in six-foot-high aerosol red letters all along the brick walls of the US-built Free University. And nobody wanted to remember Joseph Goebbels.

And it's the 51st anniversary of Crystal Night too, when thousands of homes and stores were ransacked throughout Germany. The synagogues destroyed, the tombstones uprooted and graves violated. Bonfires made of precious books and delicate carvings. And the Jews pissed on.

Afterwards, the pavements glistened with the shards from the shopfronts under a cold moon. The Jews made to pay for it all and packed off.

And one year later on this arcane night, in 1939, Georg Elser, arrested on suspicion of smuggling, close to the border with Switzerland.

Guards surprised not to find alcohol or cigarettes or at least sausages in the knapsack belonging to this Swabian carpenter.

Instead, a pair of pliers, a few unidentifiable metal parts and a postcard of Munich's famous Hofbräuhaus, where thirty minutes later a bomb exploded, blowing off its roof and killing eight people.

But Elser's target cut short his speech on that occasion, and was already in a limousine with heated seats, heading for a train back to Berlin.

In Munich there's a Hofbräuhaus – one, two, down the hatch…

Hidden in the beerhall every night for over a month, hollowing out a pillar behind the rostrum, betrayed by chafed knees and elbows from his tunnelling. That was all the evidence required.

Taciturn, nevertheless something of a ladies man, Elser, like Rainer's father. Would neither vote in sham elections, nor give the salute. Played the zither and loved to dance.

His dancing days ended that night.

And let's not forget too, Holger Meins, or Germany's Supreme Court President, Günter von Drenkmann.

Holger Meins, on the slab, November 9th 1974, the new martyr to the cause. A Benno Ohnesorg for a changed world of bombs and kidnappings and the alternatives of going underground or prison.

It could not go unacknowledged, or without retaliation, Holger's passing. A line had been drawn in the sand much earlier. The following day, von Drenkmann, celebrating his 64th birthday, took three shots to his person.

A last entry in the prison diary of Holger Meins:

Handcuffs around the ankles, straps around the waist, along the arms, wrist to elbow. The doctor on his stool puts the little crowbar between your lips, pulling them apart with the fingers at the same time, then between the teeth. As soon as your jaws are far enough apart, the medical orderly pushes, shoves, forces it between your teeth – a red stomach tube the width of a middle finger.

Either a pig or a man
Either survival at any price
Or a fight to the death
Either problem or solution
There's nothing between.

If I should die in prison, it was murder, whatever the pigs say. Don't believe the murderers' lies.

The head of a six-foot man, swollen by beard, on the body of a five-year-old.

And I read later that Rudi Dutschke – much of his brilliant brain shot away long ago – appeared unexpectedly at Holger's funeral, raising his fist to the sky.

'The struggle will continue,' he shouted down at the coffin.

Holger Meins was the first really, before Baader and Ensslin and infatuated, compromised Ulrike Meinhof, and all the others primed to follow.

I miss the haze over the waves, the hammock on the porch, the sluggish, fabric-topped box on which I played those scratchy old Fleetwood Mac records again and again. Of course I do. I should have stayed in Miami.

But it's November 9th 1989, and a wall is coming down. And there is history in the making once again. Whatever happens, this date will never make a holiday in Germany.

16. NOVEMBER 10th 1989

A soundtrack of murderous slide guitars and Dieter Kunzelmann, his eyes wild and teeth bared, wraps his arms around Klaus and Lotte, who are still children. Dieter's nails are six inches long and black I see, and there's a medical pad taped crudely over his left eye. He picks up the kids and starts to run with them along crooked Berlin streets and then past burning Miami shacks and 24/7s and surfer stores. And Annalise looks at me from the window of a coffee shop sadly as I try to catch up. Turning her spoon so loudly in the cup the whole building starts to shake, but she just looks at me, pityingly. And the guitars are keening and lurching and they make me breathless, rip barbs from my lungs. And as I get closer it's not Dieter now, of course it's not, but I can't see who it is. Though I think I must know.

And an explosion jolts me awake. Bombs one to seven, I must consider them, I tell myself. And then I also remember that my children are grown up now.

Too much brooding, too much isolation. Bad, bad dreams.

I decide to move hotels, call their bluff. If the fear's real, the only thing to do is find it and confront it.

Take a risk, brazen it out, I tell myself, spend some money, stepping out of the taxi off the Strand now, under the statue of Peter – *fisher of men* – whose palace on this spot was once razed to the ground by Kentish peasants.

If they know where I am, let them find me. No more hiding. Might as well paint a blood-red target on my chest, a black bullseye over my heart, and have done with it.

The Savoy, England's first luxury hotel, haunt for the past century of monarchs and maharajas and celebrities too: Marilyn and Elton, Dietrich and Sinatra, Chaplin and Taylor. Home of the Peach Melba and the hydraulically raised dance floor; of silver plate polishing machines for Shahs and dictators and half-acre carpets woven by children.

Where back in 1381, as the country still reeled from the ravages of the Black Death, Wat Tyler marched with his men to demand an end to an unfair tax, and ask: *What social distinctions existed in the Garden of Eden?*

Back in the days when the Bible stories were the music, drugs and revolution. Another time, another struggle.

So the Savoy it is, a simple leap from one to five stars with a peel from the fat roll – a splinter from the coal – where high profile only makes you less visible. Here in London, a city that now belongs to Margaret Thatcher and some bankers and oil companies.

Tossing down the passport in the name of Peter Novak, I memorise the lantern-jawed face of the Chinese receptionist. Pay cash for two nights. The heavy-set doorman dashes to open the door for an elderly couple laden with shiny parcels. A suave concierge looks quickly down at his ledger when I glance over at him.

I feel all of their eyes following me as I walk to the lift.

Novak is not my real name, of course; but like me, he was born in Gorzów, Poland, and has been a naturalised US citizen for the past twenty years. It's close enough.

Next, I have my ponytail spliced in a salon of chrome and thick-veined marble, acrid with the smell of setting lotion and fouled with a tinny new strain of pop music which chugs and pings like some kind of feeble machinery. Music of the new leisure generation, for the non-workers. Music for shopping.

A starchy technician of a stylist called Angela drags my new, sparse crop into spikes with her tarantula nails and sets it with gel. The unconscious push of her breasts against my shoulders and the loose fall of her cold, flat palms against the nape of my shorn neck brings me alive, for a time.

Alive again. Final destination Berlin.

'Seems a shame,' she says. 'Must have taken time to get that long. They're coming back now anyway. A lot of the rich people have them, the bank people. And it's not like you've got much on top to do anything with.'

Some kind of vain attempt to cut away from the past, even as I move towards confronting it.

'Do what you can,' I tell her. 'Use all your special powers. I'll wear a hat again anyway, like I used to.'

She laughs like a stick trailed along metal railings.

'Where are you from then? You're not London. We get so many passing through from all over, sometimes it's hard to tell.'

I shrug, semi-captive under the black plastic cape.

'Poland, originally. Then Berlin.'

'Really?' she says. 'That's amazing. Amazing. Really. It's certainly the place that's in the news. They're really having a party. Didn't you fancy going back to see it all? The Wall coming down? All the excitement?'

'I might do yet. I've been in the States for many years now though.'

'We've been watching it every night. It's fantastic, what's happening. Like some really good news instead of all the usual doom and gloom. Unbelievable. The Russians have changed though, haven't they? That's what it seems to be all about. They want to live like we do now, have all the things we've got.'

'You're probably right.'

'That Gorbachev. He's different to the ones before. Not just with that weird birthmark, the hammer and sickle thing. Looks like he means what he says at least, like you can trust him. Kind eyes. So which part did you live in?'

'What d'you mean?'

'In the East or the West?'

'Both,' I say. Her scissors pause. 'The West mainly.' The scissors resume.

'Phew, eh? It must have been awful for the others.'

'For some of them, but not for others.'

'No, I know, but… You're all so serious you Germans, d'you know that? It's not just a cliché. What I mean is there was nothing in the shops for them, y'know? Only crappy stuff. You can tell from the films of them. No proper clothes, and all bad teeth and terrible hair. People who look like they haven't had a decent square meal for years. Poor.'

'It's been a very poor country, East Germany, in some ways, that's true.'

'Now they can have everything we've got,' she says. 'Democracy and freedom. That's got to be good, hasn't it? Oh listen to me, getting all political, sorry.'

Falls silent, scoops at a few wisps of stray hair to justify the exorbitant bill she'll doubtless present to my room.

As she busies herself with plastic bottles and silver implements along the tiled sink under the mirror, I stare at my beaten face under a helmet of tinfoil and try and remember when it actually appeared, the snake of hair, the thick rope, which defined me for a time, over there. Like the hat once did, the hat that vanished forever when I left Berlin. Who knows where? I'll buy another, here in London.

The beach bum with the ponytail in the hammock, that was me, waiting for the call back to action, which never came.

'It's like a really romantic place, the way they show it in films,' Angela continues, pressing back into position and massaging my scalp again. 'Like that old film. Have you seen it? *Cabaret* with Liza Minnelli? Even all the war thing, it was kind of romantic. And of course, all the history. The uniforms. Sexy really, though I shouldn't say it. They've been showing all the old films of when it was put up. Doesn't seem like it could have happened in this century. The women and kids crying and that. I can't believe it was only a few years before I was born. But what do you think, coming from there? It seems like it should never have been up in the first place, if it can come down so easily now.'

'I liked it where it was, in one way,' I tell her. 'We were used to it. Reminded us not to get too comfortable or take things for granted. But I've been away for a long time now.'

Back in my room, I make use of the complimentary gown and slippers as advised in the faux-leather-bound guide to services, look out at the boats on the Thames, at Big Ben and the Houses of Parliament which belong to Margaret Thatcher and some bankers and arms dealers and oil companies now.

Don't get too comfortable or take things for granted, I tell myself.

And I look again at that first old leaflet – once plastered on the walls and doors along the Ku'damm and dumped on the tables of the Republican Club, the Zodiak, the Underground Shelter for Travellers and the rest:

SHALOM & NAPALM

Shalom – Peace between man and God and also between countries, at a price. Completeness. Quietness and rest, transcendence. Both hello and goodbye.

Napalm – The petrol turned to jelly by thickeners. Supplied exclusively by Dow Chemical to the US Army in Vietnam back then. Some 400,000 tons of it. *Sticks to kids*, the young Yankee soldiers used to sing.

The Crystal Night of 1938 is now being repeated daily by Israel, this old leaflet from twenty years ago alleges in its dense black type:

For four years, the left movements in the United States and Europe have demonstrated in support of the liberation struggle of the anti-imperialist Vietnamese people.

But the victorious end of the war in Vietnam is the beginning of a Vietnam war on all fronts.

135

On the 31st anniversary of the fascist Crystal Night, several Jewish memorials in West Berlin have been sprayed with 'Shalom and Napalm'.

A fire bomb was placed in the Jewish synagogue.

Both actions are not to be defamed as the work of the extremist right, but as gestures of international socialist solidarity. Until now, the paralysis of the left in dealing with the Middle East conflict is a product of German guilt:

'We have gassed the Jews, and now must save the Jews from Jew genocide.'

True anti-fascism is simple solidarity with the struggling fedayeen. Our solidarity will no longer be satisfied with the verbal, abstract methods of enlightenment as it was with Vietnam, but will fight the close interweaving of Zionist Israel with the fascist Federal Republic of Germany through concrete, unindulgent actions.

Every hour of celebration in West Berlin and in the Federal Republic of Germany underlines the fact that the Crystal Night of 1938 is repeated daily by the Zionists in the occupied territories, in the refugee camps and in Israeli prisons.

The Jews displaced by fascism have themselves become fascists who want to eradicate the Palestinian people, in collaboration with Amerikan capital.

Let us destroy the direct support of Israel through German industry and the German government, prepare for the victory of the Palestinian revolution, and force the renewed overthrow of world imperialism.

We will further our struggle against fascism in the mantle of democracy, and begin to build up a revolutionary liberation front in Berlin.

CARRY THE STRUGGLE
FROM THE VILLAGES TO THE CITIES!
ALL POLITICAL POWER
COMES FROM THE BARREL OF A GUN!
BLACK RATS, T.W.

The phone rings in my Savoy hotel room. Nobody can possibly know I'm here.

'Mister Novak?'

I can't answer. I recognise the voice instantly.

'Hello? Mister Novak? Peter, is that really you? It's Rainer.'

I can't answer.

'Is anybody there?' he asks. 'Peter?'

I can't answer. Cut him off quickly, put the phone down on the cradle and sit on the bed, thinking fast.

The past, waiting down those wires, like I always knew it was, because you can never just cut it, once there are connections.

It's brilliant, really. *They're* brilliant. Using Rainer, of all people, as the messenger.

But so soon. Letting me know they know exactly where I am. No need for threats. They can afford to play with me, have a laugh at my expense, stretch it out as long as they care to.

But using Rainer, of all people.

Rainer, who was sometimes an attention seeker and egotist, sometimes forceful and sometimes spiteful, but often also gentle and considerate. And often just so funny and one step ahead of everyone else with his ideas, especially about the media and where the ultimate control would finally move. Spokesman for his generation and half of Germany's most glamorous alternative couple at one point, with Uschi. While I tried as much as I could to keep under the radar. But I was always a firm believer in telling people what they wanted to hear, and so, of course, was he.

How much does he know? Are they using him, and if so, does he know? And if he does, what does he get out of it?

It's brilliant, but it's too soon. I don't even want to hear the things I need to know from him yet.

Action is everything though, isn't that what we used to say?

The phone rings again.

'How did you get this number?'

'Peter Urbach,' Rainer exclaims. 'My God, it really is you. After all these years.'

'How did you get it, the number?'

'Well, it was odd – some walking corpse from a filing department over in the city hall just phoned me yesterday out of the blue and gave me it,' he says. 'Incredible, really. He phoned again today, told me you'd moved and gave me this new number. I had to try and describe you to the receptionist, though, they seem to have got your name wrong. Or are you still underground? Incognito, playing the games?'

'Incredible,' I say. 'It is, isn't it? Why would that happen d'you think? They just phone you yesterday, of all days?'

Suddenly he's uncertain.

'Well, just, I've tried to get in touch before, made enquiries about you over the years. Put it down to German efficiency.'

'It's usually preceded with the word ruthless,' I say. 'So you're back in Berlin then, are you now?'

'Only for a while. I'm making a film,' Rainer tells me. 'It's a long story. But guess who with? Really, just guess.'

'No idea.'

'Marina.'

'Marina?'

'Marina Waldmann? *That* Marina. She's directing. You remember her?'

Of course I do. They know I do. He knows I do. But what else does he know? Can they really make all this happen? Using Rainer, of all people, as the messenger. And bringing Marina into it too. Brilliant.

'How is she?' I ask weakly.

'Oh, she's doing really well,' he says, oblivious. 'She's found her calling behind the camera. And good at contacts too. We're having such a great time here. In some ways the place hasn't changed much at all, still plenty of rubble, and now they're making even more. I really have been trying to get in touch with you for ages. How are you, anyway?'

'Confused,' I admit.

'I can't believe you're only in London,' Rainer says. 'Just London. We heard it was South America. Why don't you come back over? Let bygones be bygones. You simply have to. It would be great to see you. It's a laugh a minute at the moment anyway. I'm back in the Zum Schotten. Can you believe it's still here? Do you have your TV on there? They're tearing it to bits, Peter. Not the Ossies, of course. They're just hanging around in their hellish knitwear as always. It's Miele's men themselves with the drills. Can you imagine?'

'I know,' I manage to say, and I can imagine too, very clearly, many things that Miele's men could do with drills, and what they are likely to do again, if the order to stop the madness that is currently happening is given. As it just might be, before too long.

Rainer continues to gush, although it could be to anyone now – just sending the optimistic messages I remember so well out into the ether, to be picked up by anyone, whenever.

'Don't you see, it just proves we were right all along?' he is saying. 'In some ways at least?'

He means, of course, that he was right, and the others who turned against him were wrong. And who can blame him? Justification – is that what this is all about for me too? Rewriting history?

'The new currency of communication, remember saying that?' he asks. 'That was you. You got it completely. It didn't take guns and bombs. That was always the wrong path. And it shows that the media and the authorities can keep sending out what they think are the right messages, but the real meaning is passed on regardless. People find each other, networks connect. And it will only become more open and easy.'

'And you think it was just a coincidence,' I say. 'Somebody phoned you yesterday and gave you this number?'

'Come on, Peter, you think anyone cares after all this time? You think they're still playing with us, even now? Sounds like paranoia to me. Too much time on your hands.'

A long pause, too long to let this signal continue. Long enough for taps and intercepts.

'I should hang up now,' I say.

Another long pause.

'What really happened?' he says, eventually, finally. 'I never understood. Why did you do it?'

Why did I do it?

Nobody died, anyway.

'There were too many things going on,' is all I can think to say to him. 'Too many sides to take. When it all went wrong – which let's face it, was always going to be the case – I was going to carry the can for the lot of you.'

Another long silence, as if we can read each other's thoughts now.

'I had to deal with feeling like a traitor myself, too,' he says. 'But I'd still like to know what happened.'

'What *happened*?' I want to scream down the phone now, pour all of these things out of my head, get this old black dog off my back forever. 'Well, where should I start, Rainer? What about, an explosive device was placed in West Berlin's Jewish Community Centre? That's what I've been thinking about. What about that?'

Dieter flirting with disguises, sculpting his hair. Dieter trying on hats and glasses. Dieter primed for one last charge.

'That was nothing to do with me, with us,' he says.

'But someone just called and gave you the number yesterday? Twenty years ago to the day? Remember that? And on the anniversary of Crystal Night too?'

'It wasn't going to go off, though, was it?'

'I'm not sure I knew that at the time. I'm not sure anyone did. Maybe I wigged the detonator, maybe I didn't. Maybe they did.'

'Who do you mean? Who are they?'

'What does that matter? Either side. The people who wanted

it to happen and those who didn't. I couldn't tell them apart by then.'

'Well, I don't know.'

'As far as I can remember, everyone else concerned was totally okay with it.'

'Nobody was okay with it, nobody wanted it,' Rainer says. 'Nobody asked for it.'

I close my eyes, clenching the phone too tightly. I wedge the receiver on my shoulder and pull the blood back into my fingers, one by one.

'You know that's not true. All these years later and I'm still trying to work out why exactly it was deemed necessary for me to put it at the disposal of those friends of ours.'

'They weren't too friendly by then, as I remember.'

'The timing, for whatever reason, just seemed right, didn't it? To aid the struggle against fascism, wasn't it? Terror in the name of worker solidarity and international socialism? Praxis? Bringing the struggle to the inner cities? I know it wasn't you. Shalom and Napalm, eh? How is Dieter anyway?'

Rainer says nothing for some time.

'Haven't spoken to him in years,' he concedes finally. 'Old wounds go deep.'

What else should I tell him, I wonder? How much does he know? What have they fed him? Where's the bottom of this dank pond?

'Really, if you only knew the extent of it all,' I say. 'But there was me and Bommi really, wasn't there, at the end of the day? Just the two of us prepared to get our fingernails dirty. Workers at your coalface, like it's always been. Just the two of us actual workers, in your revolution?'

'It wasn't my revolution,' he protests. 'None of us wanted violence and I'd washed my hands of it all long before all that. And you were never really an actual worker either, were you? You were nothing like Bommi.'

Bommi Baumann – an apprentice to Dieter, Fritz and Rainer, back in the early days of the commune, cutting out the clippings of their actions from the newspapers over the breakfast table at Stuttgarter Place. A street kid, always on the front line and always ready to throw a rock.

But when he embarked on his own personal action – slashing the tyres of over a hundred cars along Hollander Street, a well-known police enclave – they deserted and denounced him. A pointless action, they declared, without motive or manifesto, betraying a lack of discipline. Because he was never really one of them, not really. The old, old hate again, formless and unwilling to submit to theory. Frightened them to death. They jailed Bommi for nine months after the tyre slashing.

'If you only knew,' I say again. 'But while I'm here in London, I'll tell you what else I'm going to do. I'm going to find Peter Green. Remember him?'

'Sure.'

'I don't even know why. That day at High Fish, remember?'

Nobody suffered any long-term damage.

'You should forget about it all,' Rainer tells me. 'Really, what does it all matter now? Even if they are still playing games with us, their days are numbered.'

'You really think so? All these years I've been sitting it out with nothing else to think about.'

'Come back to Germany, then, come back to Berlin. Come and join the party.'

Using Rainer, of all people, as the messenger. And Marina too. And so soon.

'Well, I don't know.'

'But what was it then?' Rainer asks, with a new urgency now. 'Tell me that, because I know you know. What was it we were all feeling at the start, can you remember it? That feeling?'

'I can't answer for you, or anyone else,' I say. 'I wasn't feeling anything very much, most of the time, I don't think, just trying

142

to fix things, keep people happy. You lot had the luxury of being giddy. And well off. Protected.'

'Come over,' he insists. 'It's party time. We deserve it. Because we're still here. We survived. Let's get that feeling back. Please, Peter. Marina would love to see you too.'

I take a number, tell him I won't be staying here, don't know where I'm going.

'Maybe someone will phone and tell you where I'll be next,' I suggest. 'That would be another coincidence wouldn't it? What's the next big anniversary? So I might see you soon and I might not. But take care. And say hello to Marina for me.'

On the TV, a sledgehammer crashes into some more bricks and concrete.

I wanted to ask him more about her, of course, but what difference would it make now?

Marina who was going to be a doctor and heal the sick. Marina who taught me that everything to do with desire is right, and everything is sometimes wrong. Marina who never became a doctor and changed into somebody else, making films. If Rainer was telling the truth. And if he was, it seems she warmed to his concept. If everything's being documented, then we'd all be better protected. If everything's on film they can't get away with anything.

But of course they can still get away with anything they want. Until Marina's children or her children's children film them in their secret places and record every off-the-record remark. Until they all know there's no remaining currency in being corrupt. Until we create a world without secrets. A new and original world in which imagination will seize power, wasn't that what we thought would happen?

As if.

In my wallet is another totem, an old article folded into quarters from *Stern*, Axel Springer's glossy consumer trivia magazine.

Its publication was also on November 9th 1969.

What's in a date? What's a coincidence, Rainer?

There he is staring out from the fading centre-spread: Rainer Langhans, betrayer of the revolution. Is he betraying me right now?

But then there are very many levels of betrayal. Even Jesus understood that.

Unmistakable with his golden curls and John Lennon granny glasses. With his thousand-marks-a-day supermodel girlfriend Uschi, and with Holger Meins too.

And the rest of them. Bare-chested, arranged into angles in front of a violin and a blanket. Rock stars. In the final days on Stephan Street.

Declaring to the world that the revolution would not be armed.

Well that was very bad timing indeed.

17. NOVEMBER 18th 1989

I don't run, I wait.

I tell the Chinese receptionist not to put any more calls through to my room, under any circumstances, but to take the names and numbers of anyone who does call. Tip him lavishly. I have a discrete word with the concierge, stressing my need for absolute privacy as I fold a twenty into his palm. This behaviour is not so conspicuous or surprising here, I convince myself. Share cigarettes and jokes with the doormen, memorise their faces.

And nothing happens.

The bad dreams continue, but I start to realise I won't disappear without ceremony now, without them making a point. Because I'm a symbol. Of what, I can't be certain.

And I'm soon drinking in the American Bar, putting it around that I'm a rock journalist on assignment.

With almost immediate results.

Someone in a back-slapping, red-faced banking crowd I get talking to swears he has an old schoolmate called Ollie. A bit of a loser, this Ollie, but drinks regularly with Danny Kirwan – Fleetwood Mac's third guitarist on those records. I express an urgent desire to meet him.

But this Ollie hasn't shown up tonight, even though I made it clear it would be worth his while and a certain donation was made in advance. A vague, late-night arrangement though – cigars and now-crumpled notes, scribbled reminders on a torn bank statement – could have been forgotten with the morning. Deliberately or otherwise.

I explain this situation to Chris the barman, who promises to be straight on the case, should Ollie arrive or leave a message.

I've tipped Chris well for three successive nights running.

'Let me fix you something special while you're waiting, Mister Novak,' he suggests, flicking at his white lapels. His eyes have a coke-bulge to them. Do I detect a fix twitch, too? That's okay, either way, or both. Perfect for a barman – keeps things moving along. He's what, between thirty and thirty-five. No paunch, face that moves from an empathetic grin to a blank question mark in a micro-second. Listening's not really listening when it's part of the job. No kids, no ties.

Noted and filed.

'Okay, thanks Chris,' I say, sliding onto the stool to wait. Phil Collins is playing, pleading for one more night. 'Have you got any other music? I hate this shit.'

'Me too.'

Pulls a pile of the new CDs from behind the bar. I shuffle through them – Dire Straits, Chris Rea, Simply Red, Madonna – the kind of music this new, shrunken, mean format deserves.

'Anything you fancy, Mister Novak?'

Fleetwood Mac, *Tango in the Night*. A tidy square of airbrushed fauna on the little plastic sleeve. Giving absolutely nothing away.

'Will you put this on?'

He picks up the CD, grins.

'Your special subject. Fleetwood Mac.'

I look up sharply.

'What d'you mean?'

He lifts a hand limply, dramatic. *What, me?*

'I'm right here,' he shrugs. 'Can't help hearing what you all talk about.'

Slides the CD into the centre of a squat rack of black equipment behind him by the fridge.

Snazzy acoustic guitars and a melodramatic man singing about a house on a hill, and then a husky woman asking for big, big love in return. The guitar turns classical, then flamenco. It doesn't make any sense. I can hear the crushing, punishing chords of 'Green Manalishi' in my head. How did that change into this?

Chris is watching me, amused.

'You look like it's the first time you've ever heard it.'

'It is really,' I admit. 'Properly.'

'And Fleetwood Mac are your specialist subject, Mister Novak? They're a platinum-selling band. Biggest of the decade.'

'I know that,' I say. 'Of course I know that.'

He nods.

'Come off it. What Walkman do you use anyway?'

'I don't.'

Chris folds his arms, tilts his head.

'You don't?'

'I need to hear the twist of the spindle, the needle falling on the plastic,' I tell him. 'Accompanied by contemplation of some work of artistic labour big enough for me to roll a joint on.'

He laughs.

I give him a *whatever* shrug.

'That's in Miami, anyhow,' I say.

'A purist,' he nods. 'Old school.'

'Something like that.'

He grins again, shakes his head.

'But how do you stay connected to it all then? What you want is…' scans the room, dips quickly in the back, '…one of these.'

Plonks down an ugly little Sony tape machine with a pair of tangled earphones attached.

I sniff, scowl.

'That's for Phil Collins,' I say. 'For Simply Red and Dire Straits and…'

'Fleetwood Mac?' he suggests. 'I can get you one for twenty quid no questions asked Mister Novak.' Another wink.

'Twenty quid?'

'Top of the range. A collector's item. The future's portable. You can take the music with you anywhere. It won't be cassettes for long though, they'll make it even smaller.'

'Those clever Japanese.'

'Clever Japs,' he concedes.

'Thought you were fixing me a drink?' I say. 'You're on, by the way. I'll have one.'

Chris starts to slice a grapefruit with a sharp knife, grinds the two halves onto a crusher, pours the juice into a silver shaker.

'Twentieth anniversary of this, to the very year, no less,' he informs me. 'The Moonwalk, that's what it's called. Joe Gilmour himself created it. *Joe Gilmour.*'

Scratches behind his ear and turns to select a stubby brown bottle with a red wax seal from the shelf.

'A legend here. Belfast boy. Best head barman from the Fifties right up to when he retired in '76. And I was here by then, just starting – straight from school. Honour to have worked with him. Wouldn't trust me in front of the famous customers of course, back then. Too wet behind the ears. I was getting to know the ropes, watching and learning, fetching and carrying. Anyway it was some send-off for him, I can tell you. First time I ever really got drunk, I think.'

Produces a plastic bottle full of pink liquid that would look more at home on the tiles under the mirror at Angela's salon.

'A real legend, he was. Served them all – our Queen, Prince Charles, Winston Churchill, the Duke of York – your presidents too, Truman, Nixon.' Shakes the bottle at me. 'Rose water, that was Joe's secret, Mister Novak.'

Stops shaking, looks thoughtful.

'What?' I ask.

'You know, I once shared a flat with this Persian guy, back in '81 it was, maybe '82 and he used it in just about everything he cooked. Don't think it's always to our taste, but... Turkish delight, marzipan – all those sweet things, you know, dusted in white powder. There's this in all of them. And a shit-load of sugar, I guess. Perhaps it's because they don't drink. Or not supposed to anyhow. They have a sweeter tooth over in the Middle East, don't you think?'

'I've never been there,' I tell him.

He raises an eye, pouring the contents of the silver shaker into a tall wine glass.

'Now that really surprises me,' Chris says. 'You have that look, you know? As if you've been around.'

Thinks I'm an arms dealer or something then. Nobody died from anything I did. Nobody suffered any long-term damage.

'Around the block?'

He grins, locking himself back into careful customer service mode.

'I didn't mean that, of course, Mister Novak. Well travelled is all I meant.'

Does he know something? Is he being paid?

'Okay,' I say, nod at the glass, 'and is that it?'

Shakes his head.

'Then you top it up with champagne.' Fiddles around under the bar, struggles, pops a cork, brings up the bottle foaming over his fist. 'The Savoy sent a flask of this to Ground Control at Houston for Neil Armstrong's return back in '69. That was some achievement, wasn't it?'

'I bet you can even remember where you were,' I say.

'Of course.'

Tilts his head at the glass, squints like a surveyor. Pours in the champagne.

'Et voilà, the Moonwalk. Well I was only nine years old at the time, but me and my brother – he's a couple of years younger – we were allowed to stay up to watch it live on the old black and white. That was unheard of. A first and last. It was about four in the morning wasn't it, when they finally did it? Latest we'd ever been up of course, but…' Puts his elbows on the bar. Thinks for a moment. '…I remember the old man going on and on about it. How for so many centuries the human race had looked up at the moon and stars and felt such, you know… what would you call it? Maybe wonder, or distance, impossibility, I don't know… Are you going to taste it then?'

'Sure,' I say. Take a sip. Smile at him. 'It's good, very good.'

It's okay, nothing special.

'Moonwalk,' Chris says, nodding. 'Moonwalk. Joe Gilmour. Legend. There are pictures of him all around the place, take a look when you've finished your cocktail… one over there with him serving Sinatra. That's my favourite. Sinatra looks half cut. Imagine that then, what it was like here in the Fifties, the early Sixties, if you were loaded, I guess, as usual…'

Gestures across the room – carpet with a pattern of unwanted Christmas cardigans, mustard Doric columns, lived-in leather-studded chairs around glass-topped tables, grand piano in the centre, fluttering veils at each window, blocking out the taxis on the Strand.

'Never see anything like it again, my old man kept telling me. History in the making. Unbelievable that it's happened in my lifetime, he said. And I still remember it, those fuzzy shapes in the static at the hatch, all the scrambled messages, and then, what was it? One small step for man?'

'One giant leap for mankind…'

Something like that, we both nod in agreement.

'And, you know, I think he was right about that. It's all been a bit of a disappointment since really. An anti-climax. Can't think of anything else that anybody's done since to match it. Only…'

'Only what?'

'Well, right, I don't believe in any of these conspiracy theories or anything, but last year I was in America – Washington, the Space Museum there – and I got a look at the capsule they came down in. It was just so tiny, and so flimsy-looking, and I just thought, you know, *never*. No way. So what about you then, where were you Mister Novak?' Chris asks. 'I need a cigarette, actually.'

'There's nobody in,' I suggest. 'I'll watch it for you. Here…'

Palm him a small wrap.

He looks at me once. *Well travelled.* Blinks, and exits.

So where was I then, as they were preparing to put the first man on the moon back in July, twenty years ago?

Bringing the restlessness of the cities to Germany's villages, I could tell Chris.

Holidaying with the blessing of Mao Tse Tung, I could say, with the peace-breakers, the rioters and the ringleaders. Tripping out of my brains in a Bavarian field with no ultimate reason for being in Ebrach.

And nothing the Americans could do – not even staking their flag on the moon – could ever win back the affections of those assembled in that field for those days. The USA had long since turned into a bad step-parent for these children of the economic miracle.

And it was all over by then anyway, mission accomplished, so to speak – the German Emergency Laws had been put in place at the end of June a year earlier, paving the way for the Allies to hand over control to Bonn.

Or so it seemed.

In the end, it took one last push for Nixon's visit in February to ensure the laws were used to the full extent of their potential. Kurt's man and his office were well pleased with all my running around in the build-up to that – from the SDS headquarters on the Ku'damm, to the first commune's new block on Stephan Street and over to the second on Wieland – weaving between the Zodiak and Mr Go's, from Pan to the Unfathomable Shelter for Travellers. Offloading my things. Hatching their plans.

Kurt's man warning me to withdraw completely from the scene by then, but something made me hang in. Because you can never just cut it, once there are connections.

Under suspicion from virtually every quarter – aware of the whispers behind hands, the averted eyes, the double-speak, the paranoia – still I persisted. Addicted, and looking for Marina.

Who would never show again on my radar. She wasn't part of this, couldn't be.

By July 1969, the extra-parliamentary opposition, the APO, was finished, especially in Berlin – had been really since Nixon's visit – the Socialist Students' Movement of Germany splintering into small cells, at loggerheads and lacking common goals, a spent force. The lost tribes had covered the Free University of Berlin red with their Marxist slogans and routinely pelted its lecturers with eggs, but their haunts were now overflowing with clink.

Cheap heroin with the lethal morphine base, out of Istanbul and up through Marseille. My toolbox was full of it. Left to turn to mould in cans and bottles and re-cooked with acetic acid – first by clever students, but soon by others looking to expand turnover rather than their experiences. Clink was now jacked up nightly on the steps of Kaiser Bill's bombed-out church. Berlin's APO dropping like flies.

But as Neil Armstrong prepared to make his few small steps, they were all in Ebrach.

Fucking Ebrach – a few hundred residents, 2,000 cows and a prison, currently accommodating one Richard Wetter of Munich. A stone's throw from the birthplace of Dieter Kunzelmann, the backward drinker's town of Bamberg, where it starts – a fitting location for his last stand – Dieter and his revolution, Dieter and his actions, Dieter and his festering clink habit, which, admittedly, was partly my fault.

Dieter exhorting the faithful to descend on that rural hell for Richard Wetter – West Germany's first political prisoner under the new laws – handed down an eight-month stretch in Munich for impersonating a police officer.

And so they descended, from Munich, from Frankfurt and from good old West Berlin, the last stragglers of the APO. For one last party, one last protest before all the other prison sentences came down and those not keen on doing their stretches were obliged to go underground.

Bring musical instruments, blankets and sleeping bags, Dieter's leaflets had demanded. Bring cameras and films. Bring weather-proof clothing and stout shoes. Bring spray paint and megaphones. Bring hash and slingshots. Bring riot police uniforms, judges' robes and grenade launchers.

So it starts in Bamberg, with scavenging in the stores. There are reports of old ladies terrorised, of screeching tyres, of iron bars and billy clubs, of shitting in the streets and fornication before children.

There is a storming of the town hall – a protest against hastily introduced new bye-laws to prevent the camp taking place. Files are thrown from the windows and the local police move in. Thirty-nine arrests.

Bamberg has never seen anything like it – the elite students from the big cities at their leisure – even though the papers have already issued warnings. Residents look on, getting angry, making plans. The press reporters fire them up, spread their rumours.

Shitting in the streets and fornication before children. The slaughter of a sheep with the word 'Pig' sprayed across its flanks.

Those arrested in Bamberg are taken to the neighbouring court prison where they attempt to flood the building, windows are smashed, sheets are set on fire.

The authorities of Bamberg load up their charge sheets and bid Dieter and his entourage adieu the next morning, pack them off to Ebrach. Bamberg's residents watch them leave, getting angry, making their own plans – watching Dieter, a barefoot, drugged-up dervish, heartbreakingly one of their own.

Dieter, thrown out of the first of the new communities a month earlier, desperately trying to proclaim himself leader of a new movement – the Wandering Hash Rebels.

Their leader is Bommi Baumann, the old commune apprentice, out of jail for his tyre-slashing campaign and by July 1969 feared and revered in equal measure, with his friends Georg von Rauch and Thomas Weisbecker – always dressed in black leather and bandanas.

Back in West Berlin, they turn over the cars of the Maltese dealers, keep the streets clear from fear. They demand free entrance to any happening, free transport through the city of West Berlin. They have their skeleton keys, with which they can enter any building or prise up the paving stones for an instant action, and they have their lumps of dope. They live on the coins from ransacked cigarette machines. And they're up for my plans.

The Wandering Hash Rebels gather at a commune on Wieland Street paid for by the lawyer Otto Schily, but they move from place to place – an extended community of floors and sofas in Kreuzberg, Mitte and Wedding.

They are younger, less well informed, more suggestible in one way, but at the same time tougher, with little interest in Dieter's initiatives. Only his girlfriend, Ina Siepmann – poor Ina, the chemist's assistant who eventually disappeared in Lebanon – seemed to listen to him by then.

And Andy Baader and Gudrun Ensslin are in Ebrach too, also prison hardened, withdrawing further into each other, surveying the circle of moth-eaten tents on the meadow with contempt.

Everyone who's been around for a while is tiring of their rants and tirades, but they are finding new listeners.

Like Brigitte Mohnhaupt, like Irmgard Möller and like Rolf Heissler, who are all in Ebrach and whose faces will stare down from posters across Germany before too long.

But Andy and Gudrun haven't forgotten me, and in Ebrach, let me know they expect more of what I can do.

Rainer Langhans isn't present, although all the papers report he is.

But it all comes to an end without him anyway, in that farmer's field, with the police surrounding the tents and the villagers surrounding the police with their heads full of new horror.

In the sleepy hamlets and remote cottages, cartridges are being pushed into shotguns and barrels oiled and primed. The dogs are kept hungry. They will not get out of this unscathed tonight, the disaffected children of the economic miracle.

The night drops very cold for July. Cold as the moon, which the Americans are finally stepping on. I never want to be back there.

★

Back in my room, I call the maid, buttonhole her for details of the staff rotas, who has access, let it be known nothing is to be touched unless I'm there and specifically request it. A handful of change is sufficient to secure her devotion, to galvanise an entire invisible army by word of mouth – the exploited, the subservient, the stranded – united only in their utter powerlessness and knowing their place as never before.

And looking again at one of those old leaflets, it seems safe to conclude now that they never really responded to the message:

PANT-SHITTERS AND RED-CABBAGE EATERS

Build Up the Red Army!
Let the Class Struggle unfold!
Let the Proletariat organise!
Let the Armed Resistance begin!

Comrades – there is no point in trying to explain the right way to the deceitful people. We have done this long enough. We don't have to explain the Baader-Release Action to the intellectual prattlers, the pant-shitters, the know-it-alls, but rather to the potentially revolutionary segment of the people. To those who can immediately grasp the deed, because they themselves are imprisoned.

You have to convey the Action to those who get no compensation for the exploitation which they suffer, who get no compensation through living standards, consumption, savings agreements, personal credit, middle-class cars. To those who cannot afford all the junk, to those who don't care about it. To those who have exposed as lies all of the promises of the future by their nursery teachers and school teachers and property managers and welfare workers and foremen and craft masters and union functionaries and district mayors, and still fear only the police.

Behind the parents stand the teachers, the Youth Authority, the police. Behind the foreman stands the master craftsman, the personnel office, the factory security force, the welfare service, the police. Behind the building superintendent stands the administrator, the landlord, the bailiff, the eviction notice, the police. They manage with censorship, dismissals, notices of termination, with the bailiff's seal for seized belongings and the nightstick.

Of course, they grab for the service pistol, the tear gas, hand grenades and machine pistols if their advance is held up.

Of course, the GIs in Vietnam were retrained in guerrilla tactics.

Of course, the Green Berets were given a course in torture. So what?

Of course, the execution of sentences for political prisoners is intensified.

You have to make clear that it is Social Democratic garbage to assert that imperialism would allow itself to be infiltrated, to be led around by the nose, to be overpowered, to be intimidated, to be abolished without a struggle. Make it clear that the Revolution will not be an Easter Parade, that the pigs will naturally escalate the means as far as they can, but also not further. In order to push the conflict as far as possible, we build up the Red Army.

Without simultaneously building up the Red Army, every conflict, every political effort in the workplace and in the courtroom degenerates into reformism. You set up only better means of discipline, better methods of intimidation, better methods of exploitation. That only breaks the people, it doesn't break what breaks the people! Without building up the Red Army, the pigs can continue, they can go on locking up, dismissing, seizing, stealing children, intimidating, shooting, ruling. To bring the conflict to a fever pitch means that they can no longer do what they want. Rather they must do what we want.

Don't sit around on the shabby, ransacked sofa and count your loves, like the small-time shopkeeper souls. Build up the right distribution apparatus, let the pant-shitters lie, the red-cabbage eaters, the social workers, those who only suck up. Get out where the homes are and the big families and the sub-proletariat and the proletarian women, they who are only waiting to smash the right people in the chops. They will assume the leadership. And don't let yourself be nabbed and learn from them how one keeps from being nabbed – they understand more about that than you.

Let the class struggle unfold!
Let the proletariat organise!
Let the armed resistance begin!
Build up the Red Army!

Most of the authors are dead now, of course – Baader, Ensslin, Ulrike Meinhof. I can imagine them agonising over their precious text, the lovers reunited, dizzy with adrenalin, trigger happy, and rounding on Ulrike. Ulrike whose career was certainly over after the Baader–Release Action. Ulrike who escaped that first criminal act by jumping from the window of Berlin's Institute of Social Studies.

Ulrike who didn't understand how far she still had to fall.

I can picture them picking over her prose, the women shorn of their wigs. The Beretta employed to fire the very first bullets into the security guard Georg Linke would never be found. Inside an abandoned silver Alfa Romeo, KriPo discovered gas canisters and a copy of *Das Kapital*.

The rest of us wanted to invent a new and original world in which imagination would seize power. Not just a few of us, millions.

It never happened.

What did *they* want?

18. NOVEMBER 19th 1989

Chris calls me over to the side of the bar and hands me a small package.

I know what it is, of course – my passport to the future, which is ever-connected and at the same time mean and meaningless, and becoming ever smaller.

'Enjoy it,' Chris says, with another wink. 'Your business is valued. And this too, on the house.'

A smaller package, in glittering Christmas wrapping paper. Reindeer and church bells.

And then Chris fixes a new cocktail for me and Ollie, Danny Kirwan's acquaintance, who's a day late.

Ollie is around forty and has also kept his hair long. It hangs in grey feathers to the collar of his denim jacket. It's instantly clear Chris doesn't like the look of Ollie. It's true there's something shifty, something ratty about him. His eyes dart constantly around and he swallows down huge gasps of air before he speaks.

I tell him about the research for the American magazine.

'Well I don't think Danny's got anything new to bring to the party if I'm honest,' Ollie says. 'I mean, I can take you down to see him easily enough, but you'd have to be early. Soon as they turf him out of the hostel he's in the pub and all you'll get for time is the first three pints really, if you want it to make any sense, but he'll probably keep going as long as you're paying.'

'Is he still playing guitar?'

Ollie snorts, gasps down another draft of air.

'He'd probably say yes if you asked him, but I don't see how.'

Raises his hands and shakes them violently.

'Always liked the old vibrato in his playing, Mister Novak, but I think he'd over-egg the pudding these days.'

Chris puts two glasses down.

'The Link-Up, another one of Joe's,' he informs me. 'Southern Comfort, Russian vodka and fresh lime. Created this in '75 to mark that Apollo-Soyuz project, when the Russians and the Yanks came together.'

'Like they're doing again now, with the Wall coming down and all that,' Ollie says. 'Don't at all mind if I do.' Drains it in one, smacks his lips theatrically. 'Not bad, but I'd rather just have a pint.'

I nod at Chris, whose face tightens before he turns and pulls down a pint glass, sulkily prodding it under a pump.

'Jeff said you'd pay my expenses,' Ollie continues, 'make it worth my while. I don't like to bring it up so soon, but my means are limited, if you know what I mean. I'm fucking skint is the truth. And he said to get a taxi here, which is hardly my regular means of transport.'

I guide him with his freshly pulled pint to a table in the corner. Push two twenties across to him.

Ollie's eyes widen.

'They must be generous with the expenses on your magazine,' he says. 'Must be great. A job like yours. Travelling around. Writing about something you love.'

'What do you do, Ollie?'

'Nothing much right now, to tell you the truth…'

He pauses, as if suddenly remembering something, goes across to the window and stares out onto the street.

My arms start to tingle, things slow down. The room lurches. 'Green Manalishi' chords are grinding around in my head again, banshee slide wailing.

This is it. Something's wrong.

He comes back to the table, still smiling.

'What was that about?' I ask him.

'What?'

'What were you looking for?'

'Nothing,' he protests, startled by my sudden change of tone. Swallows five or six times in rapid succession and winces, as if trying to keep something big down. A secret?

'Well why did you go over to the window? What were you looking for?'

'I don't know, Mister Novak, really.' He shrugs. Eyes dart down to his pint glass but he's unsure whether to touch it now. 'Sometimes I just do things. You know how you do? Things I can't explain. I wasn't meaning to be rude or anything.'

I gesture to the chair opposite. He gingerly sits down again.

'Wait here,' I tell him.

I walk out to the foyer. The Chinese receptionist is on the phone, no sign of the concierge. A doorman walks in blowing into his hands, smiles and waves across at me.

Back in the bar, Ollie is still sitting there. I walk across to the window and look out too. Nothing. Not even a cab waiting.

I go and sit back down opposite him. Stare him out for a while.

A gaunt, overly made-up woman in a glittering low-backed dress walks in, shakes her shoulders with a pained shiver and throws her coat to Chris.

Where did she come from? Nothing out there. Not even a cab waiting.

She sits down at the piano and flexes long spidery fingers. Produces a book from nowhere. *The Satanic Verses*. Salman Rushdie. *Noted and filed*.

Got them all in a quandary, did Salman this year, and now there's a fatwah out on him from the Supreme Leader of Iran. Probably not what was intended, but how can you guess with that lot? Iran, where there's no longer a Shah to dispense shares in fields and factories to the workers, or to issue discrete directions on oil reserves down a golden telephone.

I look across at Ollie. He's nervous now, flicks at his hair, fumbles with a button on his jacket and waits.

'You were about to tell me what you did,' I say, reassuringly.

He brightens, relieved, finally feels he can pick up the glass and has a long drink.

'Well,' he begins again, eyes darting left and right, 'like I was telling you, I was in publishing myself, you could say, until about three years ago. Fleet Street. Then they built Wapping and all of us got our cards. I don't know how many exactly, but a shit-load. I was only a gofer anyway really, but there were people who were really skilled. And it was hot metal and linotype, not crappy litho. The writing was on the wall wasn't it? We all took the piss, to be honest.'

'How so?'

'Closed shop, Spanish practices. Got away with murder at one time. For years, to be honest. Never touched the drink before I started there. Then the shit hit the fan. And now, well, you look at it and think, there's just a guy sat at a desk doing it all. I never bothered with the picketing, waste of time as far as I could see. Not with her behind Murdoch. But new technology, that was the real killer.'

'You've got to keep connected,' I tell him, and smile now.

'Anyhow,' he sighs, resigned, 'I get by.'

The pianist puts her book down and tinkles the keys, begins to play 'Have Yourself a Merry Little Christmas'.

'So how long have you known Danny Kirwan?' I ask Ollie.

Thinks for a moment.

'A few years now, around about the time *The Sun* did that story on him, or was it *The Standard*? "Twenty-one pints a day and I'm all right." Most of the people he drinks with down in Covent Garden, the regulars, don't know much about who he was before, or don't care, but I was always a fan. Weren't you though?'

'Of course I was Ollie,' I say. 'So where's he living?'

'Up at the St Mungo's Hostel in Holborn most of the time. They've offered him a flat but he's not interested. You only get thirty-seven quid on the dole though, so that doesn't go far. But I think he still gets royalties from time to time. His mum still does his accounts for him, so he's luckier than the rest. And there are always fans coming around to stand him drinks. You'd hardly be the first.'

Noted and filed.

He puts his empty glass down, licks his lips with relish.

'I could use another of those,' he says.

I motion Chris over.

'Can we have…'

'Tell you what I fancy Chris,' Ollie interrupts, 'a Car Bomb. Do you know how to do those? Irish whisky, a pint of Guinness and a shot of Bailey's Irish Cream.'

Chris sniffs, looks down his nose.

'This is the Savoy Hotel,' he says, whisking a towel over his shoulder waspishly. 'We'd hardly have anything to do with something named after Irish bombs.'

★

Night sweats, flashbacks. Bad, bad dreams.

'Did you place a bomb in the fridge of the communal dwelling at 60 Stephan Street in the Moabit?'

I cannot answer.

'Was that bomb actually supplied by West Germany's Office of the Constitution itself?'

I cannot answer. They have instructed me not to answer.

It started with Rudi. He was the first to accept something from me. On March 2nd 1968 he flew from West Berlin to Frankfurt with the package I handed him in the Republican Club. The plan was to take out a US transmitter, but he was arrested in Frankfurt as a matter of course. While in police custody he was allowed to leave his bag in a locker and gave it back to me when he returned to Berlin. Things were relaxed, back then.

Number Two was hidden beneath a briefcase under a bench on the top floor of the Criminal Court of West Berlin four days later. The long-running trial of Fritz Teufel and Rainer Langhans was once more underway.

A burning department store with burning people conveyed, for the first time in a major European city, the sizzling Vietnam feeling.

Fritz and Rainer were found not guilty of incitement to arson.

Bomb Number Three was placed on a shelf in the ladies' clothing department on the first floor of the Schneider department store in Frankfurt on the evening of April 2nd. Number Four was placed in a replica antique cupboard in the furnishing department. Like the device found in the Berlin courtroom, these two consisted of plastic bottles and petrol, alarm clocks, torch batteries and detonators embedded in a home-made explosive. Held together with sellotape and plastic film, their timers were set for midnight.

Number Five was discovered dismantled in the boot of a hired VW on the outskirts of Frankfurt a day later, along with the fragments of a new poem:

When will the Brandenburg Gate burn?
When will the Berlin stores burn?

★

Back in my room I pull out the smallest package from Chris, tear off the garish wrapping. A cassette of Fleetwood Mac's self-titled first album. A dog running through tipped-over dustbins on the shrunken sleeve. I slot the cassette into the new Walkman as I sit down on the bed and put on the earphones. Elmore James slide guitar. It can only be Jeremy Spencer, who one day in February 1971 wandered off from Fleetwood Mac's Los Angeles hotel and found himself some new friends. They gave him a new name and helped him be happy.

What did he have to say of his time with the group later?

I remind myself again:

GET OUT OF HIS HOUSE OR HE'LL KILL YOU

The world of Rock and Roll is a slime pit! Aside from the pitfalls of pride, drugs & money in the Pop music world, the most shocking thing is the widespread acceptance & prevalence of sodomy amongst the musicians, managers & producers. This was what shocked me most when I first entered the music business.

I was a simple country boy when I joined Fleetwood Mac, I had been living in a very small country town & I had a rosy idea of the Pop music scene.

When I first arrived in London, Mick Fleetwood, the drummer of Fleetwood Mac, was living with three or four Sodomites! Then I found out that it was pretty common for guys in the Pop world to be what they called AC/DC or bisexual – practising sex with women and men!

Many of the male managers and promoters were Sodomites. One of the oldest Pop music agencies was called 'Stable' and it was run by Larry Parnes who would 'groom' Pop singers, meaning he would prepare them to be stars. He was a Sodomite. So was Brian Epstein, the manager of the Beatles.

Then I found out that Robert Stig of the Robert Stigwood Organisation (RSO) was a Sodomite! The RSO is one of the biggest Rock music organisations of them all, managing such big groups as the Bee Gees. Bands could not become members of the Robert Stigwood Organisation unless a member of the band consented to be Robert Stig's lover-boy. In the Bee Gees it was Barry Gibb, the lead singer, the handsome one.

Ahmet Ertegun, the President of Atlantic Records, who produced our ill-fated album when I backslid in the Family, once saw a Russian ballet troupe and took a fancy to one of the male ballet dancers. So he literally bought him for thousands of dollars to be his personal 'bugger' – the old English word for Sodomite!

I encountered one of the most shocking examples of gross Sodomy when I was in Fleetwood Mac. Mick Fleetwood's wife and the woman who was George Harrison's wife at that time were sisters. (George Harrison was the guitarist of the Beatles.) Often these sisters would go together to the big parties that the Beatles threw. One morning while I was talking to

Mick, his wife came into the room & was bragging about the party she had gone to the night before & how groovy it was & said that Eric & Paul & George were having a 'scene' on the couch. (A 'scene' meant having sex together.) That meant that Eric Clapton, George Harrison & Paul McCartney (famous rock singers) were having a homosexual threesome on the couch! I was shocked! I looked at Mick Fleetwood & he said, 'What's wrong with you? What's the matter with you?' I said, 'That's disgusting! I don't think that's right!' He said, 'Come on! I wouldn't mind having a nice "scene" with Eric, George & Paul!'

Around that time Sodomy started creeping in more and more between the members of Fleetwood Mac. I would sometimes find Mick Fleetwood in bed with Peter Green, the leader of Fleetwood Mac. The way they would talk about themselves and about other men was disgusting to hear. They would comment on some man's body & say, 'Oh, he's cute. I wouldn't mind blah, blah, blah...', like normal System men would talk between themselves about women. What it comes down to is I was living in Sodom. I'm thankful that while I was involved in Fleetwood Mac I was married & had a child. I believe this & my wife's (Fiona's) prayers for me helped keep me from getting into Sodomy myself. Thank the Lord!

Success Means Paying the Devil His Dues!

Witchcraft is also prevalent in the world of Rock & Roll. Peter Green was fascinated by the Devil & he hung around with witches. He wrote the song 'Black Magic Woman' which was later recorded by a band named Santana. That one song made Peter Green a millionaire & put Fleetwood Mac 'on the map' in England. It was the first hit song we had, but why? Simply because it gave glory to the Devil. Remember the Bible says, 'And the Devil, taking Him up into an high mountain, showed unto Him all the kingdoms of the World in a moment of time. And the Devil said to Him, "All this power will I give Thee and the glory of them: for that is delivered unto me; and to whomsoever I will I give it. If Thou therefore will worship me, all shall be Thine."' (Luke 4:5-7)

After the huge hit 'Black Magic Woman', Fleetwood Mac came out with a beautiful piece of music called 'Albatross' (written by Peter Green) which was also a Number One hit. If you were to hear this number you could easily think, 'Wow, that's such a sweet piece of music. It's so nice.' But I'm sure if Peter Green hadn't first paid the Devil his due, given him the glory & the credit he wanted with his previous evil Devil-glorifying hit, then 'Albatross' wouldn't have had a chance of being a hit.

I saw Peter Green, who actually founded Fleetwood Mac, after I joined the Family & I asked him if he ever talked to Jesus. He answered, 'Yes, but I talk to other spirits too.' I told him that I had a dream that he had evil spirits bothering him. He said, 'Yes, that's right.' So I told him, 'You can get rid of them in the Name of Jesus.' He said, 'I don't want to get rid of them because they're my friends.'

I saw Peter Green a few years later in Los Angeles – he had been imprisoned for beating up his wife (he married a Jewish-Christian girl and she was pregnant & he beat her up one night, saying she was trying to control his mind. So he was sent to prison.) He was on the phone for two hours at the prison talking to Mick Fleetwood, asking him to bail him out, so Mick did. But then Peter Green complained about leaving the prison & said he would have liked to stay in prison because he felt those were the people he belonged with! How true!

The last time I talked to people who knew Peter Green, they told me that now his fingernails are two inches long, he doesn't wash & he sometimes crawls around on his hands & knees like Nebuchadnezzar did. (Daniel 4.33) One time he was scratching at the door of an ex-girlfriend's house late one night. She thought there was an animal outside her door but when she looked, she saw it was him on his hands & knees scratching at the door & making noises like an animal!

The kids named him 'the Werewolf of Richmond' because he prowls around at night in this horrible state & scares people. It's pitiful to think that a man who was a millionaire & had all that fame & glory is now just a beast! – Those are the wages of sin & entertaining the Devil & his evil spirits!

And he's waiting out there for me somewhere in this England, to tell me something I need to know. The Green God.

19. NOVEMBER 20th 1989

Barks from the stallholders out in the street, the rattle of handcarts on cobbles. Razors of Monday morning Covent Garden sun through the window make us squint. This is where we find Danny Kirwan. In the pub, as early as possible.

'The first time we saw them was at that free concert in Camden,' Ollie says, riffing on the Fleetwood Mac theme, eyes darting in every direction just as they did the other night, 'wasn't it, Karen? Hard to believe it's twenty years ago. Unbelievable. Totally blew us away, though.'

'Blew us away,' Karen, his girlfriend, presumably, agrees, crossing her legs and pulling a slice of lemon from her gin and tonic. Like Ollie, she's all in denim, half-moon slides pushing lank hair back to pixie ears, round face, livid green eye-shadow. Her tongue darts from between small, jagged teeth at the lemon shard.

'Probably because they were shitting themselves,' Ollie says, hoovering up the air again. 'That was the night with the skinheads, Karen, remember?'

'Skinheads. Yeah, all those skinheads,' she agrees, biting into the lemon now and scowling. 'Parliament Hill Fields. Animals.'

So they've been a couple for twenty years.

Noted and filed.

'The thing is,' says Martin, 'what made Fleetwood Mac so unique at that time – one of the things, I should say – was the interplay between Peter and Danny. It gave them something really special. Then of course, Jeremy was the third element. The joker in the pack, if you will.'

I don't know Martin, don't think anybody does. Why is he here? He's a Fleetwood Mac fan, he says, and they say. But they don't seem to know him from Adam, it's just accepted he's here at the table with us. Then again, they don't know me either, and that's the thing about England. Nobody questions why someone's there, what they really want or why they would want anything. They've been the victors for too long, got too comfortable.

What you know protects you against what they know and can use against you, but they haven't realised that for some time here.

Martin's words hang in the air. He half-stands and brushes at the creases in his trousers self-consciously, sits back down and pushes his glasses up his nose. Stocky and swarthy, in the uniform of an off-duty trader – striped shirt open at the neck, sleeves rolled back, fat Rolex on his wrist.

Noted and filed.

The silence grows longer as Ollie and Karen both turn frozen smiles to me, blocking Martin out in some barely discernible way. Or is it me?

Danny Kirwan, pale, his girlish features now gaunt and obscured by a heavy beard, chuckles, seemingly to himself. Puts his pint to his lips. Martin has pushed a battered copy of Fleetwood Mac's double album *Blues Jam at Chess* in front of him to sign.

'Chicago, January '69' Martin says to Danny, 'can you remember anything about it?'

Danny doesn't reply, opens the gatefold sleeve, finds a picture of himself and shows it to Ollie and Karen.

Karen dowses her lemon slice in the ashtray, takes hold of a corner of the sleeve.

'God, yeah,' she says. 'You were a good looking fella, Danny. But just a boy. Such a baby. So young, look at you.'

I glance over at a small portable TV behind the bar. Latest footage from Prague. Students with their arms full of flowers on Národní Street. Visored police beating them back with nightsticks.

'There were about 25,000 there, it was a free concert,' Ollie is saying, 'but they weren't bothered about that. They were everywhere by '69, skinheads, and you suddenly had to watch your back if you had long hair. They were out for you. Soccer types with a new uniform, like a new army. Police were no longer the problem. Hunted in packs, looking for queers or pakis mostly. But it was really tense, that night on Parliament Hill Fields.'

Martin starts to rock in his seat, looking for a way back into the conversation.

'Big red boots,' Karen says, 'sixteen-hole Doc Marten's, granddad shirts and braces. But that was after.'

'After,' Ollie agrees. '*Clockwork Orange* and that, though. A bummer. Fleetwood Mac blew us away. You were brilliant Danny, that night on Parliament Hill Fields.'

Karen nods.

'Parliament Hill Fields.'

Also known as Traitor's Hill. The peak from which Guy Fawkes planned to watch the destruction of Parliament in the Gunpowder Plot of 1605.

'Have you personally offered pistols, machine guns, mortars and grenades to certain individuals standing before this court?'

'We shouldn't have…' Danny starts to say something and we hang on his words. He shakes his head, puts the record on the table, inching further down into his army greatcoat and looking out the window.

'Danny, you see, played more like Buddy Guy,' Martin explains to me, 'while Peter was more influenced by BB King. All that sustain, the simplicity. Which is obviously why he used the Les Paul mainly. Danny though, you used more tight flourishes of notes, didn't you? More suited to a Fender Strat? And with more of a jazz tinge, a little Django Reinhardt?'

Danny continues to stare out of the window.

'Well the music speaks for itself,' Martin says, responding to an unspoken objection, 'and Peter's on record as saying he couldn't have written any of the great songs without Danny.'

'And Edgar Broughton was stirring the skinheads up,' Ollie says, 'seeming to make them even more angry.'

'Even more angry,' Karen agrees. 'Out demons out,' she growls. 'Remember? It went on forever that song. Out demons out.'

The last time I talked to people who knew Peter Green, they told me that now his fingernails are two inches long, he doesn't wash and he sometimes crawls around on his hands and knees.

Ollie needs another huge lungful of air before attempting his own rendition.

'Out demons out.'

One time he was scratching at the door of an ex-girlfriend's house late one night.

'And they were throwing bottles and cans.'

'Bottles and cans…'

The kids named him 'the Werewolf of Richmond' because he prowls around at night in this horrible state and scares people.

'Tearing out the fencing posts.'

'Tearing them out…'

They say he was never the same after one time in Germany when he took too much LSD.

Martin goes to the bar to order another round.

Karen rolls a cigarette from a tin with a skull and crossbones on its lid, passes it to Danny.

'Is it bothering you, all this harking back to the past again?' she asks him, brushing the fringe from his eyes. 'They always want to know about it, you know that. What are we going to do with you?'

He shrugs, blinks. Beautiful pale blue eyes. Looks across at me, suddenly lucid.

'We shouldn't have done what we did,' he says to me. 'I know that now.'

'What did you do?' Karen asks him, oblivious to the look, still stroking his hair.

'Stole it all from the blacks. Stole their music,' he says, still staring straight at me. 'That was all wrong. That was our problem. Ask Peter Green about New Orleans. Ask him about that. Went to Chicago like heroes and they treated us like the thieves we were.'

'But who, Danny?' Karen asks. 'Who was it?'

He flinches away from her, runs his fingertips across his beard.

'The blacks, the proper blues players, like the guys in the studio, at Chess.'

'Chess?'

He picks up the record again.

'Willie Dixon,' he points out with a nicotine-stained nail. 'Huge guy, must have been six foot six, about twenty stone. Decorating the studio when we got there, slapping whitewash over the walls with a broom. Needed the money. And we turned up in limousines.'

'Your drink, maestro,' Martin says, putting another glass down in front of him. 'Who are we talking about?'

Danny continues to avoid his eye.

'Willie Dixon,' Karen tells him.

'Ah well, one of the greats, Dixon. Everyone rifled through his songbook. Little Red Rooster, Hoochie Coochie Man, Back Door Man, Spoonful…'

'It was scary, America,' Danny continues. 'Scarier than those skinheads on Parliament Hill. Always scary, never knew what was going on. Gunshots in the night and shouting round the clock. Voodoo and tarot cards. Fucking anarchy.'

'Who didn't cover Willie Dixon songs back then?' Martin muses, bridging his hands in prayer at his lips. 'The Stones, Dylan, Cream…'

'That's Otis Spann,' Danny shows Karen. 'Died of liver cancer about a year after the picture was taken. Always sliding down his piano stool, shaking dice out the back in the drains with kids, like in an old movie. And that's Buddy Guy, who I was supposed to sound like, only I'd never heard of him. Looked like he was with the Black Panthers then; shades and a French beret. Never said a word to me anyhow, could tell he thought I was a cunt. Uppity white boy, but…'

Drains his pint in one, strokes his beard again, puzzling something out.

'…gunshots in the night and shouting round the clock, people screaming at each other. The world's in a tangle. That's when it started getting to me. Started locking myself in the hotel room, just drinking and drinking to get through it. Don't think the others even noticed. That's why I smashed the guitars and had those tantrums in the end. I just… really couldn't stand it.'

His eyes brim, swatting the air in front of his beard, at invisible flies.

'Jerry had the right idea. Just get out of it. Turn yourself into someone else, anything to get out of it. And get away from him.'

Karen puts her arm around his shoulder, strokes his hair.

'Don't Danny, it doesn't matter all this stuff. You're not in Chicago now,' she tells him. 'It was all years ago. It's all fine here.'

Danny gets to his feet unsteadily.

'Just going for a walk,' he says.

We all watch him leave, sit for a while in uneasy silence.

'We've got to get going anyhow,' Ollie says eventually. 'I hope you got what you wanted. Told you it was difficult.'

'Going anyhow,' Karen says.

Leaving me alone with Martin, who slumps back with a sigh of mingled disappointment and relief and lights a cigarette, pursing his lips, exhaling through his nose.

'It's a shame,' he says. 'A real shame. Are you a guitarist?'

I shake my head.

'They'll never bring him back now, he can't function properly. At their peak there was nobody to touch them, but God knows what happened. To him, to Jeremy Spencer, and most of all to Peter Green, of course.'

We fall silent for a while. Suddenly he brightens.

'You know,' he says, 'I heard there's this guy going around London passing himself off as Peter Green at the moment. Can you believe that? His name's Patrick Himfen. A lot of people know him as the Egg and Potato Man.'

'The Egg and Potato Man,' I repeat sceptically. He nods.

'Also known as Patrick Harper sometimes, if I remember this right. And also known as Beetroot.'

'Beetroot?'

'That's right. Wanted to be Jimi Hendrix at one stage, but obviously, that proved a little more problematic. Suspension of disbelief and all that. So he settled for Peter Green. Even had a collection of nice Les Paul guitars at one time. Rumours started to spread about him lighting cigarettes with royalty cheques.'

'That's completely insane,' I say.

He shrugs.

'Not really, when you think about it. A naughty boy, I suppose, the old Egg and Potato Man – he'd do some real damage if he got the chance. Gives people the runaround. He's already taken in a few starry-eyed chancers who want to believe he's Peter Green. Even some who *knew* Peter Green.'

'Why would he go to so much trouble?'

'Your guess is as good as mine. Who knows – a few small lies turn into bigger ones don't they, build their own momentum? The trick is remembering who you've told what and what lie you told where, isn't it? Consistency, that's the key. Or maybe it even began as a joke, then a few people started taking him seriously. Once people start believing you're what you say you are, well, this is it isn't it? You're halfway there.'

Noted and filed.

'Maybe it's the prestige?' I suggest.

Martin leans forward and stares at me now. I hold his gaze.

'It's not that,' he says. 'He wants to be Peter Green. He believes in himself. Self-belief is everything. Suppose that kind of thing's inevitable. It's just such a story. Imagine. Fleetwood Mac, now one of the biggest bands in the world. How many copies did *Rumours* sell? Something like twenty million? One of the biggest albums ever. And here he is. Multi-millionaires – the old bass player and drummer who used to back *him*,' a thumb flicked at the door. 'Danny. Mick Fleetwood and John McVie. You just couldn't make that up, could you?'

He picks up his copy of *Blues Jam at Chess* and spreads his hands. Sighs.

'He didn't even sign it,' I tell him.

'He won't have gone far,' Martin replies. 'Maybe we can find him.'

'It's Peter Green I really want to meet though,' I say.

Martin raises his eyes, draws on his cigarette.

'I don't think he'll talk to anyone. Probably a waste of time.'

'He'll talk to me. I just know. I met him only once, a long time ago.'

Martin looks unimpressed.

'He's supposed to be in Essex somewhere now,' he says. 'Left Richmond. Maybe I could help you.'

And we drink some more together, me and my new friend Martin, and the morning becomes the afternoon, and the afternoon the evening.

★

Josef Bachmann shot Rudi Dutschke on April 11th 1968, just a week after Bomb Number Five was discovered.

Josef Bachmann, a no-mark. House-painter. Short, carefully parted hair, pale face. Avid reader of the output of Axel Cäsar Springer.

Soot-black marks on the fingers, word-traces smeared on knives and spoons, on linen and door handles.

Arrived at the Zoo station from Munich just after nine with one pistol in a shoulder holster under his suede jacket, another in a green hold-all, along with ammunition, a radio and a cutting from the *Deutsche National-Zeitung*:

Stop Dutschke and the radical left revolution now!

If we don't, Germany will become a pilgrimage for malcontents from all over the world.

Sold the radio in a second-hand shop for thirty-two marks, breakfasted on sausages on a park bench.

Confronted with what is happening today, one simply cannot go about one's daily business, nor should one leave all the dirty work to the police and their water cannon.

Went first to Kaiser-Friedrich Street and rang the bell to the flat on the fourth floor of the communal block. Rainer Langhans came down to speak to him briefly. Took the bus back to the Zoo and lunched on meatballs and lentil soup, then up to the SDS Centre, 140 Ku'damm.

Are our judges asleep? Are our politicians asleep? How long are they going to permit our young people to be incited by red agitators and our laws to be called into question, made hollow, and disregarded.

And out came Rudi on his bike, on an errand for medicine for his three-year-old son. Rudi looking for an escape from being the symbol of this revolution, contemplating even a move to the USA.

Are we a banana republic in which one can trample justice and law underfoot on the flimsiest of pretexts...

'Are you Rudi Dutschke?'

...make a fool of the law-abiding citizen and a hero out of the lawbreaker...

'Yes.'

...and smash the windows of the Americans with impunity – those same Americans who protect us militarily – a protection which is a precondition of being able to demonstrate in freedom in our country?

'Filthy communist swine.'

The first shot hit him in the right cheek, knocked him off his bike and into the road.

A second shot hit him in the head, a third in the shoulder.

Bachmann fled to a nearby building site and swallowed twenty sleeping tablets.

Rudi managed to get back to his feet, leaving his shoes in the road, staggering back in the direction of the SDS Centre before collapsing.

It set the tone for 1968, the shooting of Rudi, and I had no part in the planting of any other devices for the best part of a year. Surplus to requirements. Not until Nixon's visit.

The night after Rudi's shooting, though, as the Springer vans burned, I drove Bommi and Fritz around the city with a basketful of molotovs. We talked about taking a trip to the newspaper chief's villa, looking for a better target, until the drugs and adrenalin started to wear down.

Rudi fighting for his life in the West End Hospital, a chalk circle around his shoes on the Ku'damm.

Bachmann taken into custody, claiming affiliation to no political party and inspiration from the assassination of Martin Luther King the previous week.

Lone gunmen. They're always alone. No ties, driven by inner voices. The public always prefers it that way. As if everyone is free to think for themselves. As if.

20. DECEMBER 30th 1989

I don't run, I wait. Nothing happens. I can feel myself starting to thaw, to loosen up. Maybe they have other things to worry about.

And from my room, I look out at the Tower of London, where once Wat Tyler's men beheaded the country's Lords Chancellor and Treasurer.

I skirt the pool, the bar, the lounges, crash business convention meetings that are held in plush conference centres, have suits tailored on Saville Row, buy some shirts from Pink's.

Very quickly, it seems, London could belong to me too, as well as to Margaret Thatcher and the bankers and oil companies. It's infectious.

Martin turned up in the American Bar the night after our meeting with Danny Kirwan, acting as if we'd arranged it and reminding me of conversations I didn't recall. I try to remember what was said now, how much I told him. Seems I said I was thinking of staying here, looking for business opportunities. There are lots of parties in the build-up to Christmas – important for new contacts – and he proves instrumental in helping me break the ice.

Together, we also visit the places where the famous London clubs used to be – the Flamingo, the Bag o'Nails, the Marquee on Wardour Street. I try and imagine what it was like, this city, when you could drive around it as you pleased, see Peter Green and his blues bands for pennies. The music of the victors, stolen from the sons of slaves.

I top up my tan in the solarium, have a massage from a slender Indian girl kept in the basement. Once or twice sleep with the frosty hair stylist, Angela.

Chris, she tells me – once only, smoking a thin menthol cigarette as if dreaming she's in a film – is not to be trusted. He's not who he seems.

Noted and filed.

But too late, really. Too late for everything now.

Face that moves from a grin to a question mark, Chris. Listening's not really listening when it's part of the job.

Noted and filed.

But too late. Too late for everything.

Looked at me once. *Well travelled.* Blinked and left.

★

Tonight the lobby is deserted.

I walk through the bar. Carpet with a pattern of unwanted Christmas cardigans, mustard columns, leather-studded chairs around glass-topped tables, grand piano.

Chris is away – a squat, unfriendly looking guy with greased grey hair in his place.

No cocktails tonight.

Chris is not to be trusted. He's not who he seems. But then, is Angela?

I fold myself into a corduroy sofa in front of the muted TV, watch the last of them falling.

Nicolae Ceausescu. First shown being examined by a doctor, then in a camel-hair overcoat, glancing at his watch, as if late for another appointment. Gaunt and unshaven. In a bare room, his wife Elena at his side, headscarved. Peasant stock. The camera curves to a panel of military officers and back to the couple.

He makes wild gestures, thrusts his shoulders forward, pulls his head back with a sneer. Sent to work in the factories at eleven, agitator by the age of fifteen. Climbed through the ranks. Never quite got to grips with the payback clauses in Western economic development programmes. Laid waste with punishing export drives, austerity measures, birth control.

The Ceausescus are charged with the genocide of more than sixty thousand people, of hiding more than a billion dollars in Swiss banks.

Nicolae and Elena, shouting as the soldiers take their arms.

A subtitle:

'I was like a mother to you.'

The last of them falling.

Out on the streets of Bucharest, the rioters ride on tanks with the soldiers, brother with brother. Waving flags – the Communist coat of arms ripped from their centres. More proles in their hellish knitwear. In Palace Square, and skirting the crumbling tower blocks all around it.

Then a camera at waist height in a courtyard pans in on a pair of hands being bound, the cuffs of a brown overcoat.

The last of them falling.

A wash of static and the staring, dead eyes of Nicolae Ceausescu – Genius of the Carpathians – the stone wall behind his head dashed with his blood.

The last of them. The last of them falling.

★

Back in August 1968, something of a hero, Nicolae Ceausescu. For a time. Waving a defiant fist at the Soviets as their tanks pounded Czechoslovakia's fields. Two hundred thousand Warsaw Pact troops – Russians, Bulgarians, Poles, Hungarians – flooding in to take the airport and television station, the government buildings, the industrial centres.

The Czech villagers painted out the names of their pathetic outcrops, turned all road signs hopefully back to Moscow. What had they done? Maybe the coming troops would be disorientated, turn back. Maybe they'd be scared and completely powerless too.

Broken eggs, small potatoes.

But back in Berlin, the appetite for such things from some of the members of the first of the new communities was diminishing by the day.

They wanted to turn the clock back even as they continued to move forward, even as their ideas were adopted and adapted by others. Get back to the self, back to the revolution of the revolutionary. Back to exploring feelings, to minutely examining personal behaviour patterns. Psychoanalysis, group interrogation.

Rainer and Dieter and the others who remained, along with some new faces, moved into the new place on Stephan Street, a crumbling former factory close to the Moabit court they'd come to know so well.

Perhaps unable to face such proximity and the prospect of a return to either navel-gazing or further incarceration, Fritz Teufel packed his bags for Munich, where more direct action was happening.

But I was there for them, trying to track down Marina, find out where she was, and mistakenly believing Kurt's man had forgotten all about me.

And I was there for them as Rainer increasingly started to talk of the first of the new communities as a brand. As a corporate identity.

K1. Commune One.

This was dangerous talk back then, subversive even, going against the grain. Selling out, it was called. *Selling out to the man.* Opening a gash right up, for salty accusations of bourgeois double standards to be poured in.

K1, a brand.

And I was there for them as they created their book, *Steal Me.* Sold it to the publishing house Edition Voltaire, edited by Bernward Vesper, father of Gudrun Ensslin's two-year-old son, Felix. Son himself, of the famous Nazi poet, Will Vesper.

K1, a brand. Selling out. Fraternising with the enemy.

Overpriced at ten deutschmarks, *Steal Me* sold 20,000 copies towards the end of 1968. Enough to fund Rainer's dreams for Stephan Street for a time.

K1, a brand. Selling out. Bourgeois double standards.

Stephan Street was a shell, but Rainer had a vision. It would become a cultural centre, with a club on the ground floor. A place where music and films were made, where people could come and go as they pleased, explore their ideas – be free. They would move in sound equipment and printing presses; establish a new falsehood to sell to the world as the truth.

So in the name of freedom, I had to teach them how to mix and lay concrete, how to thread electric wiring through the eaves and skirting boards, how to skim the walls, lag the pipes, connect and seal. How to be practical.

And it struck me, of course, that some things always remain the same.

When Josef Bachmann shot Rudi Dutschke back in April, the action moved – to Hamburg, Essen, Cologne, Frankfurt, Munich and Esslingen. Protests and actions in London, in Paris and in Amsterdam. Oslo, Rome, Milan, Belgrade and Warsaw too.

Taking the shine off their crowns.

K1, a brand. Selling out now, even as they continued to wage war against the judiciary, to turn the Moabit courtroom into more theatre. Playing with the wigs of judges, addressing the crowd directly, vaulting over aisles, being clubbed and cuffed by the guards. Building up the list of charges against themselves.

And riots in 167 cities for Martin Luther King. In the US, 46 dead, at least 2,600 injured and over 21,000 arrested.

So Rudi Dutschke – once the long nights of the Easter Riots in Berlin and West Germany had passed and the Springer trucks burned – was small potatoes too, in the end.

A refugee from the East and a conscientious objector, allowed to study in West Berlin thanks to its master, the USA.

Opened his eyes on Easter Monday and asked his wife where Vietnam was.

During May, sixty thousand people gathered to protest peacefully and pointlessly against the Emergency Laws for West Berlin and

West Germany, which were to come into force in July. While over in France, a general strike was called following riots in Paris. Eleven million people responded to that call.

I was still there for K1 – this new brand, this anti-capitalist corporation – when Marcuse the philosopher returned to Berlin on the night the French Army laid siege to Paris. And talk of the great refusal was somehow not on the agenda.

Didn't he start the ball rolling? Wasn't he calling for action at all? Was it all just words, empty gestures?

We tore down the coat of arms of the Free University – its emblem: Truth, Justice, Liberty – and set fire to it in the grounds. I was happy to supply the petrol personally.

I was there for them too, when with around forty friends, they occupied the Germanic Studies block of the Free University. In solidarity with the French – which was something of a first – renaming it for Rosa Luxemburg.

Mattresses in and desks out. Up against the doors to muffle the pounding truncheons, the place swimming in water, reeking of body odour and rot. Rainer wiring together a transmitter on the top floor.

And Karl Pawla blasting out the music of the victors.

Karl Pawla. Sweet little guy, running wild with us all. A few months later he would clamber onto a judge's desk like some kind of bespectacled insect in the Moabit courthouse. And full of laxatives, crouch like a beetle and empty his bowels. And wipe his arse on the files. Ten months for that.

I was there for them at the last of the happenings – right up to the battle of the Tegeler Weg in November, when the tables were finally turned and the protestors – well marshalled by Bommi Baumann, Georg Von Rauch and their troops from the new Wieland Street Commune – got the upper hand. Not only students now, but Märkische rockers and thugs too, borstal runaways and school truants, wide boys, rogue apprentices, casual workers, waifs and strays.

Suggesting, to those receptive to these things, a new front line – raining down a hail of stones, torching cars, smashing windows, splitting noses, breaking jaws. On the day that our new friend and champion Horst Mahler was ejected from the bar.

Horst Mahler, who looked exactly like the enemy, stamped in the mould of the hierarchical Order of the secular priesthood, in his dark uniform, with his thinning hair, his heavy-framed glasses.

No match for Rudi, too old to take the reins of the revolution, surely? Denied access now too, to the old books and files, the sacred texts.

Son of a Silesian dentist, family fled the Red Army in '45. A rabid anti-semite and fanatical Nazi, the dentist; shot himself in '49.

But with Rudi out of the picture, Horst Mahler was steering himself into the frame as the spokesman for a disparate collection of suddenly excited parties. Maybe even then, he didn't realise he was going to jump. Like Ulrike did.

'Have you personally offered pistols, machine guns, mortars and grenades to certain individuals standing before this court?'

I couldn't answer. I had been instructed not to answer.

Horst Mahler just stared at me.

But the rules had changed. The Emergency Laws were in place. Anyone taking part, violently or not, could now be pursued and arrested with impunity.

After Tegeler Weg, the police were provided with new tools, with special helmets and face-guards. With plastic riot shields and even longer truncheons.

And K1 – the new brand – no longer wants to take part.

But I was there for them as the actions ran their course.

There for them as other cities took the shine off their crowns.

There for them with the new music – Rotary Connection, Pearls Before Swine, Vanilla Fudge, Frank Zappa, the Moody Blues. New codes now, a new language, but still the music of the victors, in their language, being listened to.

I was there for them with hashish and with STP – *Serenity, Tranquility and Peace.*

The enchantment.

There for them with the first of the LSD batches.

The rapture.

Haggling with the new unscrupulous barons like Zoff, as they cruised up to Stephan Street in their big Yank cars. With their giant speakers and cases, their new bottles and phials, their blotting sheets and bullshit ceremonies, their test tubes from the Free University.

There for them, in the end, with the Berlin clink and its morphine base, cooked up right under Rainer's nose, at my suggestion.

Something really different is happening to us now isn't it?

Stephan Street was a shell, but Rainer had a vision. It was where the revolution of the revolutionary would finally take place. And Rainer spoke of finally getting off the treadmill, and of establishing a deeper form of community. K1, he asserted, was indispensable. Its members were now exotic cadres for political action, catalysts, symbols, a new brand representing new freedoms. Not for them an existence as seminar Marxists with grandchildren and slippers, of being party functionaries on a merry-go-round of wages and discussion groups.

What they wanted, he declared, what they couldn't settle for anything less than, was BIG WONDERFUL ECSTASY.

And some listened.

Others, however, were sharpening knives and tinkering with soldering irons and timer devices.

And Dieter, more than anything, wanted to kidnap a judge. State terrorism can only be answered with counter measures, he was telling anyone who'd listen – and there were still plenty. Judges were fair game, he told a packed meeting at the Republican Club, whacked out of his mind on LSD. Then fell over and gashed his head wide open on a radiator.

The meeting had been called to discuss the danger to politics of the new drugs.

This, then, was 1968 for me, with Kurt's man seemingly off my back after Easter.

And Uschi Obermaier arriving after the Essen music festival, hand in hand with Rainer. Essen, so pure, with its straw mattresses, its tents and bonfires. The Fugs, Pink Floyd, Brian Auger and Julie Driscoll, Tangerine Dream, Frank Zappa. And Uschi, shaking her maracas with the droning Munich band Amon Düül. Part of a women's commune. A very new idea that many did not take kindly to. Uschi, a focus for Rainer's ideas.

The revolution of the revolutionary. K1. The brand. The corporation. Fraternising with the enemy.

Uschi Obermaier, bare-breasted, poured into her denims.

Sex. The kind of sex the pack with the pads and pencils demanded.

With Axel Cäsar Springer – shaking off the feeble opposition to his craft after the shooting of Rudi Dutschke. Gazing down from his tower, still ready to reject all forms of political extremism and uphold the principles of the free social market economy.

Sex.

But some of the women no longer wanted to play. They had penis envy, they started saying, wanted to be part of the action too.

This, then, was 1968 for me.

The trips to Stephan Street. The trips *at* Stephan Street.

The absence of Marina.

And Karl Pawla.

Karl Pawla shitting himself on a courtroom desk, wiping his arse with the judge's file.

For Hans-Joachim Rehse, who nobody remembers in 1989.

Rehse, who put the charges to Karl Pawla, of trespass, slander, coarse mischief and resistance to state authority.

And four months later was acquitted himself, of 231 murders during the war.

Tense still? Yes it was tense.

You wouldn't believe how hungry the Allies are for information Peter.

A constant stream of information. Bloody insatiable they are.

Paranoid?

And then, of course, you've got to pass it to the other side too. Even unintended gaps lead to mistrust.

There had been good reason all along.

That was 1968.

It's all got to be seamless. Truth doesn't even come into it, one way or the other.

★

I return to my room.

My clippings are not where I left them, I'm certain of that. They were on the bed and now they're on the table.

I look out at the Tower of London.

Chris is not to be trusted. He's not who he seems, I was told. Somebody's not to be trusted, that's for sure.

I sit down, put the lamp on, look at the first:

SHALOM & NAPALM

On the 31st anniversary of the fascist Crystal Night, several Jewish memorials in West Berlin have been sprayed with 'Shalom and Napalm'.

A fire bomb was placed in the Jewish synagogue.

I didn't leave them on this table.

I glance at the second:

BUILD UP THE RED ARMY!

Don't sit around on the shabby, ransacked sofa and count your loves, like the small-time shopkeeper souls. Build up the right distribution apparatus, let the pant-shitters, the red-cabbage eaters, the social workers, those who only suck up, lie.

Look out at London Bridge, and then down at the third:

THE WICKED WORLD
BEHIND THE SCENES OF ROCK & ROLL!
I saw Peter Green and I asked him if he ever talked to Jesus. He answered, 'Yes, but I talk to other spirits too.' I told him that I had a dream that he had evil spirits bothering him. He said, 'Yes, that's right.' So I told him, 'You can get rid of them in the Name of Jesus.' He said, 'I don't want to get rid of them because they're my friends.'

Think things over, make certain. They were on the bed and now they're on the table. And I told the maid under no circumstances to move anything. On instinct, I check my wallet. The clipping is still there. *Stern* magazine, November 9th 1969. What's in a date?

Martin said he could organise it for me, set up a meeting in Essex. Don't really know Martin, don't think anybody does.

Things have been moved here, and it's a warning.

21. JANUARY 3rd 1990, 11am.

Essex from a train window – breeze-blocked rears of warehouses, elders sprouting through piles of tyres, rail slats dumped in nettle banks. And every available flat surface coated in graffiti – splashes and tags, symbols and code. Mysterious. The day cold and bright, the view enhanced, illuminated.

Jeremy Spencer singing about a hellhound on his trail over tumbling piano on my new Sony Walkman.

Martin arranged everything. Told me of course he'd been working on it, pulling strings. How could he forget? But didn't want to say anything in case it didn't come off. A wink and a shrug.

Martin with his business contacts and deals. His Filofax and plans, his networks. And a Fleetwood Mac fan, or so he said, just accepted at the table that day, with his copy of *Blues Jam at Chess.*

Nobody questioned why he was there, what he really wanted or why he would want anything. I let my guard down with him, we toured the city together, trawled the bars, discussed opportunities.

Didn't want to come today though.

'Just couldn't,' he said. 'Saw him play a couple of times as you know, but it's not there anymore, and it's just too sad. Good luck with it though, I hear he changes like the wind.'

Gave me a train timetable, marked the station where I should get off, said he'd be waiting there for me and knew what I wanted.

And he is waiting now, finally – no drum roll, no fanfare.

Across the tracks by a battered Land Rover in the deserted backwater station as the train pulls in. Lone figure squinting in the winter sun, blowing into fingerless gloves, shifting from foot to foot.

The Green God.

The anger and sadness in his songs, the self-pity and the rootless longing are mine. And the other music, his guitar crying, screaming, dying is mine too.

The kilos have rolled off Peter Green since his last photo, but he still looks nothing like he did back then. Why would he?

The train pulls off. I walk across the tracks holding out my hand. Take in his oiled jacket, patched and stained, a frayed tartan shirt over an off-white tee, wild bushy beard. Thin hair dancing in Hassidic curls, but not as bald as he looked in that last picture I saw of him.

'You're him,' he says, shaking his head sadly, ignoring my outstretched hand.

I consider returning the remark. His voice doesn't sound anything like it did. ECT and almost twenty years of medication. I find myself avoiding eye contact for some reason.

'Peter Novak,' I begin, 'I can't tell you what an honour it is for me to finally meet you and I really want to thank you for agreeing to see me.'

'I didn't agree to anything,' he replies sharply, sneering through his whiskers. Tilts his head. 'Sometimes we just have to do what we're told don't we? Anyway, another Peter is it? Fishers of men, we are. Come on, let's go. I've a few things to sort out but we can talk on the way.'

'I didn't expect you to be on your own,' I say as we climb in.

He laughs again, an abrupt bark. Turns and examines me.

'What did you expect then? Personal assistants? Bodyguards? An entourage?'

A few teeth missing, I notice.

'Well, I don't know…'

'Where will you stay?'

'I haven't planned anything yet.'

'It won't be a problem,' he tells me. 'There are places. We've met before somewhere haven't we?'

Tone laced with suspicion. It's too early for me to say anything. He smells earthy, close to the land at my side.

'I'm pretty sure we haven't,' I say. Guarded. 'I'd remember.'

Continues to stare at me.

'A face in a crowd then, with a pen and notebook.'

I shrug.

'Very probably.'

'Where would that have been?'

He turns the ignition, jams into gear as I start to list off a few plausible dates.

Glance in the rear-view mirror. Trays of eggs and milk bottles with swollen cream tops in racks.

I start to outline the ideas for Peter Novak's story, with Fleetwood Mac at its centre, making it up as I go along. About that journey – the 1960s and what people were expecting by the end of them, what music meant and how little it all seems to mean now. How easily all those big ideas for change evaporated. Marx and Mao kicked in the gutter. And now the end of the 1980s. How the great refusal turned into an even greater kind of complicity.

But I can't tell if he's listening. He's not a driver isn't Peter Green, surely never passed a test. And I'd read he was still on heavy medication.

Eventually he lurches to a stop at a scarlet phonebox on the edge of a village.

'Just need to make a call.'

I watch Peter Green in the phonebox. The conversation is long and animated and he looks over and gestures angrily at me on several occasions, pumping in coins.

And I know I should be wary, but instead feel emboldened, serene. I turn and look in the back again. A can of petrol and a box of shotgun cartridges between the egg trays. Arrested once, I remember, for illegal possession of a firearm. I should ask him about the shotgun at some stage.

'So I know what you want to know,' he says unbidden as he gets back in, turning the ignition again. 'The stuff about the guitar, how it used to speak for me in the olden days but I can't let it do that for me anymore, right? All that olden days stuff. Can't let it break my heart again, break me in pieces. Yeah, cue the violins, old Peter's feeling sorry for himself, but the whole thing, see, was that it used to be a bit of a show and I could get up and sing those sad songs. I meant some of it but not all of it.'

The Land Rover putters erratically across the cobbles of the pretty village main square. Buttery cottages, hanging baskets, wrought iron.

'Well if you want to talk about that, fine,' I say, 'I'm happy to listen, of course, but that's a story everybody who's interested already knows.'

'The others weren't getting broken by making the music, which was good,' he continues. 'That's why they lasted it out. Mick's got his mansions and all those deals going on, John's got his yachts, but he was okay. Straight as a die. Always blamed how things went on something that happened in Germany. But not me.'

'No?'

'My wheels just fell off,' he murmurs. 'One by one.'

'I suppose so,' I reply.

Suddenly he turns with that sharp look again, the suspicion, irritated by something.

Changes like the wind.

'You're not taking any notes,' he says. 'How can you be accurate if you're not taking notes? Are you just another one who twists everything around? They said you were different.'

'You haven't really told me anything yet,' I laugh. 'You want me to write down that your wheels fell off? Is that a quote? A neat headline? I won't publish anything before I let you see it, anyhow.'

Shakes his head, sniffs, seemingly satisfied.

'Better not then, now you've given me your word.'

Hand extends from the gearstick towards me. Butterfly tattoo between thumb and forefinger. Never mentioned anywhere, as far as I recall. His fingers not the sensitive instruments they once were.

'But I don't really want the facts as they've come to be accepted either,' I say as we shake. 'I suppose I'm looking for something else.'

'Something deeper, eh?' Another abrupt laugh, more of a cough.

'I suppose so,' I say. 'No, not suppose, definitely. That's exactly what I want.'

We pull up outside a general store, its frontage stored up with sacks of coal, bundles of sticks, string bags of turnips, onions.

'Give us a hand then,' he says, turning the engine off, slapping the roof. 'We can leave her here for a while.'

'Okay.'

He opens the back doors and pulls out a milk crate.

'You bring the eggs,' he says, breath spiralling out in the cold. 'Two trays at a time.'

We enter, start to unload our wares. An unsmiling young girl – thirteen or fourteen – watches us behind the till without a word. When we're done, Peter Green stands at the counter, holds his hand out. The girl rings the till, counts out the coins.

'Over the road,' he says, blowing into his gloves again, jerking a thumb.

Some kind of antiques shop, most of its wares obscured behind dimpled glass panels. Closed sign on the door.

'He'll be in the back,' Peter Green tells me, rapping insistently.

A shape emerges behind the glass and the door opens with a cascade of oriental chimes.

'My good friend, how are you?'

A North African, at a guess, grinning at us. Egyptian? Moroccan? Gaudily embroidered dressing gown with a ribbed turtle-neck sweater underneath, heavy glasses bobbing from a chain around his neck. Shakes Peter Green's hand.

'Come in, come in,' he urges, 'you'll catch your death. Who's your friend and what treasures do you have for me today Peter? Let me get the boiler going, fill the kettle. Take seats, please. Our usual spot.'

Scurries off.

A dim light sputters on eventually as we weave our way around pulpits carved with eagles, stained-glass panels, a kaleidoscope tangle of school pews and restaurant chairs. Beer pumps and scientific instruments, the chrome shanks of antique motorbikes. And threaded between them all – stuffing every crevice like makeshift mortar – piles of newspapers.

'What's with all the papers?' I ask.

'No use for even wrapping chips in now,' Peter Green says as we stumble forward. 'It'll take diggers to empty this place out when he goes. Then they'll have to fumigate it. Watch for the rats.'

We arrive at some kind of centre, a bar billiards table with its skittles missing, a dented tin ashtray with the pattern of a dartboard balanced on its arm. The Green God inches down onto a decrepit stool, lifts the billiard ball from its chain, sends it soaring in an arc around the edges of the light.

'Here we are then.'

Lights a long brown cigarette which illuminates his face. Dark wash of beard, eyes scrutinising me again. Grin of missing teeth. I find another chair, sit beside him.

A tray with three steaming cups is set down on the baize and the little man holds out his hand.

'I'm Alwyn,' he says.

His name doesn't fit either, I think.

'Peter,' I say. 'Peter Novak.'

Alwyn pulls a third chair from a nest in the shadows, sits down with us. Spreads his palms across his thighs as if smoothing out a napkin. Smells of camphor.

'Well then, what have you got for me today, Mister Green?' he asks, in his amused tone.

The Green God turns to me.

'Alwyn's a connoisseur,' he says, features wreathed in smoke. 'But to get the right price from him there has to be a story. Maybe you can even help me with it.'

'If I can,' I say, emboldened, serene.

'What I've got for you today, Alwyn, is this.'

Drops something between tin cups onto the felt.

I pick it up first. Small owl carved out of stone. Pass it to Alwyn.

He sniffs, sighs, takes off his glasses, brings out a magnifying glass, turning the object in his hand as he examines it. Sets it down and takes a deep draft of thick black tea.

'Well I have to profess my first feeling is of disappointment,' he says. 'Unless you can give it some kind of value.'

'Oh I think I can,' Peter Green replies.

Alwyn smiles, drums his fingers against his cup.

'Then of course, by all means illuminate me.'

Peter Green tilts back on his stool.

'What do you know about Owsley?' Looks at Alwyn, then at me. Turns back. 'Augustus Owsley Stanley. The Third, to give him his full title. Or the Bear, as they all called him.'

Alwyn shrugs and grins.

'Less than zero,' he says.

'Interesting bloke.' Peter Green stares at me through the smoke expectantly now, shadows dancing behind him. 'Soundman for the Grateful Dead at one time.'

'Ah, of course,' Alwyn says. 'Now I'm making a connection.'

'The visual stuff that you see when you take acid is like noise, Owsley said. Stuff that's there all the time, but you ignore it, see. It's filtered out. What did he say, Mister Novak?'

'The background noise of your visual system,' I can't help myself saying. Emboldened, serene. 'Both in your eye and your brain. Opening up all the portals. Deactivating the filters, that's what he thought it was all about.'

'Deactivated mine alright,' says Peter Green. 'The guitar used to speak for me, as you know. And I was over at Owsley's place once, across the bay in San Francisco, with Suzy, on acid of course. Suzy Wong took care of us back then, knew everybody out there. All the heads, the freaks. And of course, we were swimming in it, melting into each other and the furniture. Nobody had a clue what was going on. And there were owls everywhere, pictures and coffee cups, forks and spoons, salt and pepper pots. Owls on the blotting paper. Melting owls in the curtains, on the cupboards, in the carpets, Even in the toilet – you know the flusher thing? Had an owl on the end of it. I remember pulling and it would stretch out of shape, and then standing there for a time. And eventually, it came off in my hand, put it in my pocket, forgot about it. But somehow things stay with you. That's what I've brought here today.'

The Green God looks at Alwyn.

'A toilet flusher,' Alwyn says solemnly.

'Exactly. But a very special one.'

'Tell me more then, about this Owsley character.'

Peter Green leans forward, lowers his voice conspiratorially, glancing into shadows.

'A fridge full of meat Owsley had,' he says. 'Nothing else – not chops and steaks – sides of the stuff like we used to shoulder when I went up with our Len to Smithfield. And then later at Dave Gregg's. The sides I learned to break down. Shanks and heals and flanks and sirloin tips. Cross ribs, chuck shorts and blades.'

'And who might Dave Gregg be when he's at home?' Alwyn asks.

'That's the butcher I used to work for on Fulham High Street.' Peter Green takes a drink, frowns. 'Very strong this. Stewed. Worked for him for about two years. Was never really any good at it. Sliced his thumb off, Dave, in the end. I think that's right. Long time ago. Had to retire.'

'You were telling us about Owsley though,' I remind him.

'I know, I know,' he says, a dismissive wave of his cigarette. 'Well, you see, Owsley didn't believe in eating anything but meat. No vegetables or potatoes, no things from out of the ground. They were poison. Buried things, spread among the corpses waiting to grow again. Not fully formed or developed. And I'm pretty sure I was already a vegetarian by then.

'Humans were meant to be strictly carnivores, that was his

thinking. To run and to hunt and kill and eat their fill and wake up and start running again. Before the grave got them and they were buried. With the potatoes, I suppose.'

Looks at me and chuckles.

'To run and to hunt and kill and eat their fill,' I repeat.

'That's what he said. I'll never forget that. You just accepted these ideas then. If that's the bag they were into, where their trip was taking them. The Eskimos only eat fish and seals and live the longest. So as I said, there was this fridge full of sides of meat. He'd just slice off a piece and fry it, eat it straight from the pan. And the place just smelled like Dave Gregg's. Only full of these owls. Knick-knacks, what do you call 'ems.'

He gestures for Alwyn to pass him the small stone owl.

'Toilet flushers?' Alwyn suggests.

The Green God holds the owl up to catch the light.

'More than that,' he says. 'Owls are supposed to have the most sophisticated sound equipment in their brains. That's why they can hunt at night, just like bats can find their routes or how the dolphins move around. Sonic waves, echoes, radar.

'And Owsley had this idea that all the sounds have to come from a single place because the human brain is carrying around an even more sophisticated sound processing system, the biggest going. What he was trying to build for them, the Dead, was something that could amplify that, and his acid would open it all up to us, see, all the other stuff that was there. It was always about total freedom then, and that's all forgotten now. Nobody wants it really, just watch the telly. Opening up all the portals. Deactivating the filters. The background noise of your visual system. So we'd become superhuman, man and owl and bat and dolphin. *Eskimo* and owl and bat and dolphin.

'He really thought about sound and how you could move it to a new level. That was as important as the acid. Got all the stuff about radar and electronics from the air force. Wife was actually the chemist, I think. Never met her.

'So Garcia and the Dead played in front of this huge bank of speakers that Owsley put together, where they could hear everything just the same as the audience. His wall of sound. It was all coming from the same place, the one source, that was the idea.'

'You won't find him on many photographs,' I tell Alwyn. 'I think there are only about two, and both over twenty years old.'

Peter Green nods.

'Drooping walrus moustache, he had, sideburns, but wouldn't stand out in a crowd back then. Wore one of those fringed suede jackets at that time, sort of *Easy Rider*, Dennis Hopper look. Well there were thousands of them...'

Falls quiet, lost somewhere else.

Alwyn takes back the owl, subjects it to further scrutiny with the magnifying glass.

'They say he made something in the region of two million tabs of acid in his time,' I say.

The Green God nods, lights another cigarette.

'In front of this huge bank of speakers, his wall of sound from the single source, but he was never in it for the money, never. Made the sound system for locating and separating one sound from everything else, to equal the bats that fly by echoes, the sounds the dolphins hear, and the owls.

'It was the journey, that's all that mattered. Freedom. And the guitar used to speak for me in the olden days. Opening up all the portals. Deactivating the filters.'

'His grandfather was a Kentucky governor,' I tell Alwyn. 'So he came from money. And he made even more money, of course.'

'Piles of it,' Peter Green agrees. 'More than any of us. You'd find thick wads of dollar bills in drawers. But then when he made some, he had to move it along to make more. Felt uneasy, just like I did. And then he was into giving a lot away to keep the price down on the street. That's what it was like. He was embedded. Tangled up in it. "The World's in a Tangle" – that was one of Danny's songs –

sort of slow blues. But not like a complaint, just shrugging, really. Obliged. We all were.

'He just got the recipe for acid from the library at Berkeley. Swiss guy wasn't he, the original?'

Looks to me for confirmation, threading me into his story.

'Albert Hoffman at Sandoz,' I say. 'Lived to be a hundred and two.'

'Your friend's obviously up on his stuff,' Alwyn tells Peter. He nods, stares at me again.

'First the cops tried to get Owsley for meth possession I think,' he continues, his voice moving between registers now, becoming higher as the talking clears his lungs. 'Ended up suing them over that and got his lab equipment back. Sold it for lysergic to make a bigger batch. Balls on the guy. *Big* balls. Thought he was untouchable I suppose, on his mission. We all were. Barrow boys on acid, that was us all.'

'Hendrix was playing on his stuff at Monterey,' I say. 'A special batch, Monterey Purple.'

Peter Green nods again.

'And the guitar used to speak for him too. Owsley made a lot of money, but gave a lot away as well. Or that's what he'd say anyway. Suppose you would, wouldn't you? Papers all calling him the LSD Millionaire. They said I was trying to give all mine away didn't they? They got him in the end, of course, put him on Terminal Island for a couple of years. Don't know what happened to him after that.'

'He's out in Australia,' I tell him. 'Thinks the end of the world's coming.'

Alwyn has closed his eyes.

'He was like a priest or something,' Peter Green continues. 'Religious with it, preaching. If you want to develop you have to do it, that was the message. The Dead were all tripping all the time and they were a lesson for me. As players. Lovers of complete freedom, could feel each other, where they were going. Like schools of dolphins and owls and bats. Never played the same set twice or the same song the same way. It all seemed to stand up, what Owsley was saying, or it wasn't without some kind of sense anyway. And the guitar used to speak for me. We had to do it if we wanted to get to the next level. That became pretty clear.'

'*Sergeant Pepper* was kind of a big advertisement for it as well, wasn't it?' I say.

'But we were just from the blues clubs, couple of beers was about it. Scared to go out on the streets in New York the first time.'

'Can you remember much about that?'

He sniffs, Alwyn snorts.

'Owsley gave me a drink, just a little sip and I knew it was spiked. Then later he'd done the water cooler at the bar and it all kicked off. That was in New Orleans.'

Gunshots in the night and shouting around the clock. Voodoo and tarot cards. Ask Peter Green about New Orleans. Ask him about that.

He leans across and taps Alwyn on the arm. Alwyn starts, smiles dreamily.

'I'm listening, don't worry. It's all going in.'

'Nobody knew which way up their instruments were and the police came after him again that night,' Peter Green continues. 'At the Gorham Hotel in New York we got him on the phone to talk us down. It all went very dark. Everything. Danny was crying his eyes out, Mick talking about skeletons – the thirteen-star lightning bolt that came to him in a dream, damaged chromosomes. Take lots of sugar. I think that's all Owsley said. And then we were at the Fillmore in front of about five thousand people and Jerry…

'…Jerry came on to do his turn and dropped his pants again. Like we were still at the Flamingo or Bag o'Nails or worse – up north in Sunderland or Middlesbrough in some shitty working men's club. And Garcia and Owsley were looking on from the wings that night, kind of expectantly. Like they were questioning, where are you going to take it to?

'But Jerry, Jerry, filling johnnies full of milk and hanging them from his machine heads, hurling them out beyond the banks of lights. Out at the five thousand now. A New York five thousand, a New Orleans five thousand, a California five thousand – the most turned-on crowds you could get. And Jerry, Jerry, Jerry…

'…Jerry dragging us back to cobble-piss, wet places, sooty places, beery, sticky tables and bare boards. With skinheads and hell's angels. Gangsters and hooligans. Dragging us back to the time of sleeping six to a room in some Welsh pit town, and Mick with his fucking gangly arms and endless legs…

'…they used to stretch him on a board you know, when he was a kid? To make him grow. RAF family. Or in the van on top of the amps. Like we were still just another turn for the fucking Gunnell Brothers. How many copies did their album *Rumours* sell? One of the biggest albums ever wasn't it? Multi-millionaires – the old bass player and drummer. And Garcia and Owsley – it was as if they were just waiting for me to show them something.

'And Jerry, Jerry doing Sieg Heils around the stage then, in that crumpled suit. Silver, shiny, never washed it, you'd peel it off the floor of the bus. The Dobro banging down on the boards. The hairspray glistening from his Little Richard. The sneer that couldn't stay long on his face without bursting into a grin. A turn and a secret sneer. That was him. Jerry, Jerry, Jerry, saying one thing and meaning another.

'And the crowd going mad for Jerry, Jerry, Jerry, because he was a twelve-bar joke, and once it was a good joke, a good laugh. We always had a laugh back then. It was only when Danny joined that everybody suddenly had a straight face all the time. Harold the Dildo crawling out of Jerry's pants. At the Flamingo and at the Bag o'Nails. In Sunderland and Middlesbrough. In Manchester and Lichfield and Bath. But after you'd heard it every night for three years, it was hard to smile.

'And Garcia and Owsley were just looking on. Suzy Wong too. Like they were disappointed in me, expecting more. And I remember thinking, *I'll show you where we can take it*. But not with Jerry.

'Back in England he was one person. With his child bride and his Bible. Had one stitched into his duffel coat. Bloody tramp he was. But on tour he was somebody else. Dobro banging down on the boards, doing his Sieg Heils around the stage in that crumpled silver suit. Harold the Dildo crawling out of his pants. And the filth that came out of his mouth.

'Sometimes he was like that girl in *The Exorcist*, you know? You expected his head to start revolving, the green puke to come gushing out. And he'd be reading his Bible on the bus as she was sucking him off, the child bride, and his first kid, crawling around among the wires between the amps.

'That's when I decided everything was going to be different, that it all had to change. Not just the music, the whole approach. Not in Germany, like where everybody keeps saying it happened.

'Garcia had these ideas too, like how things would get beyond money if only everyone had somewhere to live and enough food. That all of the stuff that was created would be free and you'd do it just because you wanted to. And the people who were on your wavelength would just find each other, one way or another. Like dolphins and owls and bats.

'No business, that was the main thing. It was the businessmen who were killing it all, Garcia thought. So they let their fans bootleg the shows and sell the things they'd made at gigs. Talked about the free economy of the future. They hated money. Even let people get away with ripping them off so they wouldn't be burdened with too much of it. Karma would get the moneymen, that's what Garcia believed. That's what a lot of us believed back then. We were wrong though. But he just didn't want any stuff. Didn't have goals or plans and he didn't want to be a leader either. And I could see it was where I was too, or where I wanted to get to.

'So it all had to change for me. And not with Jerry. Not with Jerry, laughing at me from the shadows.'

The light above us sputters. I glance around. Piles of newspapers pushed into spaces in dark wooden alcoves. Three-quarters shadow. Alwyn's eyes are closed again. Peter Green has finished his story.

'Alwyn?' I say.

'Hmmm?' Shifts forward, eyelids fluttering, drops the stone owl down on the baize, puts on his glasses. 'Most interesting. Fascinating. And of course, now that I know the story, highly collectable. Another little piece of history.'

'I might even be interested in buying it,' I say.

They both look at me. The Green God has contempt in his eyes.

'I only sell to Alwyn,' he says. 'Ever. Will you wait for me outside now?'

★

January 1969. Fleetwood Mac went to Chicago like heroes and were treated like thieves, Danny told me. Willie Dixon decorating the studio, slapping whitewash over the walls with a broom. Otis Spann, dying of liver cancer, sliding down his piano stool, shaking dice out the back. Buddy Guy, in his shades and beret. Never said a word.

Stole it all from the blacks. Stole their music.

January 1969, and Kurt's man re-established contact. To let me know – in no uncertain terms – that I was far from forgotten. Summoned me back to Alexanderplatz to the office under the shadow of the new television tower.

'Your wife must be happier now,' he said, gaze unflinching. 'I told you it would work out. And it has, hasn't it? Everything's worked out for you now. A family reunited.'

Watching my eyes.

'We don't forget our people, we look after them, all of our people. You know that Peter.'

With Kurt's man, my best response was always silence, and what he was letting me know was that you can never just cut it, once there are connections.

'Nixon will visit Berlin in a couple of weeks' time.'

The USA had a new president.

I nodded, said nothing.

'Why, you might ask, is that important?' Kurt's man continued.

Hair slicked, raw white like the snow on the window's sill, links glistening from starched cuffs. It snowed and snowed, that winter, never stopped.

'The eyes of the world will be on Berlin, and Berlin should provide something spectacular,' he said. 'Berlin should not disappoint in this respect. Nixon's a man to get things done, and needs to know he has enemies here, that not everyone is singing from the hymn sheet provided by our wonderful liberators. That there are some who don't give a shit for the twentieth anniversary of the city's blockade.'

We have files on them all.

'Nothing will shake the resolve of the West to defend their rightful status as protectors of the people of free Berlin.' Kurt's man shrugged. 'That's what he plans to tell us, President Nixon. Well we'd like him to think again.' Unflinching, watching my eyes. 'You'll need help, of course, but there appear to be no end of willing heroes still.

'The Emergency Laws are in place, yes that's true, but what's required is for them to be applied more – let's say – rigorously. The Battle of Tegeler Weg can't happen again. Nothing like that. It's gone too far, all of it. Bommi and his boys are out of control, think they're invincible. I was right about Rudi Dutschke, now watch what they do to the lawyer, this Mahler. The police have their new equipment but it's not enough on its own.'

BePo, KriPo, PoPo or SchuPo? Sixty thousand of them on tap in the West Berlin bubble. With special helmets and face-guards now, new plastic riot shields and longer truncheons.

'Has to be a political will, that's the point,' Kurt's man said. 'At the highest level. Action down there on the street prompts action from above. It's time to put an end to all of this. Over two years it's been going on. Remember when we met that Easter, '67? We were at the start of a story unfolding, only we didn't know it back then. How could we? It all seemed insignificant then, and it still does now. But somehow, they've opened the door for Willy Brandt.'

And then it was his turn to listen. He drummed his fingers, tapped and scowled as I talked him through the key events of the past six months as I saw them. My information, of course, carefully selected.

What you know protects you against what they know and can use against you.

Kurt's man affecting boredom, exasperation, as he absorbed my impressions of the mood at the Republican Club – funded, he reminded me, *specifically funded* for results – and at the Wieland Community, in the clubs and out on the streets.

Missing nothing. But his annoyance became tangible when I told him of the developments at the first of the new communities – K1. The plans for exploiting the fame, building on its momentum, turning it into something more, something self-perpetuating. Effortlessly. Being famous simply for being famous. No achievement, I told him, was deemed necessary.

'A corporation?' he spat. 'A brand? Fan mail?'

Consumerism, the economic miracle, invented to stop us thinking about our fascist past…

President Nixon's time in Berlin should be explosive, Kurt's man emphasised in no uncertain terms.

'Are you up to the task, Peter? We don't forget our people, we look after them, all of our people. You know that Peter.'

Nixon's time in Berlin should be explosive, he instructed me.

★

Alwyn emerges from his shop in a tight-fitting duffel coat, hood pulled over to the top of his glasses, giving him the air of some cartoon character.

'Peter wants us to take a walk,' he says, 'give him a bit of space. Probably for the best. He'll be fine in there, work it out in his head. He's a bit locked into his Jerry thing at the moment. Said we'd meet him in The Bells in half an hour or so.'

I shrug.

'Fine, let's walk then.'

We turn off the square, down a tight, flinty lane, catching our breath against the cold.

'Does he talk to you a lot, Alwyn?' I ask.

'I'm there to listen when he needs me,' he tells me. 'Not too many people he trusts, and who can blame him? So I know the whole sorry tale, believe me.'

'Have you lived around here long?'

Sniffs, glares at me.

'Born and bred, why? It's a good place for him too. Away from it all.'

'And he's sold you a lot of things?'

Smirks.

'Oh sure. Made me millions.'

'Well someone's made a lot of money from him.'

'Plenty of people made money from Peter Green, but not recently,' he says. 'No, I don't mind playing the game, giving it all a little value, the history. Still not sure what to make of it all though.'

'No?'

Shakes his head sadly.

'Well, just what's real and what's not. The memory, you know. Unreliable at the best of times, but in his case...'

We enter a small churchyard. Headstones and withered flowers.

'The thing is,' Alwyn continues, 'he got to be Jesus, you have to understand that. I don't know if you're religious at all Mister Novak?'

'No, can't say I am.'

Mist across the black stones. Bare trees.

'No matter, really, but for him, it wasn't any delusion or anything.

That's too ungenerous if you're to make any allowance at all for faith. Jesus had returned and Peter was him. He had the belief and he was talking to God. Right from the start his group was selling a thousand copies a day, just in England. That does things to your perspective even without drugs. So he started to believe it wasn't just in his head. What would you call it?'

We pause at a tilting Maltese cross, the tomb under it collapsed. Broken Latin inscription.

'I really don't know.'

Alwyn kicks at a patch of crumbling stone.

'I'm a believer myself,' he says. 'Not just any old believer either. A Creationist.'

'Creationist?'

Alwyn squats down on his haunches, pulls back his hood and takes off his glasses, starts to clean them with a finger. Standing above him, I put my hand on the cold stone cross, pull it away.

'Sure, why not? It makes more sense than anything else. God created the world in an instant, but he gave it a back story, because what story works without them? If you're going to create the world, why not give it a history at the same time? Make the history too. You can't just start from nothing. That's what the rationalists and the scientists don't seem to understand. But why would they? They have no imagination.'

Stretches to his feet, still polishing his glasses.

'Has to be a story,' I say.

'Peter Green had the power to do things. Big things. To make miracles. But with power there should be responsibility, and nobody wanted him to be responsible for anything very much. A few songs are not miracles, Mister Novak, but can you remember existing before them?'

Puts the glasses back on, pulls up his hood. Examines me.

'But what was he supposed to be responsible for?'

Alwyn gestures scale, spreads his arms wide, swoops them together, makes pincer fingers.

'Who knows? Sometimes nothing, sometimes the lot, everything. You tell me. Third World debt, the starving millions or a bus that was an hour late, a broken guitar string, a plaster on a finger. It was in the interests of everyone that he take no responsibility, that his group just keep performing like monkeys, keep counting the cash. And talking about big things, infinite possibilities. New creation. What they were going to do, how much they were going to change. And then something else instead, and then nothing changed.

'All the time Peter was looking for him, he *was* him, or the closest you could get to it on this earth. I don't know how else you'd explain it. How did Jesus feel? Pretty much the same I bet. They were all wanting something, but he wasn't told anything either was he? So for Peter, it was a case of just keep counting the cash. People listened to him as if what he had to say mattered. Just because he played guitar and sang a few songs.'

'Why him though?'

'Well, he wasn't alone in it, it was part of that time, but they weren't that interested in what Jerry or Danny had to say were they? Pushed their microphones and cameras in his face, hung on his words. They chose him. That's why he needed time to read more, to find out things. To find out what the others who'd been put in that position had learned. But at the same time, he could just point at a place on a map and save lives there. That's real power. If pictures of starving children made him feel bad he could send money to feed them, pack it off to Biafra or Palestine. He could have done the five loaves and two fishes trick, no problem.

'The group's manager bought him a map, and some films of it all, he told me. And he really was Jesus then, wasn't he?'

We skirt the small church now, feet crunching on a shale path.

'And the money kept coming in, just like that,' I say.

'Let me show you down there.'

Alwyn indicates a flight of stone steps. We descend, he pulls open the oak door. Some kind of crypt. Damp wood, linger of incense. The cold follows us in.

'Where it's all been over for a long time.' He's whispering now. 'If you think in those old straight lines. Peter bought his mum and dad the house, *Albatross* in New Malden, dropped his brothers Len and Mick anything they needed. I guess they got to like it too. That's what a chosen one can do, change fortunes. Invent a story with a history. For anyone. So he was chosen. Some days he said he could really feel that, as if he were invincible, as if he was being guided.'

'That would be the mescaline mainly,' I say, my voice too loud, echoing, 'that made him start to feel so holy and righteous.'

'And the things he was reading.' Alwyn still whispering, into his cuffs now, fists bunched. 'Teachings, philosophies. Trying to find out what the others had learned, what they'd picked up along the way. That's when Sandra – she was his girl for a bit then – made the robes for him. A red one and a white one. And he grew the beard. It was all a joke and it was deadly serious. But then other times I guess he didn't feel like a god at all. Felt like the lowest thing on the planet at those other times, terribly small, I should imagine. Insignificant. Just so terribly small. Crushed. Or even like he was some kind of devil. Everything went from up to down like that for him. Can you imagine? He was God or he was the Devil. A joke, or totally serious. All extremes. With acid, from what he's said, you were high and god-like and wanted to hold on to that feeling forever, promised yourself you would, and then you were down again, and there was another big block of something missing inside you. Seems to me every time he was shown something more, it tore something out of him too.

'So the serious things made everything even more of a joke, and the jokes got too serious, until they were never funny. Just twitches at the corner of your mouth, just something glimpsed from the corner of your eye. Twitches and glimpses. You were standing on the stage in front of the five thousand, as he said, and then you were back in a room, alone, with another big chunk of something missing and your lonely cock in your hand.'

'Twitches and glimpses,' I say.

'Another joke, that's what he was, or somebody too serious for this world. And he wanted to tell people about it but they turned it all around and tried to shatter his faith. And that wasn't acid, that feeling, that was coke and that was journalists, who are never interested in the world's back story, only the now. Sometimes he was really aware he had the gift and that it was going somewhere, and the group too, sometimes they were all flying.'

I nod at him in the half-light of the crypt.

He spreads his hands wide and I start to shiver.

'Shall we go?'

We make our way back through the churchyard. Alwyn concludes his story.

'So all this was going on inside him at that time, from what I gather, and by the end of that summer of 1969, when it all started falling apart for them, he was being pretty difficult, I suppose. Fleetwood Mac were recording a third album and there was a lot of pressure from their new record company. He did most of the music himself because he didn't really want the others around too much by then. I don't think poor Jerry played a note on it. By then it was like he wasn't in a group at all. But most of all, he was just really tired of all the attention.'

*

Rainer and Uschi were basking in attention over in Berlin, but tiring of just about everything else. And building up the black marks against themselves. Suddenly, they too didn't want the others around so much. It was no place for sad grandfathers of that old revolution, who still shouted for the bayonets and beer, for assassinations and slow marches, committee meetings and sub-committee meetings too. And the old, old hate.

And 60 Stephan Street quickly became a hothouse for jealousies and new tensions.

STP.

But to Rainer and Uschi, the others in the new community were no longer newsworthy, no longer in tune, and they knew it.

STP. Serenity, tranquillity and peace.

Rainer and Uschi needed beauty. Beauty and youth and new ideas around them. Part of the package, essential to the new brand.

STP. Side effects – substantial perceptual changes. Blurred vision, multiple images, vibration of objects, visual hallucinations, distorted shapes, enhancement of details, slowed passage of time, increased contrasts.

Rainer and Uschi, dropping back in, when everyone else was dropping out. Selling out, making love not war. Traitors, enemies now, of the revolution. If you're not for us, you're against us.

Rainer and Uschi, courted by pop stars and actors, film directors and writers, philosophers and photographers, hip lawyers and architects – all visitors to the new K1 corporation on Stephan Street. From the USA and England now, from France and Holland, Switzerland and Italy.

A new drop-in, multi-media happening centre – Berlin's tense answer to Andy Warhol's New York Factory.

Rainer and Uschi flew to London, saw what was going on. The music of winners, the Happenings in a country ever so proud of itself. Swinging London.

Blurred vision, multiple images.

Attention came, inevitably, from the Springer Press, but now it was friendly, playful, hiding its claws, welcoming them with cameras and pads back at the Tempelhof, eager for their findings, their *bon mots*.

'We only need to do a little work, very quickly to earn a lot of money,' Rainer unwisely told them. 'This is the future.'

And he spoke also of the female as the real core of the revolution. Instinct, sensuality, gentleness. An antidote to all the violence. An end to guns.

And across Europe, the men were gripping the stiff guns in their pockets as they gaped at Uschi's fabulous tits.

Uschi had tried to read her Mao and Marx, she told Springer's scribblers, but politics was boring. Not a thought in her head, other than to her own immediate needs. The real core of the new revolution – instinct, sensuality, gentleness, selfishness.

Vibration of objects, visual hallucinations.

We charge ten thousand marks a day for our services, Springer's papers reported Rainer had said. And told Berlin. And Berlin told the world.

Attention now for Rainer and Uschi from the spoiled children of the economic miracle across Europe who were hearing something else. The bravest of them would make the pilgrimage to Berlin, to Stephan Street, where some would stay, subjecting themselves to this new transformation, this promise of turning themselves into something else, lured by the potential of what this new K1 brand was offering.

Something's happening now isn't it? It's hard to explain, just that something feels exciting and good.

And there was also too much attention, of course, from the BePo, the KriPo, the PoPo, the SchuPo. The men in bare rooms with wire taps and those making clandestine plans – English, Russian, French, American – in the cafés. And the leaders, behind closed doors – smoking their pipes, drinking their brandy – referring to the old books and files, the sacred texts passed down from one generation to the next. Books of order and authority. Essence of the machinery of the state.

Distorted shapes, enhancement of details.

Attention and black marks for Rainer and Uschi from the new drug barons of Berlin, plying their Red Leb and phials and clink. Cleaning up.

And from Dieter Kunzelmann and the Wandering Hash Rebels, who after the APO's last stand at Ebrach had first driven through Italy, with the addled plan of hijacking a boat to liberate Sicily, and then on through Yugoslavia, Bulgaria, Turkey and Syria, and finally to Jordan. Where they were housed in splendour, kept under observation and came back full of new ideas on just how their revolution would come about.

Slowed passage of time, increased contrasts.

Attention and black marks from Dieter, lost to his old comrade now and shanking up my clink. Thrown out and pleading to be let back into his former home.

No place for sad grandfathers of that old revolution.

Still intent on kidnapping a judge, but also now seeing parallels between his destitution and that of the misplaced Palestinians.

Imperialism attempts to prevent its next decisive defeat by a show of all its force in the Near East, where European and US capital has established a strong military base. It actively supports the Zionists in their aggressive expansionist moves into Arab territory. Several thousand US specialists are already working as military advisors in the Israeli Army and over 40% of the Israeli budget is used for defence expenditures.

Golda Meir travels throughout the Western world and returns home with Phantom jets, dollars and napalm. The tarnished billions from the Federal Republic of Germany – given as reparation payments and foreign aid – are planned into the Zionist defence budget.

After the USA, German investors are the biggest investors in the Israeli economy. Under the guilt-conscious cloak of overcoming the fascist acts of horror against the Jews, Israel is now allowed to carry out its own against the Palestinian Arabs.

In packed Israeli prisons, Gestapo torture methods are employed. The houses of Arab civilians suspected of sympathising with the armed resistance are blown into the air, and the inhabitants chased out or murdered. In rebellious villages where nests of resistance are suspected, the Israeli occupation army uses terror. Surprise attacks, massacres and mass arrests are carried out daily.

The victims of Israeli napalm bombs lie in Jordanian hospitals.

Once again, the German public knows nothing. Springer lets himself be draped with honorary doctorates in Tel Aviv. The Palestinian people have fought for their independence for over fifty years. The three million Palestinian refugees who've vegetated for more than twenty years in pathetic tent camps have begun their struggle. For ten years they have organised the armed people's war against Amerikan imperialism. Racist and Zionist Israel defends the oil interests of the world police with napalm, Phantom jets and German tanks throughout the Arab region. The fascist expansion move of Israel in June demonstrated that imperialism can only be fought through a lengthy armed revolutionary people's war. The exploited masses in the feudal sheikdoms and the revisionist Arab States no longer expect anything from the radical phrases of their government leaders.

The struggle of the El Fatah has shown everyone how imperialism, Zionism and the system in their own countries is to be fought. The Palestinian revolution is the starting point for all-inclusive change in the Arab world.

Dieter flirting with disguises, sculpting his hair. Dieter trying on hats and glasses. Dieter primed for one last charge.

Substantial perceptual changes. Blurred vision, multiple images, vibration of objects, visual hallucinations.

Attention for Rainer and Uschi too, from the Horla Commune – fans of Wilhelm Reich – who simply turned up one day and demanded to be let in, fed and watered – having been hounded out of Cologne for a series of publications advocating the sexual liberation of children.

You have money, share it with us, they said.

And all those circular conversations with the Horla about Reich.

Wilhelm Reich, labelled a Jew pornographer for his ideas on sexual liberation, forced to flee Europe to the USA.

The Horla with their manky dogs and snot-nosed children on the concrete of the ground floor of Stephan Street, wanting in on the attention, a share of the fame. The smells of shit and hash and burned food. The piled sinks, the broken, charred sticks of furniture, the soiled mattresses and thin sheets. The pipes and paraphernalia.

Those endless conversations with the Horla about the orgasm as the body's emotional energy regulator and society's sexual oppression.

Distorted shapes, enhancement of details, slowed passage of time, increased contrasts.

Meandering dialogues about sexual development as the origin of mental illness, about the source of sexual repression being bourgeois morality and the socio-economic structures that produced it.

About the dissolution of the body's armour, about bio-electricity and orgasmotherapy.

About orgone accumulators.

The Horla with their dogs and children and their humourless monologues about orgone – a primordial cosmic energy.

Orgone was blue in colour, according to Reich, omnipresent, and could be seen with the naked eye. Orgone was responsible for the weather, the colour of the sky, gravity, the formation of galaxies and the biological expressions of emotion and sexuality.

And the Horla wanted to build some of Reich's orgone accumulators – alternating layers of ferrous metals and organic insulators with a high dielectric constant – on the concrete of the ground floor of Stephan Street.

And they wanted Rainer and Uschi to pay for it now.

'We only need to do a little work, very quickly to earn a lot of money.'

Wilhelm Reich, who died in a US prison in 1956 after several tons of his books were burned by the US authorities.

Bonfires were made of precious books…

Illness is primarily caused by depletion or blockages of the orgone energy within the body, Reich said.

The Horla had moved in to 60 Stephan Street with their dogs and children, and appeared to have misread the message.

Share and share alike, was their understanding, otherwise what was all the talk of Marx and Mao, of escaping the nuclear family, about?

You have money, share it with us.

'We only need to do a little work, very quickly to earn a lot of money.'

Attention for Rainer and Uschi from Rudi Krawallo and his Märkische Quarter boys too. Veterans of the Battle of Tegeler Weg. Appointing themselves the new security force and happy at first. Rudi and his boys, who played with chains and whips, whose currency was domination and humiliation, divide and quarter.

Who did not want to know about the future being female. Not when they had everything to look forward to.

22. JANUARY 3rd 1990, 7pm.

'Let's hope he's calmed down a bit anyway,' Alwyn says as we push through the door of The Bells.

Peter Green standing at the empty bar, tilting slightly, unfocused already. Turns to us, top lip curled.

A bored-looking kid behind the bar on a stool, long fringe, black baggy clothes, pulls off a pair of earphones, climbs up expectantly for our order.

'So come on then,' The Green God slurs. 'Ask me some more of your questions Mister Journalist. Novak, what kind of name's that anyway, German?'

Expecting me, then. Thinking about it. Remembering something?

'Polish,' I tell him. Emboldened, serene. Oh well. 'What about the shotgun, do you want to talk about that?'

God created the world in an instant, but he gave it a back story, because what story works without them?

Peter Green's response is a shrug of annoyance. Scratches his beard, swats the air, spilling off a swathe of his pint.

Alwyn orders two pints for us.

'Shall we sit down,' he suggests, peeling himself out of his duffel coat and throwing it into a corner. The Green God turns back to the bar, muttering to himself.

Alwyn and I take a table, sit in silence for some time.

There's no jukebox, but music from somewhere behind the bar. The kid's earphones, I realise. Tinny new strain of pop music which chugs and pings. Not to be shared, nothing communal anymore. No more networks connecting. People listening to music in solitary. Lone gunmen. The public prefers it that way.

Peter Green turns, hitches elbows on the bar, tilts on his stool, red cheeked now.

'I know what you're referring to,' he growls across, 'but I don't even think you could call it that, a shotgun. It wasn't. It was up at Mum and Dad's place on Canvey Island anyhow. In a box, still wrapped up really. Joe and Anne. Beautiful people, my old man and me mum, my people. Supported me from the first, the very first and through it all. Salt of the earth, which they'd never call me now.'

'You'd better finish the story about Jerry,' I suggest.

'Don't think that's a good idea,' Alwyn says quietly, taking my elbow, putting his glasses on the table, raising his eyes darkly. 'Come on Peter, sit down now.'

Peter Green comes across meekly, sits down next to Alwyn. Bows his head below the table, fingers clasped. Earthy smell and Alwyn's camphor.

'I think Jerry just fell apart after I called it a day,' he says. 'So they took him to the warehouse in Los Angeles, shaved his head and called him Jonathan. It was a start, wasn't it?'

'It was a start,' Alwyn agrees, nodding. 'We know, but there's nothing to be done. You have to let it go.'

'Shaved his head and renamed him Jonathan, like they were saying, lazy sod, you want to feel like Jesus? Couldn't ride a bike, Jerry, couldn't swim, couldn't drive. Put him on a horse one time, out in the desert for some shit photos we were doing or something, a publicity stunt anyway, and it was like he was sitting on it backwards. All wrong.'

Alwyn produces the small stone owl from his pocket, swaps it from palm to palm.

Peter Green pulls out a crumpled packet of cigarettes, fumbles in his pockets for matches, puts the cigarette down on the table.

'Well there are responsibilities, aren't there Alwyn?' he asks.

'There are Peter.'

'So they shaved his head and renamed him Jonathan, didn't they? Washed his brain. Washed out the condoms full of milk dangling on the machine heads, the Sieg Heils, washed off the grease from his quiff. Washed down Harold the Dildo. Washed out his mouth. Dirty minds need cleaning.'

'He was cleansed, then,' Alwyn mutters.

'And then they started making children for God didn't they? In Brazil and Peru, in India, Japan, Sri Lanka and Greece. Children of a bigger family.'

All institutions are derived from the oppressive character of the nuclear family. Wasn't that what we once believed too?

Peter Green lights his cigarette, leans back.

'Making children for God,' he says, spilling out a plume of smoke. 'Jerry, Jerry, Jerry. And Fiona, the child bride. Begat children for God, under a Mayan volcano.'

'Begat children for God in the jungle around the husk of Manila, as the Tamil Tigers rampaged through the seven thousand islands,' Alwyn counters.

'Begat children to make more children for God, in the Bulgarian back streets,' Peter Green fires back, as if it's a conversation they've had many times.

'Begat children in the snap of the Siberian wastes.'

'Begat children in the hot rains of Macau.'

A prayer of some kind; their mantra.

'Children to dance for God,' Alwyn says, benign look betraying some kind of rapture now.

'Children to sing for God.'

'To offer up their spirits to him.'

'To come into his heart forever.'

'Children who belonged to God.'

'Whose bodies were God's. Is that right Alwyn?'

Alwyn looks blankly ahead.

'That's right Peter,' he whispers from the corner of his mouth.

'Opening up all the portals to God,' I suggest. 'Deactivating the filters that lead to God. God, the background noise of your visual system.'

Peter Green stares up at the ceiling. Alwyn puts away the owl.

'Jerry, Jerry, Jerry and Fiona, the child bride, making children for God.' Peter Green's voice is a hoarse, musical mumble. 'Children to witness, cleansed children, children of the future, children without sweets, without Coca Cola or Mars bars, without Pop music – a few songs are not miracles – without television, without radio, without blemish. Who do not, will never need these things.'

'Children not of this time, out of this time and place,' Alwyn adds.

'Children of a bigger family.'

'Children standing in corners. Locked in rooms to reflect, to memorise their scriptures.'

'Kids to fast.'

'Kids to offer themselves as witnesses to strangers.'

'To witness in civil war.'

'To witness between earthquakes.'

'In droughts and in famine.'

'In heatwaves and in bitter winters.'

'And children to obey their sinful fathers, that's what it was all about wasn't it?'

'Children to atone for their sinful mothers. To witness in shorts and socks.'

'To witness hungry.'

'To witness in their thirst.'

'At midnight, at dawn.'

'From dawn to dusk.'

'In civil war.'

'Between earthquakes and hurricanes.'

'In droughts, in plagues and famines.'

'In heatwaves and the snap of Siberian outback.'

'To witness and obey.'

'Change their names, move them around, call them Peters, fishers of men.'

Peter Green leans across the table now, grasps my hand.

'And all the time I was looking for him, I was him, or the closest you could get to it on this earth,' he says.

'Just keep counting the cash,' Alwyn chirps into nowhere.

'Call them Mary Magdalenes, because idleness is the Devil's worship, isn't that right Alwyn?'

Alwyn puts his hand on Peter's shoulder.

'It's right enough.'

'And then… your brother's dead. That's what they told them, the rest of the kids when one left. Because the good tree cannot bear bad fruit. Your brother's dead, your sister is no longer your sister. Jerry, Jerry, Jerry, and his clean children, because the good tree cannot bear bad fruit. Cleaning his doubts in the fears of his kids. Children to recognise the sins of the father, to take back their passports, to become the bad fruit from the tree. To taunt and reject. To take back their bodies, to reclaim their souls. To break the hearts of Jerry, Jerry, Jerry, and Fiona his child bride. To refuse to bear witness…'

He stops, drained.

'What about the shotgun?' I remind him.

He pulls himself up and stares me in the face.

'I had eighty dollars and what I really wanted was a handgun, but they wouldn't sell me one, needed a licence, so I bought the fairground rifle and a couple of boxes of cartridges. That's what they put me away for. Can you light me a cigarette?'

Alwyn insists on driving him home. Away from the village, flat January Essex fields in the twilight now, a box of cartridges and empty milk crates rattle on the back seat of the Land Rover. Alwyn pushes his glasses close to the windscreen, blinks like an owl.

Peter Green coughs, stares out of the window, seemingly calmer now.

'I was on the phone to him,' he tells me. 'In Our Price Records on Kensington High Street it was – there was this money see, about thirty grand owed to me. Maybe I would have given it away, but the point was it was mine to be giving away.'

Scratches his beard, looks out into the murk.

'Just keep counting the cash,' Alwyn nods at the wheel.

'And I was thinking of all these people – when I could think straight at all then – of Rik Gunnell with his triple whiskies and cokes outside the Flamingo. Dragging in the crowds. Real characters in them days. And the beautiful girls too, in that scene. Beryl and Christine and Jenny but…

'…and Dave Simmonds, this little teaboy – tea-leaf more like – an accountant now, who was holding on to all the money, according to our manager Cliff. And I said, I don't know, maybe I'd come around to his office and shoot them both. Maybe that. And I think Cliff knew I had another gun too. A single-barrel twelve bore. I didn't know where that was, but maybe he was more worried about that and asked me if I was threatening him. I said yes I was. Maybe I did.'

We pass the telephone box where he made his call earlier.

'And that was when they arrested him,' Alwyn says.

'Picked me up round at the house of a girl called Betty. The guns were fifty miles away I think, the one I bought in Canada still in the box.'

'Here we are anyway,' Alwyn tells us.

In the headlights boarded windows and weeds around a rusting car. Bath and sink out in the yard. Broken wood, bits of furniture. As I get out I step on things – mashed parts of an old guitar in frazzled dandelions I realise, a shattered scratchboard. Splinters and wires.

We stand by the door, for a while, the three of us, sobering up in the cold. Look out over the fields, breath like ectoplasm.

'And then, next thing, I'm in Horton Hospital,' Peter Green says. 'The loony bin.'

'Asylum,' Alwyn corrects him.

'Or West Park, it could have been, I don't remember.'

'The Epsom Cluster they called it all,' Alwyn says, for my benefit.

'Huge sprawl of places,' Peter Green continues, 'with just about every nutter in London in them. About five thousand again. You name it, they had it, these people. Thought they were Hitler or Napoleon, or could only stand on one leg or had to hold their breath so they didn't breathe in anyone else's germs. All that stuff that flits through your mind, until one single idea just takes over.

'And anyway, the place was huge, and after they'd given you a bath and found you a bed they just let you wander around until they remembered you again. That could be weeks, sometimes months. There were people in there nobody had remembered for years.'

'Well there would be,' Alwyn tells him. 'They used to stick you in those places for all kinds of reasons. If you were a young girl and had a baby without being married, for instance, or if you couldn't get up or clean yourself, or if they decided you were just too much trouble.'

Peter Green laughs at this. Eerie, high-pitched, for a little too long.

'Or just if they didn't happen to like you,' he says. 'You don't know the half of it. I bet there were women in there who just didn't like housework. There were old dears there from the First World War, and it was normal to them. And to tell the truth, it was normal to me too, after a very short bit. More normal than outside, just normal people, owning up to not being gods.'

'Maybe it's just the normal state, to be completely confused?' Alwyn suggests. Peter Green nods.

'Like Jerry. Shaved his head and renamed him Jonathan, washed his brain. What do I know? What do you know? But I wasn't feeling like Jesus in there, I can tell you.'

'Things weren't just a joke, or totally serious either?' Alwyn suggests. 'There were none of those extremes anymore?'

'People did things because they just did them, and it was all just normal. Even if it was bonkers.'

They're both chuckling away now.

'Only it wasn't, of course, at all,' Alwyn says, suddenly straight-faced again.

'What is? All of my life seems bonkers now, bleeding bonkers. I don't know why things were ever in my head and why things happened.'

He looks across at me, smiles sadly. Knowing smile. Ancient-wise and long beaten. Thin hair, wild bushy beard.

'Across a ward, along a corridor,' he sighs. 'Through a doorway, hiding behind curtains, throwing voices. In the graveyard, between the stones.'

Fishers of men and diggers of graves. Like that poor fool Andy Baader, dead these thirteen years now. Him and Gudrun both. Digging at midnight in the Buckow Cemetery for my consignment of World War Two pistols. Which were never there, of course, because I didn't understand just how much they lacked irony.

I miss the haze over the waves, the hammock on the porch, the sluggish fabric-topped box on which I played his scratchy old records again and again. Of course I do. But here I am.

*

After that meeting with Kurt's man, I started to think about K1.

I was there for them for the last of the happenings, there for them as the actions ran their course, as other clans and other cities took the shine off their crowns. I laid their concrete, ran their wires, picked up the spanner and the drill on their behalf, fixed the water, fixed the heating, ran and carried, patched and fixed.

They treated me, in other words, like a prole. But now the students were the new working class, along with the Märkische rockers and thugs, the borstal runaways and school truants, the wide boys, rogue apprentices, casual workers, waifs and strays. There was talk in certain quarters of building up the troops from this diaspora, to man the front lines of Berlin and West Germany. It was an idea from South America – recruiting from the disaffected of the urban cities – finding the new proles where they actually existed. The Tupamaros.

And I thought back to that first meeting with Rainer, on the street just outside the Western. Squinting into the weak morning sun behind his glasses. A strange kind of calm assurance coming from him. I tipped my hat.

And inside, their eyes on me. *What's he doing here?*

'The false needs that are created by advanced industrial society,' Dieter lectured.

'Methods of control and the desperate need for the great refusal,' Rainer informed me.

I was there for them with the new music, with hashish, with the first of the LSD batches, with petrol and matches for these little boys.

And suddenly they didn't want to play anymore.

Dieter scratching his arms for me to arrive with the clink, then turning his back, lost in a haze. Rainer immersed in Uschi, telling everyone he'd seen the future and it was female, like a doting puppy. Leaving the action of the streets to others, even as it all grew darker and the paranoia set in.

Selling out, it was called. *Selling out to the man.* Opening a gash right up, for salty accusations of bourgeois double standards to be poured in.

So where were they then, the willing heroes Kurt's man spoke of? Who were the real Tupamaros?

I went first to the Republican Club – funded, Kurt's man reminded me, *specifically funded* for results – to see the elders of Marxist thought and word in West Berlin. The intellectuals drawing up their revolution on paper. Deniers of deed, locked in debate, frozen in their rhetoric. Blocking out history with their words.

I offered access to arms, because as every bookworm and shrinking violet kept telling me back then, the revolution must be armed. I found a few takers for firebombs, nothing more, and moved on to the newly opened News and Research Institute at 52 Ku'damm. Established to document crimes by the state against its citizens. Inside, I opened up a suitcase of fifteen primed incendiary devices for the delectation of the team.

They shit themselves first, then took the moral high ground their class and education always entitled them to. Followed me to the car, surrounding it, forcing me to hand over the keys so I couldn't make any further trouble. I returned later, with the spare, drove it away. I told them I'd buried the suitcase in the Landwehr Canal, with Rosa Luxemburg.

So where were they then?

Things were getting desperate. I went back to Stephan Street, shot Dieter up. Strobe lights, Frank Zappa blasting out again.

Rainer and Uschi, ruling the Stephan Street roost, exhibiting. Cameras and film equipment, tape recorders, fashion designers, hangers-on. Dope fug. Went into the kitchen, pulled out a package, slid it to the back of the fridge.

Bomb Number Six.

I had always been there for them and suddenly they didn't want to play. Well they started the game. I'd ensure they continued to be famous for being famous.

And President Nixon came to Berlin. Visited the Siemens factory, paving the way for Willy Brandt's socialists to take power.

But the police found nothing in their search at Stephan Street.

'Nothing will shake the resolve of the West to defend their rightful status as protectors of the people of free Berlin,' Nixon told the city.

It took another search six weeks later – much too late, after the elections – for the police to finally locate the package. Sixty thousand of them on tap, and all useless.

Rainer and Dieter were arrested the next day, detained until well into April, but just as suddenly released again.

You wouldn't believe how hungry the Allies are for information, Peter. It's all got to be seamless. Truth doesn't even come into it, one way or the other. A constant stream of information. And then, of course, you've got to pass it to the other side too. Even unintended gaps lead to mistrust.

★

Look out at the flat Essex fields. And in the foreground, broken wood. Bits of furniture, masonry and plumbing. Rotting parts of old guitars.

Peter Green nudges Alwyn.

'Says we've never met but I think he's lying,' he says. 'Somewhere, some place.'

Alwyn looks at me, puzzled.

'Fleetwood and Mac,' Peter Green adds, rattling a key around in the lock. 'Come in then, if you're coming, Mister Journalist, you might as well hear the rest of it, if you're so interested in this ancient history.'

Inside: damp on the walls, fried sockets, an old stereo with a cracked lid. Piles of papers, unopened letters.

Alwyn fusses around, attempting to tidy up.

'It's a bit of a mess Peter,' he admonishes.

Layers of dust and ash and abandoned roaches, submerged plates, sunken cartons.

'Well it would be wouldn't it? I'm a bit of a mess. A lot of a mess. And like you don't live in a junk shop anyway. Shall I make some tea?'

He falls into the sofa instead, turns on the portable TV and flicks from channel to channel, settles on *Coronation Street*.

Alwyn picks up a battered Spanish guitar – a crack down the side, bent plastic pegs.

'Where shall I put this?'

'I think it's the one I did all those bits on "Oh Well" on,' Peter Green tells him. 'But maybe not. Pass it here.'

Don't ask me what I think of you, I might not give the answer that you want me to.

Alwyn hands him the guitar. He tries to play along to the sad trumpet of the soap opera theme. It doesn't sound right.

'I'll make the tea,' I offer.

226

In his kitchen, heaped sink, dripping tap, some sodden boxes on the drainer, soil along the sill, an upturned plant-pot full of dead leaves. There's a green tinge on every paltry thing in the fridge, and I think of what he said earlier, about Owsley's fridge full of carcasses, the way he'd just slice off a steak and fry it, eating it straight from the pan. To run and to kill and to eat their fill.

I boil the kettle, find some bags. Pull the half-bottle of Scotch I bought back in The Bells from my pocket, douse the cups.

The tea seems to lift our spirits.

'That's good,' Peter Green tells me. 'Bit of a kick to it. Got any gear?'

I pull out a chunk of Red Leb, for old times' sake. Alwyn produces papers, starts to meticulously construct a joint on the coffee table.

'I'll drive you back shortly,' he tells me. 'You'll be able to get a room at The Bells.'

We drink and we smoke. Peter Green puts the guitar down, flicks from channel to channel again.

'You know that song that was a hit a few years ago?' he asks me. '"The Lunatics Are Taking Over the Asylum"? Kind of reggae thing, bit gloomy. Deep voices?'

'The Specials,' I nod.

'That's what it was. That's what it all was. Like for the first time, we were really controlled by God.'

'Maybe that was the first time you really knew God,' Alwyn suggests, passing him the spliff. Drags and grins. Blinks rapidly. Cherubic smile behind the whiskers.

'I'd talked about him of course, but he wasn't making any sense anywhere else. There was a greater power. And now God controlled things. With prescription drugs mainly. Sparine and Nardine in there. Spar and Nar. From the little plastic cups.

'And it's funny the small things you think about. The things that stick with you. Those wheelchairs with potties in them. Christ. The huge oven in the place. Enormous. For feeding the five thousand.

All of us washed up on the shore of somewhere else. And the farms all around, doing well, doing what they had done for years – feeding the five thousand.

'There was this sort of pavilion,' he continues, 'out in the grounds, and that's when I first met her, June. It was peaceful out there, even in the rain. She was damaged, sure – who wasn't? But not like the way I was.

'She didn't know who I was at all, I'm pretty sure, so that was okay. Some of the others did – I remember there was this one guy used to follow me everywhere – up and down those long tiled corridors. Wore one of those long air force coats, you know. Said he'd seen me play at the Windsor blues festival, back when I could.

'There was this big stage inside Horton, or maybe it was West Park, and he dragged me to it one time. And he had this pigeon in his pocket, and we stood on the stage, me and this guy, and he let it go and it flew up to the roof, and then sort of hit it with a shock. And he said I should be on stage here.

'But I looked at the pigeon, and that's what I feel like happened to me, I remember telling the guy. It sounds corny now, but... They let me flutter off without a plan. Like I just flew up, and then suddenly there wasn't a sky there anymore. I felt like I could keep flying forever, but instead I hit the roof.

'Me and June didn't say much for a while, just used to sit together out in the pavilion, even if it was raining, listening to the pigeons and smoking. Players Number Six, we smoked then. I don't think they make them anymore do they? You wouldn't know. Then, after probably a few weeks, she asked me why I had such a long beard. And I suppose it all came tumbling out and I told her stuff, about it all.

'And she told me about this guy called Reich who thought that everything was about repressed sexuality. That there was no mental illness really, but it was just caused by society's rules and the way they play with you. Well I don't know about that, but I can tell you she wasn't repressed wasn't June.'

'But if she wasn't ill, why did she keep cutting herself?' Alwyn asks him.

Peter Green bares his teeth at this, glares at Alwyn.

Changes like the wind.

'I don't want to talk about that.' Mood softens again. 'We were sort of a couple for about, what, two weeks I suppose. Not longer than that. But she was making me feel really good. So I don't suppose it could have lasted. It wasn't exactly a honeymoon setting was it?

'But there was a recreation room, with a baby grand piano in the middle, bit out of tune and there was this old guy used to play it, all from the wars, you know, "Roll Out the Barrel" and "It's a Long Way to Tipperary". Well it was a laugh sometimes. There was this big black nurse called Wanda and man could she laugh the loudest. Sort of infectious, like it was in your head. And then all the old biddies would be singing along, even if they were doing other things, opening or closing the curtains or knitting their shadows or whatever they thought it was. It got to being like it was all just one big normal family.

'But then somebody remembered me. And they started giving me the ECT. And I never saw June again after that, but now I keep thinking about her.'

We drink and we smoke. Peter Green flicks from channel to channel and we stare at flickering images. Eventually the remote control slips from his hand. He starts to snore gently.

'We should be going,' Alwyn says, half-rising.

'Let me show you something,' I say, take out the folded leaflet. 'What is it?'

'Something Jeremy Spencer wrote, during his time with the Children of God, after leaving Fleetwood Mac.'

I hand it to him. He reads it, passes it back. I read it again myself:

Then I had a nightmare. We were on a dark street at night in some big city like New Orleans. Peter Green's house was there and I walked into

*it. He looked normal and was very pleasant and charming. He gave me a
really nice big acoustic guitar to play. 'You can sit down and play this for a
while,' he said. I started playing, but then I heard this voice say: 'Get out
of his house or he'll kill you.' It sounded like the voice of an angel, but I
argued back. 'No,' I told the angel, 'he's being so pleasant and generous.
He's letting me have his guitar and everything.' Then all of a sudden he
walked back in and I turned around and saw that his look had totally
changed. He was a rabid Jew and on his chest he was wearing a big Star
of David and he was looking at me with hate in his eyes. He looked like
he was ready to pull a knife out and actually kill me. He was coming at
me so I jumped out of the chair and I ran out of the house. Then I woke
up. I told Fiona about the dream and she said maybe we should stop
listening to those Fleetwood Mac records because the music was sucking in
our minds. This dream kept coming back to me very strongly but I didn't
realise the full significance until later.*

Peter Green continues to snore.

'So?' Alwyn asks.

'I did see him once, but it's a long time ago,' I tell him.

Nobody died from anything I did.

'In the States?'

'No, in Germany.'

Nobody suffered any long-term damage.

'Where they keep saying it all went wrong for him,' Alwyn says.
'At a gig was it?'

'No, a house, big old house, down in a basement where they
had a studio. He was playing.'

It would have happened anyway.

'What was he doing there?'

'You tell me.'

It's not as if I can change anything, or even particularly want to apologise.

Peter Green suddenly starts, his eyes blink open. Looks around,
confused. Has he been listening all the time?

'Says we've never met, Alwyn, but I think he's lying,' he says.

'It's late, Peter,' Alwyn replies. 'We should be going.'

'He can kip in here tonight,' Peter Green suggests. Turns to me. 'If you want?'

'Sure,' I say. I miss the hammock on the porch.

'No point in paying. Other people might come round, wanting to crash too. They know me round here, know the door's always open. That's why there's nothing left. But I'm going to be a bad host now, and go to bed.'

And they leave me there.

★

To think, once again, finally, about November 9th 1969.

What's in a date?

Willy Brandt and his Social Democratic Party of Germany had been elected, to everyone's surprise, and were promising real change. There was talk even, of an amnesty, for many of those facing charges for APO protest actions. The reason for the extra-parliamentary opposition was probably over – Rudi long gone – but if you'd believed in it, given it everything for over two years, would you want to see it just wither and die?

The Free Socialist Republic of Germany, proclaimed by Karl Liebknecht from the balcony of Berlin's palace on this date.

Andy and Gudrun were the new Karl and Rosa, they believed, inspiring their Tupamaros, even as they prepared to flee on false passports to France. The amnesty would not be in time for them and their re-arrests were imminent. False passports in the names of Hänsel and Gretel Andreas were procured.

Here in West Germany we are abandoned, unable to escape from a world of fairy tales. Our stamps have illustrations from the Brothers Grimm – the Wolf and the Seven Kids, The Frog Prince, Frau Holle, covering little girls in gold and tar. Hänsel and Gretel.

In Paris, it turned out, they ended up staying at the flat of Regis Debray, who once fought alongside Che Guevara, before moving on again to Italy to be welcomed by the publisher Giangiacomo Feltrinelli. Feltrinelli who had handguns and grenades in his desk and believed a civil war in Italy was imminent. And in December, there were bombs in Milan and Rome, but of course, it didn't stop there.

November 9th 1969. The 31st anniversary of Crystal Night, it was, and thirty years since Georg Elser's simple, universe-changing plan went awry.

During the night, several memorials in Jewish cemeteries had been sprayed with the words 'El Fatah' and 'Napalm' in the black and green national colours of Palestine.

And a bomb had been planted in West Berlin's Jewish Community Centre on Fasanen Street off the Ku'damm. The centre stood on the site of the former synagogue, which for many years lay in ruins after the events of the date thirty-one years ago.

Heinz Galinski watched the synagogue burned to the ground on that night in 1938 and he was there again to speak at the commemorative service in 1969.

After his father died in a Berlin police station, Galinski, his mother and his wife were sent to Auschwitz. Unlike them, he survived, worked to the bones at IG Farben Buna, producing magnesium, explosives, methanol and Zyklon B. As the Red Army advanced in 1945, Galinski was one of the prisoners forced on the death marches, first to Buchenwald, and then to Bergen-Belsen, where he was finally freed by soldiers of the British Army and later became chairman of the Jewish community in Berlin, and was instrumental in the rebuilding of the Fasanen Street centre.

The significance of this date, November 9th 1969, he told around 250 guests – including state representatives, members of all the political parties and two classes of high-school graduates – extends far beyond the Jewish community, its commemoration is an opportunity to draw lessons from the past.

Berlin's mayor Klaus Schütz laid a wreath in memory of all victims of the Nazi regime and said they must never be forgotten, expressing hope that the world powers would soon bring about stable peace in the Middle East.

The singing of hymns was led by Berlin's chief cantor Estrongo Nachama who, like Galinski, had been active in Berlin's Jewish community for many years. In 1969, his singing was broadcast every Friday night on the radio and his beautiful baritone had once saved his life. It pleased certain SS guards to hear a rendering of 'O Sole Mio' by 'the singer of Auschwitz'.

All of Nachama's relatives were murdered in the camp.

Bomb number seven in Berlin's Jewish Community Centre did not go off. Police later confirmed that it contained a highly explosive mixture of potassium chlorate and Pattex and was similar in construction to the one seized back in March at 60 Stephan Street, immediately putting Dieter Kunzelmann and Rainer Langhans under suspicion.

The struggle of the El Fatah has shown everyone how imperialism, Zionism and the system in their own countries is to be fought. The Palestinian revolution is the starting point for all-inclusive change.

The bomb was wired to an alarm clock set for 11.30 – the time of the memorial service – but had stopped at 3.51.

Dieter in hiding, sculpting his hair, trying on hats and glasses, shanking up my clink and dropping STP.

Substantial perceptual changes. Blurred vision, multiple images, vibration of objects, visual hallucinations.

Meanwhile, the special feature on K1 in *Stern* magazine – with Uschi on the front cover – hit the news-stands that very same day.

This was particularly bad timing.

Readers were invited to admire the glamorous lifestyles of Rainer and Uschi and the other residents of the top floor of the K1 centre at 60 Stephan Street. There they were: Rainer, bare-chested with the others, a number of them visiting from Munich – Richard Wetter, Heidi Opfermann, Rolf Pohle and Holger Meins – arranged into angles in front of a violin and a blanket. Rock stars.

Dieter and the Wandering Hash Rebels were getting angry.

The Horla were getting angry.

Rudi Krawallo and his Märkische Quarter boys were suddenly getting angry too.

You have money, share it with us. They would not get out of it unscathed, Rainer and Uschi.

Tense? Yes it is. It's always tense here.

Rainer and Uschi go out very rarely, *Stern* told Germany, told Berlin, told Dieter and the Wandering Hash Rebels, the Horla and Rudi Krawallo and his Märkische Quarter boys. The curiosity of strangers was a nuisance to them, they said. They did not drink, but they smoked cannabis constantly.

On the second floor of 60 Stephan Street, unknown to Rainer and Uschi, was where Rudi Krawallo and his boys cooked up the clink. And on the ground floor, the Horla were shivering under thin sheets.

The third floor of Stephan Street was supposed to be a room where everyone could get on. So how come so many felt excluded from the inner circle?

'With a little work we can earn lots of money and live really well,' Rainer said in the *Stern* article. 'It's incredibly easy to live well here. But in all this preoccupation with political actions, we've ignored the sensual side of life, which is where personal satisfaction really comes from.'

'I tried with Marx and Mao, but never got past the introduction,' Uschi added. 'Reading is boring.'

'We embody the new leisure existence and can quickly make lots of money with our beautiful bodies,' Rainer concluded.

It was bad timing, really.

Stern paid Rainer and Uschi 45,000 marks for the interview and Uschi's modelling session, I pointed out to Rudi Krawallo and his Märkische Quarter boys on the second floor of 60 Stephan Street the very next day.

I didn't usually linger long on that floor, avoided eye contact, paid for what I needed and left. That day, however, I was obliged to stay around a while.

They're disrespecting you, I told Rudi, watching the cogs turn behind his considerably furrowed brow as he tried to read the *Stern* article. They want you as cheap muscle when it suits them, I said, but do they pay for your services?

The place was a tip – plastic drums of acetic acid procured from the Free University's labs. Sacks of lime. Thick enamel pots on each of the four hobs of the oven with their lids clamped down. A five-hour boiling cycle. Clumps of thick dark paste spread on torn sheets across the floor. Slogans daubed on the walls.

Rudi passed the magazine to the fat one, his lieutenant, Ronni.

They're laughing at you up there, laughing at everyone, I suggested.

The vinegary smell made my eyes burn.

Forty-five thousand marks, I repeated. Some of that is owed to you, surely?

The Märkische Quarter boys looked to their leader, whose single nod was enough. They pulled on their studded leather jackets, loaded up their chains and dusters.

They followed Rudi in single file up the stairs.

I remained where I was, listening. A kick at a door. A conversation, quiet at first, getting louder. A scream, a crash. Shouting.

Tense? Yes it is. It's always tense here.

Shouting, bellowing, more screams, the thud of someone, something falling, then something else. The wrenching of furniture, the splintering of glass. More screams. And the door opened and people were thundering down the stairs.

I remember looking out of the window by the bubbling pots.

Uschi was pulling Rainer along the street, followed by the others, carrying whatever they'd managed to pick up in their haste to leave. A chair crashed from the window above and splintered onto the road. Plates and cups followed in a hail.

Rainer turned and looked back up at the building just once. Blood was streaming from his nose and there were tears in his eyes.

He didn't see me.

23. JANUARY 4th 1990, 7.30am.

I look out of the dirty kitchen window. Flat January Essex fields of beet stubble, steam rising from them in the winter morning.

Shiny new Transit van next to the old Land Rover. At the wheel, Martin. Smiles and waves, as if I should have been expecting him.

Of course I was expecting them, expecting them all along, just wasn't sure where or when. Said he'd be waiting for me and knew what I wanted.

The horn hasn't roused my host upstairs. Won't wake Peter Green, or whoever it is up there.

I get out of his house.

Martin steps down from the van, takes out a small cigar, lights it. Looks me up and down, circling, grinning.

'Thought it would be about time to collect you by now,' he says, pleased with himself. 'When your time's up, your time's up. Nice and quiet around here isn't it? Isolated. Secluded. Did you get what you were looking for, anyway?'

I squint up at the bedroom, an old sheet blocking out the day. No signs of life.

'That's not Peter Green is it?'

The kilos have rolled off Peter Green since his last photo, but he still looks nothing like he did back then. Why would he?

He shrugs, glances at his watch.

'Does it really matter?'

I breathe the morning air for a bit longer.

Not as bald as he looked in that last picture I saw of him.

'We're not going to have one of those talks about perception and reality are we?' I reply, eventually.

Martin's still grinning.

I watch Peter Green in the phonebox. The conversation is long and animated and he looks over and gestures angrily at me on several occasions, pumping in coins.

'Why not?' he says. 'It's all got to be seamless. Truth doesn't even come into it, one way or the other.'

Butterfly tattoo between thumb and forefinger. Never mentioned anywhere, as far as I recall. His fingers not the sensitive instruments they once were.

Toying with me, laughing at me, enjoying my confusion.

His voice doesn't sound anything like it did. ECT and almost twenty years of medication.

Martin's not alone, there's somebody else in the back of the van.

Noted and filed.

'Shall we walk for a while? Take a little stroll?'

There's nowhere to run. Flat Essex fields in every direction. I shrug.

He bangs on the side of the van.

'We'll only be five minutes,' he says through the open window.

We amble out along the track from the house.

'I don't know what anyone's told you…' I begin, but he shakes his head, puffing on the cigar. Too late for any of that.

'You can't say you weren't given a chance,' he says. 'Why didn't you go back when Rainer called? That was quite a clear message.'

Rainer calling from Berlin. And reminding me of Marina. Marina who was going to be a doctor, heal the sick. Who turned to the camera so that everything could be better documented and we'll all be better protected.

'Surely you didn't need the gravity of the situation spelling out?' Martin says. 'Why did you come back to Europe? That really wasn't the smartest move. Was it the Wall? All the commotion? It won't make any difference to the way things are, you know that don't you? Same old people pulling the strings. Same old Nazis, if you really want.'

I say nothing.

'I can understand you'd start to feel you'd been forgotten,' he says. 'But, I mean, fucking hell, see what it's caused, all this big song and dance for a few old secrets? Makes no difference to me, you understand. I just do what they tell me to do.'

You can never just cut it, once there are connections.

We turn back towards the van.

'What you know protects you against what they know and can use against you,' he says. 'When your time's up, your time's up. I've enjoyed our time together. Shall we go?'

He drops the cigar, grinds it in the dirt with his foot. Goes to the passenger side of the van, opens the door and makes a regal sweep.

There's nowhere to run. Flat Essex fields in every direction. I get in.

In the back, the slender Indian girl who gave me a massage in the basement of the Savoy five days ago. Two of them then, maybe more, watching and waiting.

A box of cartridges rattles on the seat next to her as Martin pulls the van away, crunching over the broken wood, the mashed parts of old guitars.

Beet waste and rape stubble.

I say nothing.

'Where are we going to do it?' the Indian girl says in the back, but Martin raises his hand to silence her.

'She's very good with her hands,' he says, nodding back.

They're going to kill me, of course, here in England, where else? Shut me up for good, here in the land of the victors.

I glance in the rear-view mirror. She has beautiful brown eyes.

'How many years did you work for them?' Martin sighs. 'I really, *really* don't understand. In all that time, did they ever let you down? They look after their people, you know that Peter, take care of all of them. You were like a son to him too, that's what they said. Always telling those stories. They were worried after your wife left, but that all seemed to blow over.'

Annalise. Totally assimilated now. An all-American, independent woman. Never forgave me for leaving her mother behind that second time. When we were taken out of the picture. New identities funded by the West Berlin Office for the Constitution.

Her mother abandoned again, arranging her lucky horseshoes and grim sepia photographs along the mantelpiece, hanging her tapestries on our walls. Abandoned in the Free West where there were so many cars and long-haired students, where anything was available, but everything too expensive. And the Reds were on the wrong side of the Wall.

New identities for Kurt and Lotte too. For their own protection.

Kurt and Lotte, my all-American children, raised as regular college brats and settled now, with their own American families, their American ranch-style apartments, their perfect American teeth and big American cars and debts.

Consumerism, the economic miracle, invented to stop us thinking about our fascist past...

Kurt and Lotte, never having to worry about invasion, never being compromised. No longer Hänsel and Gretel. Kurt and Lotte who would not be interested in Bombs One to Seven.

'Were you in some kind of trouble over there, is that what it was?' Martin continues. 'They said you could handle what they gave you. Falling off a log, for you, they said. Delivery, that's all it was. Light distribution work. But I understand how the waiting around can get to you.'

With Kurt's people, my best response is ever silence.

To run and to hunt and kill and eat their fill and wake up and start running again.

'Maybe you had too much time to think about things,' Martin suggests. Turns and grins at me. 'Started to hanker after your glory days, did you? Your star performance?'

I say nothing, think back to that.

The first trial of Horst Mahler was scheduled to take place in the spring of 1971 when I would be revealed as the secret weapon of the West German Protection of the Constitution Office – a pillar of the prosecution's case against the lapsed lawyer, Mahler. Playing for them all the time – with the blessing of the Americans of course – exposing the revolutionaries as enemies of democracy, of individuality and consumerism. Wanting the revolution armed, in order to suppress it.

Which by happy coincidence, it turned out, was what the German Democratic Republic wanted too, to further its own cause, reveal it as a beacon of order and public-spirited community. For West Berlin's students to be armed – as symbols of the decadence of individualism and consumerism – was exactly what was required.

And the revolutionaries? Well, it's true, not many of them wanted to be armed, but it was their armed revolution, after all. Inevitably, it was left to the handful of crazies we could stir up.

So in the end, everyone wanted the same thing really; one big happy family.

But only Kurt's man seemed to be able to see this and was squeezing from all sides – unfortunately with me right in the middle. That was the game. I understood it.

We'd been hiding out for over a year – me and Annalise, Klaus and Lotte too. My increasingly malevolent mother-in-law – the cause of quite a few of my problems as far as I could see – was left behind in West Berlin when we went to ground.

We'd have new identities very soon, we were promised. A new life. America, just like Annalise always wanted. There was just one thing left he wanted me to do.

Testify. Spill the beans. For the West. For the East. For the revolution. Who knows? You think those doing the driving have plans, but they seldom do.

I wouldn't have to say anything much, he told me – I could refuse to answer questions about anything not relating to the arrest of Baader back in April 1970, after that farce in the Buckow Cemetery.

Mahler and Baader, digging for buried treasure at midnight. The idiots. World War Two pistols. Spades under the headstones. I should have kicked them into the holes, had done with it.

But then Mahler insisted on getting in my car on the drive back. And Baader was arrested alone.

Mahler put two and two together, and from then on, I was in the frame. A marked man, the game was up.

And his trial in the spring of 1971 didn't quite go according to anyone's plans, either.

I have always remembered them there in that courtroom where I gave evidence. Staring at me, staring at the judges in their wigs and gowns under the spread eagle, laughing at me, laughing at them, chewing gum, smirking, sprawling, smoking. Kissing. In love with themselves and each other. Beyond fear by then.

But of course, *they were never there at all.* The memory plays tricks.

Only in spirit. They had haunted West Germany for over a year by then and the trial was about them even in their absence, not sad old Horst Mahler. The Baader-Meinhof Gang, as Springer's papers were now calling them.

But they haunted me more than anyone, Andy and Gudrun – spirits in the wind, footsteps in the night, the parked cars of any stranger in the sleepy hamlet we were holed up in. Anything could set it off. The scrape of a stone from the farmer's tractor, the midnight snap of a poacher's snare, a raised voice out in the darkness, the hoot of an owl.

And Annalise drawing even further into herself and the kids bored out of their brains, away from school, away from their friends – away from civilisation as we knew it entirely.

I didn't sleep any easier, even when news got to me they'd fled Germany for Jordan, and later that the Jordanians had got sick of them, and they were doing guerrilla training with the Palestinians. The Palestinians threw them out too.

Now Horst Mahler was in custody. Horst Mahler whose front line troops I had armed at the Battle of Tegeler Weg. Horst Mahler who I drove first into Belgium, and then to Italy, to procure weapons for the cause. Horst Mahler who had abandoned a brilliant career in law to follow them underground. Fled with them, first to Jordan, and then to Palestine. And returned with them to be arrested in Berlin.

Horst Mahler in the dock.

Staring at me, staring at the judges in their wigs and gowns under the spread eagle, laughing at me, laughing at them, chewing gum, smirking, sprawling, smoking. *But they were never there.*

Kurt Neubauer, a member of the Berlin Senate, announced to Springer's scribes that a 'secret weapon' would be introduced.

That was me. I could refuse to answer questions about anything not relating to the arrest of Baader back in April 1970, after the Buckow Cemetery. But it didn't turn out that way.

'Did you personally offer to supply weapons to the left-wing circles – pistols, submachine guns – even mortars and phosphorus shells?' I was asked.

Otto Schily – sponsor of the Wieland Commune where the Wandering Hash Rebels congregated – was defending Mahler.

'I can't answer the question,' I said.

'Did you plant a bomb in Commune 1?'

'I can't answer the question.'

'Were the bombs supplied by counter-intelligence agencies?'

'I can't say anything about that.'

Laughing at me.

'Did you set fire to any vehicles on the occasion of the anti-Springer demonstration in 1968?'

'I can't tell you anything about that.'

Laughing at them.

'Were you responsible for a fire at a police stable in which a police horse was severely injured?'

'I can't answer that.'

Chewing gum, smirking, sprawling, smoking.

And then Mahler himself stood up, breaking his silence for the first time in the trial.

'I understand the restrictions which have been placed on what the prosecution witness Peter Urbach can and cannot say,' he said. 'Without them, he may have been obliged to shed light on the mysterious incident of the bomb that was found on the premises of the Jewish Synagogue in West Berlin in November 1969. Mister Neubauer would surely find it very difficult to explain with any satisfaction how that bomb could be traced back to the Office of the Protection of the Constitution. This bomb's origin could perhaps have been explained with a bit of honest detective work. Especially given the alarm it caused the Jewish community of Berlin.'

Mahler was eventually acquitted, but not freed. There were other charges.

We were on a plane to Miami six hours later.

★

Flat January Essex fields.

Beet waste and rape stubble.

With Kurt's people, my best response is ever silence, but I have to ask him something now.

'Do you actually play guitar, Martin? Are you really a fan?'

Now it's his turn to say nothing.

'All that stuff you sold me at the Savoy, you know, about how Danny played like Buddy Guy and Peter was more influenced by BB King? All that about sustain and tight flourishes of notes, about Fender Strats and jazz tinges and Django Reinhardt? Was that just background?'

He thinks about it.

'I'm generally interested,' he says, looks at his watch again. 'But you know, anybody can play guitar these days. It doesn't make you some kind of god.'

The beautiful Indian girl in the back tuts, knows it's going to be longer than she expected, with all this long-winded old man's talk.

But anyway, I tell them both about it, finally.

★

On the Saturday afternoon of March 21st 1970, Fleetwood Mac stepped down, one by one, from a plane at Munich Airport.

In Munich there's a Hofbräuhaus — one, two, down the hatch...

They were en-route from Hamburg, where they'd played a long gig at the Musikhalle the night before.

There they all were:

Mick Fleetwood first, all gaunt six foot six of him, ambling down the steps. Peter Green is not happy with Mick, thinks he can't read his signals, won't break the mould, is holding the music back.

The drummer of Fleetwood Mac, was living with three or four Sodomites!

John McVie. Lights a cigarette on the runway and stretches.

John's got his yachts, but he was okay. Always blamed what happened on those Germans.

Their manager Clifford next. Trying to hold it all together, aware the group is falling apart even as it's riding so high.

And I think Cliff knew I had another gun too.

Danny Kirwan. Peter's not happy with Danny, who's becoming withdrawn, locking himself into hotel rooms.

You were a good looking fella, Danny. But just a boy. Such a baby.

Jeremy Spencer, barely over five feet, with the Bible sewn into his duffel coat.

Doing his Sieg Heils around the stage in that crumpled silver suit.

And last down the stairs, Peter Green himself.

He wears a tailored Biba maxi coat over a Liberty shirt with a long multicoloured scarf a fan has knitted for him. His beard is almost to his navel now. He flashes the peace sign at the few journalists and photographers.

'He's very hairy,' Uschi Obermaier observes from the car park, where she's waiting to meet him with Rainer Langhans in a red BMW V8, two girlfriends in the back.

It's true, they don't look like superstars: there are blokes everywhere who look just like them – in the tap rooms and betting shops, in timber yards, down at the docks and digging the roads.

For Peter Green, things are blurring, not just places and faces, but left and right, back and front.

Last Sunday, he knew, had been Hannover, and the week before that, Belfast in Ulster?

But he wasn't over the US tour yet, Peter Green, the long bus rides and the endless planes. And all the people. Crowds with pens and notebooks, behind cameras, at mixing desks, grinning over cups, squinting through smoke. Extending autograph books, angry hippies, snarling skinheads, in the desert, in the wilderness, in front of the five thousand.

First time Owsley gave me a drink, just a little sip and I knew it was spiked.

From the Eagle Auditorium in Seattle to the Fillmore West in San Francisco.

There were owls everywhere, pictures and coffee cups, forks and spoons, salt and pepper pots. Owls on the blotting paper.

Then up to the Kinetic Playground in Chicago and back to San Francisco again.

Owsley had this idea that all the sounds have to come from a single place.

Six nights at the Whisky-A-Go-Go and then back to the Eagle.

And I remember thinking, I'll show you where we can take it.

And three nights at The Warehouse in New Orleans.

Ask Peter Green about New Orleans. Ask him about that.

He wasn't over the US tour yet, Peter Green.

Rainer and Uschi and her two girlfriends get out of the BMW and wave at him. He walks across to talk to them and they tell him all about the new High Fish Commune where they all live together. One big happy family.

It's a different way of living, Rainer tells Peter Green, a way of escaping from square society and very beautiful. It's all cool, he says, and beautiful, a far-out trip. An in-demand Uschi makes enough money for all of them, he explains, and Peter agrees she is very beautiful. All three girls, in fact, are very beautiful and this Rainer too, is attractive, fascinating – his calm assurance. They're beautiful people and they're on his wavelength as he tells them about his plans for a new kind of music, something that's totally free. Freedom is the key. Everything will be free in the future.

And they're on his wavelength as he tells them about owls having the most sophisticated sound equipment in their brains and bats finding their routes and dolphins moving magically around in schools. They tell him about the musicians who live with them and are attempting similar things. They understand as he talks about sonic waves, echoes and radar, and they invite him to see how they live so beautifully at their commune, High Fish.

Everyone is smiling as Peter Green starts to get into the BMW, but then Cliff comes across with John McVie and attempts to dissuade him. He's very tired, Cliff explains to the Germans, and partying's probably not a good idea. The atmosphere suddenly changes. Come on, you know it's not a good idea, Cliff implores him, but Peter is adamant. Rainer scribbles down the Landshut address for them and the car speeds away, leaving Cliff and John looking lost on the tarmac.

*

I'm in another car, a Volkswagen Beetle. I've just driven over from Berlin and I park up outside a house in the east of Munich. My passengers, who have been hiding out at the home of the journalist Ulrike Meinhof for some weeks, are anxious for a meeting with members of the southern resistance front, the Tupamaros Munich, including their old friends Fritz Teufel and Ulrich Enzensberger. Ulrich is working in a glue factory and Fritz is attempting to evade a half-hearted police search. There are so few of them now with the will to get things done, to see things out for the APO.

But Hänsel and Gretel need funds. And so, it turns out, do Fritz and Ulrich. The revolution must be armed, and the revolution must be adequately funded too, if it is to have a chance. The talk turns, inevitably, to Rainer and Uschi and the end of K1 back in November. Rainer and Uschi who've sold out to the man, turned their backs on their former comrades, turned their backs on the memory of Benno Ohnesorg and Rudi Dutschke and the APO.

Rainer and Uschi who have once again unwisely made appearances in various capitalist magazines, but would surely seize the opportunity to make amends.

Eventually everyone climbs into my car and we set off in search of the hunting lodge on the banks of the River Isar.

*

Peter Green can't believe how beautiful the place is, like a magical castle out in the forest.

We are lost in the forest and the past is approaching. We are threading a trail of berries backwards, trying to avoid the inevitable, covering little girls in gold and tar.

Peter Green can't believe how simple it all is, how beautiful they all are, and he can't believe the music they're making now.

Something really different is happening to us now isn't it?

This is it, he thinks, what he's been waiting to hear. He wants it to go on forever, to never stop. And he feels like he's made of crystals, thousands of crystals.

*

I could hear the awful music as we approached, with Fritz in the passenger seat and Ulrich and Hänsel and Gretel crammed in the back, smoking furiously, everyone cursing the ostentation of

Rainer and Uschi as they surveyed the majestic splendour of the scene. Domes and turrets, sculpted gardens and stone carvings. A waterfall. Not just a bourgeois, but a pseudo-aristocrat now. Betrayer of the revolution.

Andy wants to go in alone, push a piece down Rainer's throat, kick the shit out of all of them, take everything there is. No prisoners.

Build Up the Red Army!

Let the Class Struggle unfold!

But Fritz reasons with him. Too dangerous. No idea how many are in there or how quickly the bulls could arrive. And there's the risk of walking away with nothing. The revolution must be armed. Safer anyway, to keep Rainer on side for now, he reasons; the friendship goes back a long way. Gudrun agrees with Andy, but Ulrich agrees with Fritz and they still claim some kind of seniority.

Fritz and Ulrich climb out. Ulrich pulls a gun from his pants, as if to pacify Andy, underline the seriousness of his intent. A starter pistol, I think. I watch the two of them clank open the heavy gate and then sit and wait for a while. It's starting to get dark.

Gudrun complains she's hungry. Is she supposed to live on fresh air?

Andy tells her to be cool. Be cool baby.

How can she be cool, Gudrun says, when she can't even think for hunger? This is a shit plan anyway, she says. What are we doing in fucking Munich anyway? she wants to know.

Be cool, baby, be cool, you're always fucking uncool about one thing or another, Andy tells her. They both light cigarettes, smoke furiously.

It's tense, all of a sudden.

Take the car, I suggest to Andy eventually, go get something to eat, come back for us. They look at me suspiciously.

Somebody has to wait here anyway, I shrug.

Andy can't wait to get behind the wheel as always. They speed off in a dust-raising arc which sends the birds panicking from the trees.

Good riddance you morons, is what I'm thinking.

Satisfied they've gone, I move towards the heavy gates, towards the awful music. Move through the trees towards High Fish, peer through a first window. A record player on the wooden floor, two high speakers on stands. Product endorsement gifts for the beautiful people. Scattered LPs, overflowing ashtrays, empty wine glasses.

Move along the vine-covered wall around the back. Peer through another window.

Rainer, Fritz and Ulrich in a room full of clothes on hangers – more product endorsement gifts. They are deep in conversation. Rainer is still, his hands on his chin. The others circulate like a couple of coyotes, gesticulating angrily. The window's glass is too thick to hear anything above the awful music that's coming from somewhere below.

I follow it to its source now, down a winding metal staircase, and push open a door.

Peter Green is alone in a room, but seems to think he's surrounded by others. Amplifiers and abandoned instruments. His guitar is deafening. It's crying, screaming, dying now. He was jamming, but it got too much for the others.

But he's hearing something else.

He's playing along to some other music pumped through the headphones he's wearing.

And he's hearing something else.

The music of dolphins.

The music of bats.

The music of owls.

And of course, we were swimming in it, melting into each other and the furniture. Nobody had a clue what was going down.

I walk into the room and move into his field of vision.

If I were ever to meet him, he might think he recognised me, and strain to remember, but I pull out a sheet of blotting paper from my pocket, tear off an entire strip.

He smiles at me. Takes it on his tongue, chews it all up. A sacrament. It will help him on his way.

And then he closes his eyes again.

His guitar is crying, screaming, dying now.

But he's hearing something else.

I climb back up the winding stairs, peer back in the window. Ulrich is waving the starting pistol around. Rainer has his head in his hands. Fritz kicks over a table. They are all shouting, but all you can hear is Peter Green's guitar. Rainer glances up at the window. There are tears in his eyes again.

He doesn't see me.

I walk back along the side of the magical castle, through the gates, to wait for Hänsel and Gretel. Feels like the start of something else.

It was always about total freedom then, and that's all forgotten now. Nobody wants it really, just watch the telly.

REFERENCES

Background information and inspiration for this novel came from many sources, including the following key reference works:

One-Dimensional Man: Studies in the Ideology of Advanced Industrial Society.
Herbert Marcuse, Routledge Classics 1964
ISBN: 9780415074292

Die Jahre der Kommune I
Ulrich Enzensberger, Goldmann 2006
ISBN: 9783442153619

Wie Alles Anfing
Bommi Baumann, Arsenal Pulp Press 2000
ISBN: 0889780455

Ich Bin's: Die Ersten 68 Jahre
Rainer Langhans, Blumenbar 2008
ISBN: 9783936738346

Die Bombe im Jüdischen Gemeindehaus
Wolfgang Kraushaar, Hamburger Edition 2005
ISBN: 3936096538

The Untold 60s
Alex Gross, CCRP 2009
ISBN: 9780982317808

The Berlin Wall
Frederick Taylor, Bloomsbury 2006
ISBN: 9780747585541

Peter Green: The Authorised Biography
Martin Celmins, Sanctuary 1995
ISBN: 1860745075

Bringing the War Home
Jeremy Varon, University of California Press 2004
ISBN: 9780520241190

In Europe
Gert Mak, Vintage Books 2008
ISBN: 9780099516736

The Baader-Meinhof Group
Stefan Aust, Bodley Head 1987
ISBN: 0370310314

Protest Movements in 1960s West Germany
Nick Thomas, Berg 2003
ISBN: 1859736505

Joschka Fischer and the Making of the Berlin Republic
Paul Hockenos, Oxford University Press 2008
ISBN: 9780195181838

Man Without a Face
Markus Wolf with Anne McElvoy, Public Affairs 1999
ISBN: 1891620126

Fleetwood Mac Behind the Masks
Bob Brunning, New English Library 1990
ISBN: 0450531163

Hitler's Children
Jillian Becker, HarperCollins 1979
ISBN: 9780586046654

Germania
Simon Winder, Picador 2010
ISBN: 9780330536288

The Peter Green Story: Man of the World (DVD)
Scanbox Entertainment UK, 2007

The excerpt from the leaflet printed on pages 164–166 is available to read in full at: www.xfamily.org

The position of xFamily.org is neither for nor against The Family. It's a collaborative work aimed at supporting contributions from diverse individuals. Individuals contributing to this project might have taken up a favourable or unfavourable position on The Family, but through peer review the site maintains objectivity.

Acknowledgements

With love to Rainer Langhans and Christa Ritter for their generosity, trust and original spirit.

Also special thanks for much help, in no particular order, to Peter Craven, Jutta Kramm, David Peace, Michael Nath, Richard Huffman, Alex Gross, Aribert Reimann, Norm Pearce, Emma Smith, Kevin Reynolds, Emily Penn, Gary Leftbridge and Jakob Henninger.

And Isa and Ian at Route, of course, without whom...

Ada Wilson is a journalist based in Yorkshire. His previous novel *Very Acme* was also published by Route. He edited the acclaimed short story collection *Tubthumping*.

For background information on this book please visit
www.redarmyfactionblues.com

For further information on this book,
and for Route's full book programme
please visit:

www.route-online.com